WORLD AFTER
DEATH

Jason Pere

Acknowledgements

For Laura, My Valkyrie, that we may come to know a life without burden.

For My Family, Friends, and Supporters. Having an ample supply of willing spirits I was able to lean upon has made the journey far more enjoyable and much less frightening.

And most of all, for those with fire in their spirit and steel in their heart, who take arms in the name of all that is good, the true Ladies and Lords of the realm, and those yet to be and to become.

The First Law
All Challenges demand an Answer.

Chapter 1

"Will you come to the Blinding?" Mark said to Lea with a flutter of his majestic, deep green eyes. He drank in the spectacle of her fair, smooth skin that disappeared beneath the sheets of their bed as the fire cast dancing shadows across her delicate body.

"I don't want to see you do it, that horrible thing," Lea said quietly. "If you want me there, I will go for you."

"It would make it easier for me, I think," Mark responded as he observed how enraptured Lea had become by the hypnotic quality of his eyes.

"If it's going to be so hard for you, why are you set on doing this?" Lea had asked this question many times before.

"If the Blinding was meant to be easy, it would not serve any purpose, and everyone would put in to be an Arbiter." Mark looked at Lea and knew the unnatural, sagely wisdom his stare contained would rapidly bring her defiance to an end. He could see his gaze affect the spectacular woman in the bed the way it always had, making her unable to resist him. "It will help me to know that you are there when I have to do it. We don't have to talk about it anymore tonight. I don't want to upset you on the last night we have before I become an Arbiter."

"No, it's okay. I can handle it. You're the one who has to be brave tomorrow. I can't imagine…" Lea trailed off and dropped her eyes to the crumpled and sweat-stained sheets on which she lay. "Have you decided which one it will be?"

Mark gave a pause for a moment, considering the words of his beloved. He had not given much thought to that question and didn't want to respond too quickly. He didn't want to give Lea the understanding that he was far more comfortable with the impending ramifications of the Blinding than others might think. "Well, my vision is pretty even between the two. I am right-handed, so I think it would make sense to choose the left one," he said in a comforting tone. Normally, talking over morbid topics never unsettled this glorious woman. He knew Lea was not squeamish and had a stomach of iron. That was one of the things Mark loved most among the many things to love about her. The Arbiter-to-be knew that her apprehension came from the impending suffering he was about to endure. They had always protected each other from pain and hardship, but this was a necessary pain. He knew it hurt her, having to stand idle in this matter.

"It seems a crime. Your eyes are so beautiful. I hate to see them ruined."

"I'll still have one after tomorrow. Just love righty twice as much," Mark said with a smile. His humor worked, and Lea found a smile of her own.

He loved her smile, but then both expressions faded into the silence of the night. The only noise filling the quaint little country house was the crackling of the logs burring in the fireplace. Lea's words had struck a chord in Mark. He sympathized with her very much, in fact. As she would be robbed of looking into both his eyes come tomorrow, he in turn would never again be able to fully drink in the marvelous spectacle of her beauty.

He caught himself before he shed a tear. He thought of Lea when she smiled. The sight always melted his heart, and he was confronted with the reality that perhaps his left eye had witnessed its last of her smiles.

"You couldn't just have them sew it shut, could you? I mean, do you absolutely have to destroy that perfect little gem of yours?" Lea asked.

JASON PERE

Mark had needed to defend himself from this question on more than one occasion. The repetition of the task never made it any easier on the soon-to-be Arbiter's spirit when he had to dissuade Lea from protest. "No, you know it has to be the way it has to be," Mark said quietly as he rubbed his chin. "It needs to be a choice that can never be undone. Becoming an Arbiter is a forever kind of thing."

"I know. It's just so hard for me to think of what you'll have to do to yourself..." Lea trailed.

Mark could see that his lover's imagination was running rampant with a theater of bloody fantasy. He moved to comfort her with an embrace but Lea kept her distance.

After evading the arms of her paramour, Lea continued to voice her position on the matter at hand. "Mark, I don't want you to think that I'm against you becoming an Arbiter. On the contrary. I support your choice, and it's not just because I love you and stand by you. I want you to be an Arbiter because you will be a remarkably good one. You will do so much good for the village..."

"Lea, it's okay. We don't have to talk about this anymore." Mark cut her off when he saw the difficult she had in continuing. Lea was quiet again. He watched the rhythmic rise and fall of the sheets covering his woman's body as she inhaled and exhaled.

Lea finally broke the few silent moments that passed. "I'm glad you feel that way, because what I want to do now doesn't involve much talking."

"Oh?" Mark raised an eyebrow with a playful, inquisitive smirk. "And what is it you had in mind, love?"

Lea pulled the sheet from her naked body and stood. "Come to me." She said the three words barely louder than a whisper, but they boomed in Marks ears like a spring thunderstorm.

Mark wanted to go to her. He nearly leaped upon the gorgeous creature right there in front of him, longing for his touch. "You make it hard to say no. I want to, but first, please let me look at you for just a while. I want the most beautiful woman in the world to be one of the last things my left eye remembers."

"It means I get to look into those stunning emeralds of yours just

3

a little bit longer. That seems like a better trade for me. You have your-self a deal, sir," Lea said with a tearful smile that cut straight to Mark's core.

They stood without any more words passing between them. He absorbed every curve of her shapely body, her stormy, dark brown eyes, and short-cut golden hair. He did not merely flatter her when he called her the most beautiful woman in the world; Lea was breathtaking. He became aware of the way Lea was looking back at him and taking in the spectacle of his lean and long limed dancer's body awash in the firelight. It was plain to see by the unmistakable adoration making her face that she had once again fallen into the boundless wonderment of his re-splendent green eyes.

The two stood as long as they could will themselves to stay apart. They pushed their resolve to its limit, waiting as long as they dared, knowing they were saying goodbye forever to beautiful things they had come to cherish so profoundly. Mark felt he could no longer resist; he stood fast for a single breath longer, and then he went to her. They folded themselves into each other, and for a brief time, there was nothing else in existence.

The Eighth Law
Both the Challenged and the Challenger have the right to call upon a Personal Champion to fight in their stead.

Chapter 2

Leon hated the traffic on Interstate 395. Most of the cars had been moved to the side of the road on the northbound side. That endeavor had taken the village of Northeastern Connecticut much of the first spring *after* to accomplish. The southbound side, on the other hand, was still heavily congested. It stood to reason that travelers were more apt to come from Connecticut than they were to leave Massachusetts. In fact, Leon doubted that anyone other than someone of his calling would ever be inclined to travel south on the interstate. It didn't matter anymore, how the interstate used to work; most things didn't work like they used to these days. A single lane for travel was more than sufficient to accommodate anyone with business on the road.

He pumped the pedals on his trike, watching the sun starting to dip from its zenith. He had made good time from New Boston, but he had not left as early in the day as he had hoped. A late Challenge had seen his departure delayed. In the end, the Challenger had relented, and Leon had not needed to raise arms. It had been set to a simple unarmed contest to the yield. The Challenged was a fit, middle-aged man, and Leon knew that the man's opponent-to-be was far less conditioned than he, though he did boast a small height advantage and more than a small weight advantage. Were it not for his training in hand-to-hand, Leon would have found difficulty in both striking and grappling with the Challenged.

He wasn't sure why the Challenger had relented, but Leon was glad that things didn't have to come to violence. Despite his proficiency in combat, Leon never enjoyed drawing blood if it could be avoided. It gave him hope for those who had survived the sickness when he saw conflicts resolved peaceably. He would gladly endure a small delay in his travel if it meant that men could still choose to rise above coming to blows when they were at odds. Seven billion deaths in less than three years certainly gave a new perspective on the value of a life.

Leon was used to riding his trike up and down the northeast. This area was always harder on his calves than the flat, sprawling roads of New York or Pennsylvania. He did take solace in knowing that he would not have to ride the steep inclines and low valleys of New Hampshire's White Mountains until next summer. Leon knew that even if he pushed himself he would not make the Village of Northeastern Connecticut before dusk. He was not about to arrive at his destination in the late hours and request hospitality from the villagers, so he resigned to spending a night on the road. He would make his appointed arrival in the early morning tomorrow.

Once Leon had accepted the fact that he would be camping out this night, he slowed his peddling. The man needed a break. He pulled his trike and attached buggy off to the side of the road, then realized the gesture was in all reality unnecessary; the probability of encountering anyone else needing to make use of the road was highly unlikely. Still, Leon observed the proper traveling etiquette and made sure he would not impede anyone else's travel while he chose to rest his weary legs.

Leon wiped the sweat from his brow and took several long, refreshing sips from his water bottle. The heat of the sun warmed his back. Since he knew he would no longer need to observe any sense of propriety, he unbuttoned and slipped out of his charcoal polo shirt. The late August breeze felt wondrous against his bare chest, and he took several deep breaths. Soon, there would be the smell of autumn in the air. He longed for that scent—the nostalgic fragrance of burning leaves and warm cider, memories of senses from the days *before*. How he missed those simple pleasures taken for granted.

Leon got off the seat of his trike and stood for a while. His legs were sore with the trek he had made since the morning. He walked up and down the pavement of the interstate, then raised his hands up into the air. He pushed his fingertips up towards the cloudless blue sky and felt the stretch pull him up onto his tiptoes. He held that pose for as long as he could, then returned he feet flat to the ground and dropped his hands to his sides with a satisfied, "Ah," and powerful exhale.

The ride had sapped a fair measure of his strength. Leon decided that now was as good a time as any to break for his midday meal. He went to the buggy he had been pulling behind his trike and unhooked several of the bungee cords holding the blue tarp over his cargo. He filled his water bottle from the jug in the buggy, then dug out a couple granola bars and a tin of mixed nuts. Spreading his sleeping bag in the bed of a dented-up F-150, he enjoyed his impromptu picnic. The food was adequate and would provide him with the energy he needed to pedal until it was time to bed down for the night. The sun had been harsh on his back only moments ago, but now it gently warmed his body as Leon lay stretched out in the bed of the pickup. He was tempted to call it a day right then and there but forced himself to rise after letting his lunch settle. Then he re-secured his sleeping bag in the buggy with the tarp and bungee cords.

Before he got back onto the seat of his trike, he took a quick glance at his arsenal in the buggy—guns, blades, Kevlar, bow and arrow. All were accounted for. Leon knew he had no reason to expect his weapons to have vanished, but he always liked to be certain he could depend on his tools to be where he needed them. He sat atop his trike and absorbed one final bath of warm sunlight upon his face before pushing down on the pedals again. Serene moments in nature like this almost had the power to make him forget what the world had become and what had made it this way. Almost.

***

The sun had disappeared below the tree line some hours ago. Apart from the half moon and starlit sky above, the only light source Leon had were the two Maglites he had fastened to the handlebars of his trike. It was time for him to stop for the night, and he knew it. He wanted to keep pedaling and make some more ground before turning in and finding a place to sleep, but the darkness and the soreness he felt in his lower body quickly won out against his need to press on. He would have to get up a little earlier than he wished if he were the make the village of Northeastern Connecticut first thing in the morning. For this, he was okay with cutting his sleep short. While he might not get the hours of rest he wanted, the fatigue he felt now would ensure he slept soundly. At this point, his chief concern was making sure he would not be disturbed while he rested. The likelihood of anyone happening across him while he was dreaming was remote. Leon was also sure that nobody had been trailing him from New Boston; he had not felt the unease of strange eyes upon him during the day. Still, he was not a man to be carless with his safety.

Leon found a minivan on the side of the road that suited him. The doors were unlocked, and it was easy for him to stow his trike and buggy out of view of the road. He slipped into the vehicle with his sleeping bag, bringing his .38 revolver and hunting knife from his buggy to keep within arm's reach as he slept. A curious black bear would more likely be cause for any late-night alarm than another human being. In that case, the small handgun would be grossly ineffective, but having some kind of weapon gave Leon peace of mind.

He lay still in the forgotten vehicle and listened to the late-season hum of crickets outside. It was peaceful and calm. He briefly visited some of his memories from the day. They were simple things; apart from the challenge of that morning, the bulk of his day had consisted of little more than one white painted line on the asphalt of Interstate 395 bleeding into another.

He tossed and turned as he always did until finding a comfortable position on his side, facing the back of the long seat playing the part of his bed for the night. Leon let his mind wander toward the village he was traveling to and what might be in store for him there. But before those free thoughts ensnared his imagination with a limitless world of unknown possibility, he made himself quash them. Finally, sleep found the man, and he was left to his dreams.

"You don't want this. I'm telling you, you really don't want to do this. Some people see it as a privilege or something that's cool or makes you better than everyone else. I can tell you that is the farthest thing from the truth. You don't do anything but listen to people's problems and intolerance. You spend all your day trying to make the best of a bad situation. And for all that, your reward is this. Take a good look, because if you really want it that bad, you better get used to seeing a shredded iris every time you look in the mirror. Henry, stop asking me. It's for your own good. Yeah, yeah. I know. If it's so terrible, why did I do it? If I didn't, I wouldn't have been able to live with myself. You want to ask me again?"

Arbiter Richard McKenzie

Chapter 3

"**D**o you think he will make it to the red today?" Danny asked.

"What, Mark? He could push the red and twice that if he wanted. He has balls of solid steel," Peter responded. The shock on his face couldn't be hidden from the younger man seated next to him.

"What is that look?" Danny said with surprise.

"I just can't believe the utter absurdity of that question," Peter scoffed. "Make it to the red, Mark…" He trailed off and muttered a few choice words under his breath. "You know Mark, he's done—" Peter started again in a huff but cut his words short. He shifted in his lawn chair and poured himself some coffee from the thermos at his side. The beverage was now at a perfectly warm temperature after a splash of powdered creamer, and Peter had no need to blow on the beverage before sipping it. The drink offered a nice distraction from the sour chitchat Danny tried to maintain.

The sun was barely up, and the warm coffee helped both men wipe the sleep from their eyes. The banter they had engaged in was really a mutual means of distraction. The wind was calm today, and the water tower was quite pleasant to sit upon during the end of summer. Nobody in the village cared to be on watch duty when the snows came in January. Normally, none of the people in Northeastern Connecticut would lament standing watch on a fine pre-autumn day like this, but today there was a Blinding.

"I was just saying many prospective Arbiters have made it this far, but when it comes time for the Blinding..." Danny finished his thought with a gesture of his hands and shrug of his shoulders.

Peter was grievously annoyed that, of all the topics Danny could have picked to break the golden silence, the man had chosen the Blinding. "Do you have to talk about the Blinding? Damnit!" Peter snapped. "It's the most lively thing to happen to Northeastern Connecticut since *after,* and we are the only two lucky people who don't get to be there. Pisses me off."

"So you're all bent out of shape cause you don't get to see someone else stick a needle in their eye? That says quite a bit about you," Danny said with a smile.

"Oh, like you wouldn't rather be there. And it's not about seeing something grim. It's about seeing Mark do something most people will never have the guts to do. The man deserves respect, and we should be there to show it."

"Well, I can agree with that. Mark does deserve respect," Danny stated, wiggling his fingers beneath the side of his baseball hat and scratching his head. "If he makes it to the red, that is."

"He will make it to the red!" Peter nearly shouted.

"Would you—" Danny started.

"What? What is it now? I swear, ask something else about the Blinding!" Peter was nearly about to explode out of his seat.

"I just...I just wanted you to pass me the sugar packets was all," Danny said meekly with wide eyes.

10

Peter gently passed the box of sugar packets to his friend as a means of silent apology. The outburst had firmed Danny's mouth, and he remained silent. The two men sat in their chairs cn the water tower and quietly sipped coffee in the picturesque August morning. The sun continued to rise overhead. The men returned to their duties and scanned the road and surrounding tree line for any signs of trouble. Raiders had never come to the village—they tended to stay clear of the northeast— but none of the residents wanted to take any chances with the safety of the community. Wordlessly, the two passed the binoculars back and forth, taking time to look for anything out of the ordinary. It was still closer to morning than afternoon, but boredom and some legitimate pangs of hunger directed Peter and Danny to break out the sandwiches wrapped in their bags. The freezer-burned roast beef helped to liven the dull moment.

"You know, I heard about this one guy, wanted to be an Arbiter. Made it all the way to the Blinding and he went too far in. Killed himself." Danny spoke with a mouthful of sandwich.

Peter rolled his eyes. He knew getting mad would not pull him off the water tower any sooner, but he felt he'd endured his fill of silence for the day, so more conversation would be fine with him. Even if he didn't care to speak about the Blinding, it was at least something to talk about. "And how would that have happened, huh? There must have been another Arbiter there and a doctor. What, nobody thought to stop this guy before he went too far?" Peter humored Danny's musing. "And somehow this guy managed to go past the red without passing out first? You're sure you heard right?"

"I don't know. Just something I heard about one time. Somewhere down south, I think it was. Or maybe it was out west. I don't remember," Danny said with a downward glance.

"Don't remember, huh. Well, you keep on thinking about that one. Maybe it will come back to you."

"Pete, I'm not making this up. I remember hearing about it. I just don't remember any of the details."

"Okay, then. How about who told you about it?"

"Oh, I remember that. It was Steve," Danny said confidently as he took another bite of his lunch.

"And how would Steve know anything about this? The last time he was out of state was *before*."

"Steve talks to a lot of people." Danny slipped his finger under the side of his baseball hat again and scratched his head. "Oh, wait a second, maybe it was Rebeca who told me. No, I got it. It was Rebeca, and Steve was there with us."

"Danny…" Peter was about to start in on the younger man, but he never got the chance.

Danny stood from his chair and grabbed the binoculars. "I see something coming on the road," he said hurriedly.

"What is it? What is it?" Peter shifted impatiently from side to side. He put a hand above his eyes to block the sun and help focus his vison, but he could not make out the source of Danny's alarm.

"Looks like…"

"Oh, come on. Just give me the binoculars, will you?"

"No, I got it. I see. We're okay," Danny said happily.

"Well what? Tell me," Peter said, brimming over with curiosity.

"It's Sir Leon."

"Oh, is that all? I thought it would be something more important than that." Peter's excitement fell into a heavy frown.

"Hey, a Templar Sebastian coming to the village is important," Danny said defensively. He crossed his arms and squinted judgmentally at Peter.

"Templar Sebastian…" Peter muttered. "You know how ridiculous that sounds? A bunch of man-children playing at being knights in shining armor and coming to save us all from ourselves. Ridiculous!"

"The Templars are good people. I think it's great what they do. You were there right *after*. We need men like Sir Leon. They stop people from abusing challenges."

"*Sir* Leon. Ugh," Peter said with mocking distain. "Maybe, just maybe, the Templars do a little bit of good. But come on, Danny. Here in Northeastern Connecticut? When is the last time we had a challenge go to the death…let alone combat, come to think of it? No, the Arbiters keep things in order just fine."

"You make it sound terrible that we live in a village where people get along with each other."

"Danny, you know that's not what I mean." Peter shook his head and let his face fall into his hands as he tried to explain himself. There were several moments of silence, and Peter chewed on his lip, nurturing a thought before speaking next. "You know, my feelings aside, a Templar Sebastian coming to the village is news most others will want to hear about immediately."

"Well, right. I don't disagree," Danny said, unsure of what Peter was driving at.

"News enough that delivering it quickly might be considered more important than watch duty," Peter said slyly. He nudged Danny with his elbow, and his companion acknowledged him with a show of comprehension on his face.

"I see. I get it," Danny said with a grin. "But wait, we both can't leave our post. It only takes one to deliver a message," he continued. Danny's grin faded and was replaced with a childish pout.

"Well, it seems to me that one of us should greet our guest and bring him to everyone else. They would be at the Blinding, I imagine."

"And the other?"

"They should go and immediately tell everyone that a Templar Sebastian is coming to the village. I guess we will both end up at the Blinding after all," Peter said and chuckled in satisfaction.

"That's a plan, but who gets to greet Sir Leon? Rock, paper, scissors for it?"

"Oh, you win, Danny. Enjoy telling Sir Leon. I'll see you at the Blinding," Peter said as he was already three rungs down on the water tower's ladder.

***

Leon was far more exhausted than he had planned to be at this point. He silently chastised himself for choosing to sleep in a minivan. He lamented not seeking out a roomier lodging the prior night. The chain of his trike squeaked each time he pushed down on the peddles, and the noise was beginning to cause him some alarm. He had repaired the old chain twice now since last winter. Clearly, his trusty steed would require some upkeep beyond his level of knowledge, and very soon. Leon knew Lea was quite skilled with her hands when it came to all sorts of nuts and bolts for tinkering. Perhaps his appointed stop in the village of Northeastern Connecticut would provide him with more than a place to watch the leaves change into their brilliant autumn hues of red and gold.

His attention was drawn to a man running towards him on the road. The Templar's right hand instinctively released its grip on the handlebar of his trike and dropped to the butt of the .38 holstered at his side.

"Sir Leon! Sir Leon!" Danny shouted.

"Daniel?" Leon hollered back. He could not fully make out the speaker's face, but he was just about certain of the voice.

"Yes, it's me, Danny."

The Templar allowed himself the luxury of a deep sigh before working his pedals double-time. He sped towards the younger man with an agonizing shake of his head. Leon cared for Danny and genuinely liked the fellow, but he found the man's idolization of the Templars Sebastian nearly vomit-inducing. He'd come to think of Danny like a stray dog he'd fed once and now followed him with unwavering loyalty.

Leon stopped his trike short of Danny and looked at the sweat-soaked man as he gasped to catch his breath. "Is there something wrong at the village?" he asked.

"No. No, not at all. There's a Blinding today."

"A Blinding." Leon spoke the words with a measure of surprise. He paused for a moment as he thought of who in the village would want to take up the mantel of an Arbiter. "Mark?"

"Yes, it's Mark. They'll be starting soon. The whole village will be there. You should come," Danny said, nodding excitedly.

"Hop on, then," Leon said with a glance at the back stand of his trike.

Danny climbed up, and the two men were off to the Blinding.

"Mark, sweetheart, we have some wonderful news for you. We got the test results from the hospital today. You are all healthy. You are going to be just fine. Isn't that great? It's okay. I'm just crying a little because I'm happy for you is all. It's really, really great. Um, they said they need to run some more tests on you father's and my bloodwork, but the doctors are positive that everything will be just fine. Hey, you're going to be fine. It's good, right? Don't look so sad. It will all be okay. I'll make you anything you want for dinner."

Caroline Fishers

Chapter 4

A Blinding was barbaric. It had to be. The utter brutality of the ceremony was truly the only deterrent standing in the way of the men and women who wished to claim the title of Arbiter. The laws of the Challenge were easy enough to learn, and every village had a copy of them for reference. As long as a Hopeful was not an absolutely horrid excuse for a human being, it was often easy enough to secure sponsorship from a standing Arbiter. So much of the world *before* had been lost. Now, men were often judged by a different measure than where they went to school or how great a profit their company turned in a quarter. Now, the worth of a sound body and life itself were so much more profoundly understood. Those willing to permanently give up part of themselves were to be held in the highest regard. Money was of little use these days. Trade and barter was how the world went around now, and life was the most precious of commodities for those who had survived.

Mark reflected on all the teachings he had learned during his sponsorship with Arbiter Henry. Now it was time for him to take the final steps of his journey and assume his new role. Once the Blinding was complete, he would serve as an Arbiter.

***

"I'm so thirsty," Mark said to Lea as he licked his dry lips.

"You're welcome to drink something. You're the one who got it in your head to fast," Lea chided. "I didn't expect you to complain about it so much after the big deal you made."

"It's not a complaint. More of an observation," Mark retorted, nervously clenching his hands into fists. "And it *is* a big deal. You know, Henry told me that most people who undergo the Blinding throw up or piss themselves, even if they don't pass out. He did."

"Right, and nobody would think any less of you if you did too."

"I know that, but I still don't want to wet my pants in front of the whole village."

"Didn't stop you at the Halloween party last year," Lea said with a playful smirk.

"That was different, and you know it. I don't normally get that wasted…" Mark grumbled defensively. "That was a good night, though." He continued with a morbid laugh. "I know it's stupid, just…"

"It's not stupid at all," Lea said, rubbing her man's back supportively. "You know, I still have my Little Red Riding Hood costume from that year. The real slutty-looking one. I'll wear it for you tonight."

Mark looked at Lea and brushed her face with his fingertips. His breathing grew steady and even. "I love you, Lea."

"I love you, Mark." Lea tried to keep her voice from cracking. It was not easy to hide just how terrified she was. She knew Henry and Dr. Michael would be there for Mark, but it did not comfort her enough, and she fought to stay strong.

They embraced, holding held each other long and hard. Neither of them said a word. They didn't need to; there was nothing more to be said. Then the intimate moment was put to an end when a knock came at the door of their home. Lea carefully wiped away the traces of a tear she'd been unable to hold back on the sleeve of Mark's shirt. Mark did not notice the gesture.

"That's probably Henry," she said, pulling away from him.

"Yeah." Mark sighed, then opened the door.

Henry stood on the large stone landing of Mark and Lea's home. He wore his standard attire of blue jeans and a plaid flannel shirt with the sleeves rolled up. The Arbiter had dressed up for the occasion of the day; his jeans were washed, and he had managed to find a pair that were not worn through at the knee. Had times not been as they were, anyone would take one look at Henry and think, *Lumberjack*. He rubbed his bushy, salt-and-pepper beard, looking at Mark with his one light brown eye. "It's that time. Are you ready?" Henry asked.

It took Mark several seconds to respond. "Yeah, I'm ready," he rasped in a dry-sounding throat.

"Ha. If that were true, you'd be the first person ever who's ready for the Blinding." Henry laughed as he clapped one of his weathered hands onto his protégé's shoulder. "It's okay to be nervous. I'll be with you the whole way. You'll do just fine."

"You have a strange way of trying to make me feel better about all this," Mark grunted. He looked at the tired and beaten brown leather patch covering where Henry's right eye used to be. Henry was right-handed, but the vison in his left eye was much keener. That was why Henry had chosen to take his right eye.

"The Blinding is a strange thing," The Arbiter chuckled. "Hi, Lea." Henry peered around Mark and greeted the man's better half.

"Hi, Henry," Lea said, matching the Arbiter's tone and pitch. In their early days of Mark's sponsorship, Lea had found it hard to share her man with someone else as much as Henry had required. But she'd quickly warmed to the Arbiter. Despite some of his rough edges and his gruff exterior, Henry was an easy man to grow to like.

"And are *you* ready?" Henry asked Lea.

"I am. I think I'm more prepared than he is," Lea said with a blink of her eyes and a nod at Mark.

"Hey, I'm the one doing this today. Me!" Mark said defensively.

Lea was about to respond with a suitably playful and sarcastic re-mark, but Henry spoke first. "Now there's the man I came to see today.

Come on, you two kids, let's get this thing done." The Arbiter threw his bearlike arm around Mark's shoulder, and the trio headed off to the Blinding.

***

Things were always quiet on the streets, but they were never this quiet. The village of Northeastern Connecticut was small, only a population of one hundred and seventeen, but they managed to give the place the feel of a lively community. Normally, one or two people could be seen walking the streets attending to an errand. Voices could usually be heard in the village, as conversation was one of the best ways to pass the long hours of the day. Right now, though, there were no conversations to be heard and no passersby to be seen. Everyone in Northeastern Connecticut was gathered at the memorial park green across from the library. They all waited for the Blinding—the first Blinding to be held in the village, as a matter of fact.

Mark was sweating bullets. He couldn't tell if it was the heat, his nerves, hunger, something else, or perhaps a little bit of everything all rolled together. He felt Lea take his hand in hers and was immediately comforted. She must have seen is anxiety. He looked at her, and they exchanged awkward smiles. The sound of people talking filled the air as the three approached the memorial park green. The sensation spiked Mark's tension.

When they rounded the last bend in the street and Mark finally laid his beautiful green eyes on the gathering of people come to see him, he nearly broke into a panic. He swore that if he hadn't gone without eating for the last day, he would have emptied the contents of his belly right then.

"Hey, you. Little Red Riding Hood, remember?" Lea said to Mark.

Her words managed to garner a real smile and even a hint of laughter. "You're good to me, Lea. Thank you…and I will hold you to that, by the way," Mark said, trying to grasp the small measure of levity Lea had instilled in the moment.

"I'll let you hold me to whatever you want."

"Oh, now I have to make you regret saying that."

"I'm sure I'll enjoy it while you try to make that happen."

"So am I," Mark said with a smile he could no longer contain. "Didn't think I would be this nervous.

"Hey, enough of that. I'm with you, okay?"

Mark wanted to respond, but he thought it was best to stay as quiet and focused as he could manage from here on in. His eyes fixed on the crowd. The people began to quiet their conversations as they saw Mark and his entourage approaching the green. The silence didn't help his constitution, either. He felt like he might fall on his face at any second, he was so wound up.

The people of Northeastern Connecticut parted and revealed the white gazebo in the center of the park. In the gazebo stood Dr. Michael, a handful of his instruments, and an admittedly comfortable-looking, overstuffed reclining chair.

Mark met the doctor's eyes. He was not a real doctor, of course. People with that level of medical training were nearly extinct these days. Michael had been an EMT and volunteer firefighter *before*. In a town like this, that was about as good as you were going to get. Still, nobody felt bad about calling Michael a doctor; he did the job better than most would expect despite his lack of a medical degree. Michael spent a lot of his time at the library, scouring over books and honing his healer's touch when he wasn't actively practicing his craft. Mark respected the other man and was glad that Michael would be there to help today.

A few villagers patted Mark on the back or voiced their feelings of support and approval as he passed through the crowd. The encouragement of his friends and neighbors helped reinforce Mark's unsteady resolve. The Arbiter-to-be stepped up into the gazebo, where the doctor stood amidst the white, peeling paint of the structure. Mark and Doctor Michael exchanged glances laced with apprehension and masked with bravado.

"You ready for this?" Doctor Michael asked.

"It's about to happen regardless of how I feel, so I would say I'm ready," Mark stated as he wiped a few beads of sweat from his brow.

Michael waved Lea and Henry up into the gazebo. They would

provide Mark with a fount of moral support. For Mark, having his lover and his mentor at his side in the next few moments would be strong medicine. "Mark, it's all good. Last year, I handled a collapsed lung and an appendectomy. This is going to be nothing. Easy, easy," Michael said in a calm, relaxing voice. His words managed to have a positive effect on Mark's demeanor.

"You got this, Mark. We'll take care of you the whole way," Henry said as he bounded up the step of the gazebo and patted his protégé on the shoulder. Lea came up right behind the Arbiter. She said nothing, but the mere sight of her standing with him was the greatest aid for Mark's courage.

"You want to say your thing while I get him ready?" Michael asked Henry.

"Yeah, that would be best, I think," the Arbiter replied as he adjusted the brown leather eyepatch chaffing his nose.

"Okay, Mark. Just lay back in this chair, here," Michael said, patting the fluffy cushions of the recliner. "Are we doing the left or the right?"

"Left...we're doing the left one." Mark choked out the words.

"Okay. Lea, would you be okay to assist?" Doctor Michael asked. He didn't need her for much more than a pair of hands, but he seemed to want to remind his patent of his greatest measure of support as much as he could.

"Absolutely, Doc. Anything you need," Lea said eagerly. She clearly wanted to do as much as she could to help her man see it through to the other side of this thing.

"All right, then. Would you be amazing and hand me that athletic tape, please?" Mark pointed to the half-used roll of tape poking out from his medical bag. Lea retrieved the item while Michael put on some latex gloves and produced a pair for his assistant. She went to work taping Mark's left eye open as directed by the doctor. Michael put some moistening eyedrops into Mark's eye, then followed them with some anesthetic drops. The expiration on the bottle of numbing agent had passed, but the active ingredients in the solution would still work well enough.

Michael and Lea prepared Mark for the Blinding; Henry gave his protégé one final look before turning to address the village.

***

"My name is Henry Billings. I am an Arbiter," he said, loud enough for
all the people in Northeastern Connecticut to hear. All eyes focused on
Henry as he addressed those gathered. The only ones not intent on what
the Arbiter had to say were Mark, Lea, and the doctor. "I have been a
member of this village since the first days *after*. I know everyone here
by name, and in turn, every family in Northeastern Connecticut has honored me with an outpouring of respect and hospitality." Henry took a
moment to quell his emotions, restraining himself from getting sucked
into the fond memories he had collected in his time serving his friends
and neighbors. "I would now ask you to extend that same respect and
hospitality to this man, Mark Fishers," he added, gesturing to his protégé. "He is one of us. You all know him, and you all know that I have
taken him under my wing and taught him what it means to be an Arbiter."

Henry couldn't prevent himself from getting choked up with emotion. When he heard his own words crack and waiver, he allowed himself
a few moments to stop and regroup. "You will all also know that I had
to teach this outstanding young man very little about what it means to
be an Arbiter. His moral compass has always pointed true-north. Mark's
has been a sugar-coated sponsorship," Henry said. His words were
greeted by nods of approval and laughter from the people of Northeastern Connecticut.

"It is bittersweet today. Our friends in New Boston need another
Arbiter, and that has to be me. I didn't want to leave Northeastern Connecticut. This village is my home, and everyone here is my family, but I
cannot let my feelings take precedence over the needs of an entire city."
The Arbiter had to stop and recompose himself yet again. "This means
that someone has to take my place and serve this fine community as an
Arbiter. There is nobody better suited to such a task than Mark Fishers."

The crowd in front of the gazebo murmured with approval. Henry saw that several people had been moved to tears already. He was uncertain if the cause was his words, the fact that he would be leaving the village, or a showing of love and respect for the man who would become an Arbiter today. Either way, he hoped that all three reasons played a part in each tear falling to the ground. Henry heard the doctor talking to Mark behind him. The Arbiter-to-be was nearly ready for the Blinding.

"Can you feel that?" Michael asked Mark while he probed around his left eye with a gloved index finger.

"Not really. I can tell you are doing something but that's about it," Mark responded.

"Good. I think we're ready," Michael said while he looked to the other side of his patient at Lea. "Lea, why don't you hold Mark's free hand," he continued, retrieving the Blinding Needle from the tray at his side.

The Blinding Needle was something between an icepick and a fishhook—long and thin with a barb on the end of the point. It was designed to penetrate the eye in a smooth and easy motion. When the needle was withdrawn, the barb on the end would ensure there was enough irrevocable damage done to the eye that sight would be lost completely. Their Blinding Needle was a typical metallic color save for the small, half-inch band of red two inches down from the point. The red mark was the distance a would-be Arbiter needed to push the needle into their eye.

Henry drew his remarks to a close, unsure how much longer he could stand in front of the village and keep his wits about him. "It is often asked why we do what we do. Why must an Arbiter cripple themselves so? The answer to this is twofold. First, The Blinding serves as permanent reminder for an Arbiter to use their remaining sight to be objective, seeing the conflict of the people they serve without letting their personal bias enter the matter. Second, Arbiters help settle disputes between others. We oversee challenges and make sure they are conducted in accordance with the law. In the end, an Arbiter's word is final judgment. People will ask, 'And who are you to sit so high and mighty, that I must answer to you? What gives you the right?' An Arbiter will point to their patch and say, 'I put myself one eye from night for you. I have given willingly of my body for you, and I have made a sacrifice for you that others would not make themselves. That is what gives me the right.'"

Henry knew he had to stop speaking quickly if he wanted to be of any use to Mark. His heart felt about to explode out of his ribcage. "Justice is blind. Justice is blind," Henry said hurriedly before he turned his back to the crowd. Then he went to Mark and knelt next to the recliner.

***

"Nice speech," Mark said.

"Glad you liked it. You should remember it, because you might have to give one or two of your own someday," Henry responded. "Now how are you feeling?"

Mark gawked at the Blinding Needle before he spoke. "Two inches never looked so long."

The four people gathered in the gazebo stuffed the plethora of lude comments which might follow such a remark. "Is that true, Lea?" Henry finally asked with a chortle, unable to help himself.

"How should I know? Mark is enormous," Lea retorted good-naturedly. Mark give her hand a loving squeeze, and they all laughed.

"You ready to do something stupid?" Henry asked his protégé.

"Let's go," Mark responded. Mark, Lea, and Henry looked in unison to Michael.

The doctor finished wiping down the Blinding Needle with disinfectant and handed it to Mark. "Mark, I need you to look at my finger out here with your left eye and keep your right eye closed," he said holding, his index finger stretched far and away. "Then, I'm going to need you to take the needle in one hand and push it in straight and slow. Go slow, you hear me? Too fast, and that will cause pressure on the fluid behind your eye. We don't want that. Go slow, but do not—*do not*—stop until I tell you to. You got that?"

"I got it," Mark said.

"Henry will spot you. He's going to have his hands on the needle as well, and he'll keep it straight for you so all you need to do is push. If you start to freeze up, just let us know, and we will keep pushing on to the red for you, okay?" The doctor spoke confidently.

"Okay."

"When you're ready," Michael said to Mark.

Mark put the Blinding Needle up to his eye. He felt the tape pull against his eyelids as he instinctively tried to shut them. He tried to bear down, but his sense of self-preservation locked up his arm. "Damnit. Henry, can you help get me started?"

"Sure. Here it is," the Arbiter responded with the slightest of pushes. The Blinding Needle punctured Mark's cornea.

After the initial surge, it was easy for Mark to ride the shock for the first couple seconds and continue the push. Then his body took over and entered survival mode. Mark fought to continue driving the needle in; his sight became blurry and dim. "Am I there yet? I can't see," Mark said, panicked.

"Almost. You're over halfway. Don't stop. Don't stop," Michael said, cheering on the soon-to-be Arbiter.

Mark felt like he had been driving that needle for an hour. His hand holding the needle now waivered and shook. His other hand, gripping his lover's, bore down so hard that he was sure he'd leave bruises. "I don't think…" Mark trailed off, and his body overwhelmed him. "Henry…" He felt his mentor aid the needle in the final few centimeters of the plunge.

"Good job, Mark. You're at the red. Now just pull the needle out. You can go fast this time." The doctor showered Mark with positive affirmation.

Mark felt like he was about to retch, seize, or pass out. His body had nearly shut down from the shock of trauma. "I…I…help," Mark stammered. There was a beat of uncertain silence for a moment.

"Rip that sucker, Henry!" Doctor Michael shouted.

The Arbiter pulled the Blinding Needle form Mark's eye in one swift motion. Everyone in Southeastern Connecticut heard Mark scream.

"I heard there was some government that survived. Up in the northeast, I think. At least one man. He's trying to build this country back up, from what I gathered. I didn't hear his speech, but Jessica and Brian did. They said it was amazing. They said it was the first time after that they felt safe or hope or anything really truly good. They said he's offering shelter for any and all American citizens. I think we should go try to find him."

Wyatt Donaldson

Chapter 5

"Those goddamn, motherfucking, cocksucker Templars!" he shouted at the top of his voice amidst the smoldering ruins of the decimated armory. Mathew Haze kicked a hunk of scrap metal that used to be a Humvee fender with the tip of his steel-toed boot.

"I swear, we've had better hauls for weapons and ammo at gas stations and sporting goods stores," Mathew's younger brother Aaron stated dejectedly.

"Yeah, I know that. Don't need to go and state the obvious," Mathew snapped at his brother. Aaron recoiled in defense. "That piece of shit Sabastian went and set his little fuckers all the way out here to bumfuck middle of nowhere moose country Maine to dynamite this armory. I swear he has had his guys hit every military base, ammo dump, and motor pool on the fucking east coast. Fuck him!" Mathew raged and thrashed about amid the destroyed vehicles littering the former National Guard station.

"Hey, we still pulled some small arms. It's not a total bust," said

Tony Gastopie, poking at the wreckage of a burned-out truck with the tip of his rifle. Tony was one of Mathew's college frat brothers from *before*. Much like Aaron, Tony also was accustomed to following Mathew's lead.

"This trip out to this toilet was absolutely a waste. We got nothing we didn't already have plenty of. We don't need pistols and shotguns. We need some major firepower, and this shit is not it," Mathew growled. He brooded for several moments before speaking next. "Why? Why would he send his guys up here? Nobody needs to come this far north."

"We did," Aaron responded, shrinking again as he seemed to immediately regret voicing his thoughts.

"You just can't help but piss me off right now, can you?" Mathew snarled at his younger brother. "I had us come up this way because the Templars should not have had any interest in ransacking a site so far from Manhattan. Clearly, Sebastian Clarke is just an asshole."

"Hey, Matt. I know this is shitty, but you might want to try and keep it down," Tony said with a wary glance about. "Some of the other guys…" He trailed off, still looking around at the other members of their group, who had taken notice of Mathew's outburst.

Mathew was about to launch another verbal attack, but he stopped himself as he took note of the inquisitive eyes fixing on him. He calmed himself and smoothed his hair back, tucking in the shirt that had become disheveled with all his frantic arm-waiving. "You're right, Tony… thanks." He had some difficulty expressing the gratitude, but his frat brother was one of the few people on the planet who could get away with reigning in his tempter when it overheated. "This will not go over well with the rest of the guys. Promises were made, and now I'm going to have to figure out a way to tell everyone why I can't deliver. Shit, this is really like being in office."

"Hey, we got this. We'll figure something out," Aaron interjected.

"Yeah, Aaron's right. This was a good call. We're on the right track. There are only, what? Fifteen hundred Templar at most. Sebastian sure as hell didn't send his people up as far as Canada. We keep going north just a little longer. Sure, they might not have the kind of gear we were hoping to find, but it's definitely better than what we got now,"

Tony said reassuringly.

Mathew grimaced and scowled, but he did not explode again. "This is going to be hard news to break. A lot of our guys are hanging on by a thread. Loyalty is wearing real thin around here. At the start of the summer, we had numbers on Sebastian and his flunkies. Now, we're scarcely more than nine hundred. And most of that is through desertion." He paced up and down the asphalt of the lot as his mind whirred. "Feeding these guys lines about patriotism and the restoration of democracy doesn't actually fill their stomachs," he said, keeping his voice barely more than a whisper. He couldn't afford to let the thin veneer of his authority fall apart in front of his followers any more than it already had.

"The men we do have are loyal to the cause. We are the Patriots, remember that," Aaron chimed in. "We'll see this country returned to proper order."

"Damn right. Our fathers worked so hard to see us succeed. We can't disgrace them by being halted by some crazy, one-eyed dumbasses and a handful of vigilantes who call themselves knights," Tony said.

"You're both right. It's been a whole lot of disappointment the last few years. I'm still mad about everything. Tony, you were primed to take over one of the top ten Fortune Five Hundred companies in the world once your dad handed over the reins. And I...well, I was being groomed to make a run at the fucking Whitehouse. I mean, by the time 2044 rolled in, I wouldn't have had to do anything more than put my name on the ballot, and the goddam presidency would have been mine. Fuck! But no, the Sickness had to come along and wipe its ass with the entire world," Mathew rambled on. His tone now held more defeat and loss than anger.

"You don't need to remind us. We were all supposed to have top-shelf booze and blowjobs on demand, and now we're expected to milk cows and fucking farm and shit with everybody else. Fuck that. We get back on top and we stay there," Tony lamented.

"Remember, the people want what we are trying to do. They just need to be reminded that this is still America, even after all that's happened," Aaron said hopefully.

"Yes, yes she is," Mathew sighed.

The party continued searching the rubble of the armory, but to no avail. Anything worth taking had been taken or had been rendered totally unusable. Mathew Haze had regained his composure, but it was far from easy to maintain it. As he rooted through the charred remains of some kind of vehicle he could no longer identify, he dwelled on the terrible run of luck he and his so-called Patriots had been having. Not a single place where they might have been able to secure the weapons needed to reestablish democracy had yielded any fruit. The Templars had always been just one step ahead. Sebastian and his troops saw to it that any cache of arms was laid to waste. The Templars were not about to let any roving bands of raiders traveling these parts help themselves to state-of-the-art military grade equipment. The Templars were not actively trying to thwart Mathew, but they thwarted him nonetheless. In fact, Mathew was all but certain that Sebastian had never even heard of him and his attempt to bring back the America of *before*.

It amazed him how easy it had been for the people of this country to forget who they were. It was like the Sickness had wiped the minds of those who had survived. He could not wrap his head around just how the rest of the country was so willing to accept this Templar and Arbiter nonsense. Democracy had flourished for two and a half centuries, and now it had been replaced by half-blind fools and blood-sport junkies dispensing justice to anyone dumb enough to buy into the hype. There was no real government anymore, just sheep without a shepherd, but Mathew Haze would see the lost flock of the American people tended to if he and his Patriots got their way.

Mathew had just finished looking through the dust of an empty weapons locker when the sounds of one of his men fast approaching got his attention. He turned to look at the man who had drawn Tony's, Aaron's, and virtually all the other search team members' attention. Mathew felt his spirits rise as he saw the excitement plastered on this man's face. Perhaps he brought good news. Admittedly, most of Mathew's Patriots were not the brightest of men, but they had the good sense not to approach their leader directly without having something exceptional to report.

"Mr. Haze! Mr. Haze, Congressman, sir!" the Patriot shouted.

Several of the other men fell in behind the man as he ran towards Mathew like a child chasing an ice cream truck on a hot summer day.

Mathew raced to remember the man's name. The very first lesson his father had taught him about politics was to remember everyone's name. That practice alone had enabled Mathew to secure his district the very first time he ran for office. The sizable campaign contributions from his father and Tony's company admittedly played a part in Mathew's election.

He felt like he was about out of time. The Patriot was now right in front of him, and Matthew still drew a blank on the man's name. At least he knew that he *knew* the name; he just needed to place the face.

"Hold on, there. You look like you're about to drop dead," Mathew said, calm and cool. He instantly slowed the scene down to a pace he was comfortable managing. "Just get your breath. Why don't you sit down?" He placed one hand on the man's shoulder and gestured to a reasonably smooth, knee-high plateau of cement that might have been part of a wall once upon a time.

"Congressman Haze," the Patriot started, still breathing heavily. He clearly had good news.

Mathew waived the man silent with one hand, then with a twirl of his finger gestured to nobody in particular in the group of his men that had gathered. "Can we get this man a drink of water, please?" Mathew said commandingly. Without hesitation, two of his men broke off and headed back to the coolers in their vehicles to retrieve something cold for their compatriot. "We're going to get you something to drink, and then you can let us all know what's going on."

"Thank you. Thank you, sir," the winded Patriot said.

Mathew saw his men quickly return with water bottles in hand. They gave the man sitting next to Mathew a bottle, and all watched as he nearly drained the contents in one long swig. *Travis Ross, West Virginia, gas station cashier*, Mathew thought as his memory clicked. The Patriot next to the Congressman wiped a drop of water from his chin as his breathing returned to normal.

"Now, what's all this commotion about, Travis?" Mathew Haze asked his constituent with the best empathetic and concerned look he knew how to give.

Travis looked about at the group of men bound in suspense. "Well, Mr. Haze, sir, we were searching the surrounding woodland area, like you asked us to. Me and Billy and George, just like you said. We didn't find nothing at first, but then we came up on a big ol' chain link fence," Travis said, then stopped abruptly.

All this for a fucking fence. I'm going to bash this hick's fucking brains in with a rock, Mathew thought lividly. "Okay, a fence...and then what?" the Congressman said, raising his voice inquisitively.

"Well, sir, we were about to turn around and come back, but then Billy brought up a good point. He said that it seems odd that someone would put a big fence like this out here in the middle of the woods. So we all decided to take a look inside." Travis stopped again, but this time a smile the size of the Grand Canyon haled the younger man's words.

"And? And?" Mathew pressed on. His patience for this simpleton was about at its limit.

"And it's fucking Christmas."

"I heard you lost one in the ride today. I also heard you gave defib for twenty minutes after she flatlined. She was your first, wasn't she? Mine was a forty-five-year-old man. Name was Bard. One minute he was talking and smiling fine. I took my eye off him for a second to get some fresh gloves, and then next thing I knew, he had stroked out. I gave him chest compressions until they pulled me off him in the ER parking lot. We can't save everyone, even when we do everything we can to save them, Mike. It doesn't make it any easier to deal with when you can't bring one back, but that's the facts. You look beat. How about you get a shower and then I take you for a drink? I'll tell you about some of the good ones."

Warren Thomas

Chapter 6

Lea, Henry, and Doctor Michael were gathered at the dining room table in Lea and Mark's country home. Mark was fast asleep, tucked into the warm confines of the king-sized bed next to fireplace in the master bedroom. The Blinding had been a success, if such a horrific event could be thought of as something at which one succeeded. Mark was now an Arbiter and would begin to faithfully serve the village of Northeastern Connecticut.

"He needs sleep. Sleep, sleep, and more sleep for the next three days," Michael said to Lea. He paced, increasing inflection on each subsequent use of the word sleep. "Sleep is the absolute best thing he can do for himself."

"I got it, Mike. I'll keep knocking him over the head with a log if I need to." Lea grinned while she joked.

"I think a concussion might be counterproductive. Maybe you

31

should try low light, warm blankets, and heavy peace and quiet. I think that will give you better results than blunt-force trauma." The Doctor responded to Lea's jest with a mocking tilt of his head.

"I don't know about all that. I wouldn't mind hitting that kid on the head a time or two," Henry said, rubbing his beard and adjusting his eyepatch.

"Well, I know two people I will never employ as nurses again," Michael said and garnered some low laughter from both Lea and Henry. The doctor reached into his bag lying beside him at the dining table and rooted around in it for a few seconds. He withdrew a small bottle and roll of gauze, which he handed to Lea. "Humor aside, listen, because this is important. Infection is the greatest concern for Mark right now. He needs one drop of these antibiotic eyedrops three times a day for the next month. That will end up being half the bottle at the end of it. If he sleeps through a dose here or there over the next three days, that's okay. Don't wake him. Be sure to change his dressing once a day as well. By the time he's done with the drops, we can see about getting him fitted for an eyepatch. Okay, so tell me, Lea, what are you doing for Mark the next month?"

"Plenty of sleep, eye drops three times a day for the next month, but don't wake him, and fresh gauze every day," Lea said while she burned the instructions into her memory. "Oh, and don't hit him on the head."

"Perfect. Please try to remember that last one. I know it'll be difficult," Michael said with something between a chuckle and a snort. "I'll be around if you or Mark need anything. I'll check in at least once a week and make sure you have enough tape and gauze."

"So, he'll be up and about for Labor Day?" Henry asked.

"Oh, sure. Less than a week of bedrest for something like this, but he shouldn't do anything strenuous until the eyedrops are done," the doctor responded.

Lea shifted as she pondered the subtext of Henry's last query. "Henry, I know they need you in New Boston, but are you really going to leave so soon?" she asked the veteran Arbiter.

"I really should have been there at the start of August," Henry said.

His words carried a highly evident measure of regret.

"You know you can't leave before Mark is back to normal. He would hunt you down and shave your beard off if you left without a proper goodbye," Lea said with wide, disbelieving eyes.

"Anyone tries to shave me, it'll be over my dead body," Henry said gruffly as his hand protectively went to the silver tufts of thick hair on his chin. The laughter that followed quickly died into uncomfortable silence. "I can stay until the Labor Day festival at most, but that's it," Henry said, breaking the stillness with his ultimatum. "I have to go after that."

"Thank you, Henry. It would mean the world to Mark if you were here for that," Lea said softly.

"I don't want anyone thinking I'm in some kind of hurry to leave the village. This is my home, and I will always think of Northeastern Connecticut that way, but I'm needed where I'm needed," Henry said solemnly. Again, he fidgeted with the brown leather of his eyepatch. "I did see Sir Leon hidden in the crown at the Blinding. I suppose I shouldn't leave without a good sit-down talk with him as well."

"Leon's here?" Lea and Michal said in near-perfect unison.

"Yes, he is. Really, four eyes between the two of you, and my one is the one that sees we have a Templar Sebastian come to town. You two…" Henry scoffed and shook his head as his words drifted off, but a smile snuck in there, too.

"I think it will be easier to see you go with Leon in the village," Michael said thoughtfully.

"Oh, I see. You're just going to trade on up, are you? Maybe I should head out now," Henry mocked.

"Shut up. You know what he means," Lea said in the doctor's defense, smacking the Arbiter on his arm.

"I know. I know. Only kidding," Henry said. "You're right, though." He nodded at Michael. "Having a Templar to lean on will be very helpful for Mark. Especially one like Sir Leon."

"It's important to remember that this is Northeastern Connecticut. We're not known for the abundance of challenges that occur here. We have had, what, how many this last year?" the doctor asked.

"Count them on one hand, I think. But it's not the locals I worry about. You never know when we might take in a traveler who thinks they're entitled to this or that and get the bright idea to start some trouble," Henry said.

Several sobering, wordless moments passed until Michael finally broke the silence. "I need to be on my way. I need to stop in and check on Mrs. Hurst before turning in for the night. Her Alzheimer's has been getting more pronounced. I don't know how much longer she'll be able to live on her own."

"I'll show you out. I have some soup on the stove for her. Do you think you could take it along when you see her?" Lea asked.

"Sure, I can do that. She'll appreciate a hot, homecooked meal," Michael replied and followed Lea to the kitchen.

***

Henry sat alone at the dining room table with his thoughts. He listened to the doctor and Lea chat back and forth. Their words faded into indistinguishable sounds against the backdrop of his mind as it swirled with memories. Leaving Northeastern Connecticut was going to be one of the hardest things the Arbiter had ever done. Even *before,* this place was where he had grown up, gone to school, worked, gotten married, and buried a wife and three children. New Boston was not so far—half a day by bike and a stone's throw by car—but still, it was not his home, and it never would be.

Henry was pulled back to the moment when he heard Lea and the doctor exchange their goodbyes for the fourth or fifth time, and the front door closed. He blinked and wiped his eye to clear any trace of tears that might have felt like making an appearance. Lea rejoined him at the dining table.

They had spoken about his immanent departure many times before, and both Lea and the Arbiter knew nothing could be said to change what needed to be done. Northeastern Connecticut was not big enough to warrant having more than one Arbiter in residence, and New Boston was one of the largest cities in the world—nearly ten thousand people.

New Boston needed men like Henry to help keep it relatively peaceful.

"I don't know what our home looks like without you," Lea said mournfully after several tense moments.

Henry wanted to tell her how badly he wanted to stay, but he knew it would serve no purpose to get her all worked up and emotional with nostalgia. "Things will be much the same. One man coming or going will not change the village," Henry said, even though he knew his words were a half-truth at best.

Lea put her hand on top of the Arbiter's like a daughter would to her father. "You don't need to try to soften this. Losing you will have a great impact on everyone who lives here. You're a giant part of our family. It's not a good thing, and we don't need to pretend like it is," Lea said, her words floating between anger and sadness.

"You make it sound like I won't ever see any of you again. New Boston isn't so far. You'll just need to find a reason to come visit some more," Henry said in an attempt to soothe the woman sitting next to him. "I'm sure I'll be able to get away for a few days here and there. I have no intention of saying goodbye to Northeastern Connecticut forever."

"We are...I am...just greedy, I suppose. None of us really want to share you with another community. You've always been our Arbiter," Lea said with a measure of grief.

"I know. I won't blame you. I am pretty fantastic," Henry said with a flashy smile, then adjusted his eyepatch and folded his hands behind his head.

Lea pouted in response to the Arbiter's clear display of bravado. "Hush, you."

They sat at the dining table and exchange memories both fond and not so fond. Lea and Henry both treasured this moment. Neither knew how many more times they might get to share a candid conversation with each other. Laughter and more than one tear shed accompanied the pair late into the night. They snapped their heads from their steaming cups of coffee when they heard Mark stir in the bedroom.

"I think maybe you should go check on him," Henry said before taking a sip of the warm drink he held in his hand.

"I'll take a look at his eye and make sure he gets back to sleep quickly."

"I think I better go as well. I would like to get home and lie down before the sun comes up."

"You could stay a little longer. Just a little."

Henry was slow to respond; the severity of his words struck him before he spoke them. "We are going to have to say goodbye sometime, Lea."

"I know that. I just don't want to."

"Neither do I," Henry said. He shifted his gaze from Lea back to the door of the master bedroom as Mark's groans grew louder. "Go on and take care of that big baby of yours."

"I will," Lea said as she leaned over to hug the Arbiter. "Goodbye, go home, and get some sleep."

"I will. You get some sleep too," Henry said and made his way to the front door.

Lea watched him leave her home. She stood there feeling a little bit empty inside. When she heard Mark call out, she couldn't tell if the sounds coming from the bedroom were supposed to be words or not. Lea started for the door to the bedroom, then stopped herself. Smiling, she darted upstairs as fast as her feet would carry her, bounding up to the attic and pulling out a large chest. She fiddled with the clasp for a few moments, then opened the chest to reveal a red cloak, woefully short mini-skirt, and tastelessly low-cut matching top. *A promise is a promise*, she thought and put on the costume.

"I could have let it go if you weren't so sloppy. You stole from the company. My company. Not only did you steal, you got caught. And it wasn't by the people at the FBI or the Trade Commission. It was one of our own junior fucking accountants who found you out! You want to hold the reins of my legacy, you need to be better than that, Tony, and you're not. Don't. Just don't. You're not going to jail. I took care of it. I realize now that it's partly my fault I never taught you accountability, and I damn sure never made you pay your dues. Well this is a mistake I can fix. At the end of the fiscal year, we're going to announce that you have decided to step down as V.P. I'm currently leaning towards calling it a resignation, but I might be willing to call your abdication a temporary hiatus for personal reasons...if you can convince me."

Angelo Gastopie, President/CEO American Trust

Chapter 7

Mathew's good faith in Travis' report had long worn thin and now hung by a thread. The Jeep that he, Tony, and the overly excited Patriot from West Virginia rode in had passed the fence that had warranted so much excitement nearly twenty minutes ago. So far, the only thing Mathew had seen was more trees and more back-road twists and turns. Travis had promised the Congressman that his scouting expedition had uncovered a cache of weapons to make this entire trek into the far reaches of Maine's rural corners well worth it, but Mathew had yet to be removed from his position of doubt. The simple presence of a large chain-link fence in the woods was not sufficient means to instill much hope in Mr. Haze's heart.

"And you're absolutely positive that this was the road you and the others took?" the Congressman asked his Patriot subordinate.

"Yes. Yes, sir. We passed the fence just like we did before. We should be up on the house any second now," Travis said as he looked about for familiar landmarks. Tony drove the Jeep around all the winding bends in the dirt road. The path stretched on for another five minutes before the trees thinned out and signs of something other than wildlife became apparent.

"Really? That's it?" Mathew Haze pointed at the weathered, rustic, brown log cabin to which the lengthy dirt road had led him and his two companions. Travis had made large declarations of vast arms and armament. The Congressman could not believe that this quaint little hovel might contain such a massive arsenal. Mathew wondered if perhaps the West Virginia gas station cashier might need to have himself a tragic accident out here in the secluded wilds.

"I know, Congressman. We didn't think much of it when we first saw it, but that's not what the big deal is all about," Travis said excitedly. Tony parked the Jeep in front of the log cabin. "Look over there."

The Congressman looked off in the direction the Patriot pointed with his gloved finger. Travis seemed to indicate a structure that looked like a cross between a greenhouse and a small airplane hangar, situated just behind the cabin. "What is that?" Mathew asked Travis. For the first time since he had spoken to the younger man that morning, the Congressman did not have to attempt to conceal some measure of disdain in his voice. Mathew Haze was genuinely interested in what his follower had uncovered.

"Oh, sir, you are going to love this. I can't really describe it all. You're just going to have to see it for yourself," the West Virginia Patriot said enthusiastically. The man nearly giggled like a giddy adolescent girl as he climbed out of the Jeep.

Mathew Haze hated it when people answered his questions and somehow managed to avoid telling him what he wanted to know. He also hated walking into a situation and not knowing exactly what to expect. Both such instances were precisely the sort of things with which one would expect a professional politician to take issue. Mathew unbuckled his seatbelt, opened the Jeep door, and was about to prod Travis for more information when Tony finally interjected.

"You never said if this place was abandoned. Are you sure there's nobody here?" Tony said as he pulled his shotgun from the back of the Jeep and made sure it had a full load of shells. "I don't want to be surprised by anybody who might have a problem with us being here."

"It all looks like everyone has been long gone. There was a lot of dust everywhere, and it doesn't look like things have been touched in months, maybe even longer," Travis said as he slung his hunting rifle and motioned for the other two men to follow him towards the structure.

Mathew didn't like this feeling one bit. He followed the young Patriot anyway. The Congressman and his best friend had followed Travis this far; they both figured they might as well see it through. Mathew and Tony exchanged a familiar glance. Evidently, they were both thinking the same thing. If Travis delivered anything less than an earthshattering revelation, the young man would catch one epic beating before he died. Neither Tony nor Mathew liked it when their lessers took it upon themselves to waste the time of more important men.

In a small corner of Mathew's mind—and Tony's mind alike—they hoped Travis might present them with a legitimate reason to hurt him. It had been far too long since either man had been able to force their will on another by brute strength alone. In the time Mathew and Tony had shared in the fraternity house during their collage days, every party they had thrown afforded them the chance to use some unsuspecting underclassman to satisfy whatever urges they might have felt. Now, *after*, the two men could likely count such instances on one hand. They missed that feeling of dominance in a way words could not describe. For them, power was more like a compulsion.

Mathew noticed the name placard carved beside the front door. 'Smith', it read. *Of course it would be something so bland*, Mathew thought indignantly. The Congressman was not about to entrust his safety and wellbeing to some simple country bumpkin, so he called out, "Smith. Mr. Smith." There was no answer, only the autumn wind blowing through the trees. "Mr. Smith, my name is Mathew Haze. I'm a representative of the United Sates Congress. I would like to speak with you," Mathew shouted. The wind blew in the rustling trees, and the only sounds of any living creature that might have called this place home were a few sporadic birdcalls. "Mr. Smith?" Mathew Haze called one final time. There was nothing.

"Well, I guess that's it. Nobody home," Tony said. Mathew's confidante headed towards the structure nestled behind the cabin.

Mathew fell in step behind the two other men. He felt better having a couple guns at his front to take the first shots should any hidden assailants be waiting in ambush. The Congressman let his hand fall and rest comfortably on the butt of the nine-millimeter handgun holstered on his hip.

Mr. Haze still could not make out what the structure behind the cabin was exactly. As he drew closer, he saw it was made of some kind of camouflaged netting and fabric over sheet metal. After passing the cabin, he noticed that the thing was far larger than he'd expected. In fact, his initial call of an airplane hangar had not been off the mark at all. It looked like the sort of hangar in which single-passenger planes were stored. Mathew felt a sense of hope upon seeing the thing for what it was. The Congressman was highly intrigued by this Mr. Smith—whoever he might have been—and that he would have gone to such great lengths to keep this hangar concealed. It also struck him as peculiar that Mr. Smith would have kept an airplane hangar on his property but would not have bothered to fashion a proper runway; he clearly had the land for it.

"Here it is," Travis exclaimed as he parted some of the camouflage netting and opened up a small side door into the hangar. The West Virginia Patriot disappeared into the darkness of the hangar and left the Congressman and his right-hand man standing outside.

"What the fuck is going on?" Tony leaned over and quietly asked Mathew.

"The shit if I know. This is all kinds of fucked," the Congressman responded in kind.

"Uh, sir? Come on in, Congressman. I got the lights," Travis said from inside the building. After he finished speaking, there was a pop and a quick flash before light emanated from inside the sheet-metal structure.

Mathew nodded to Tony, and the Congressman's man took the

cue. Tony readied his shotgun and entered the hangar. Mathew was quickly behind him with his finger on the trigger of his weapon.

"Holy fuck!" Mathew said. The sight before him rendered him incapable of censoring himself in front of Travis.

"Fuck!" Tony said, obviously having much the same reaction.

Bathed in light from a jury-rigged series of work lights, jumper cables, extension cords, and car batteries was an impressive stockpile of weapons. Even the word impressive failed to completely illustrate just how grand the contents of the armory was. Handguns, shotguns, automatic rifles, and a plethora of ammunition were only the tip of the iceberg. Weapon racks filled the entirety of the hangar with top-end police and military-grade ordnance. High explosives, full head-to-toe body armor, large-ammo-capacity machine guns, anti-armor rocket launchers, long-range sniper rifles, night vision and thermal imagery targeting lenses—it went on and on. The place was filled with anything a professional soldier could ever dream of.

In the center of the space, a massive tarp covered something. Travis stood in front of it, wearing the haughtiest of smiles. As much as Mathew had wanted to wring the young Patriot's scrawny little neck for dragging him all the way into this terrible, backwoods hole, he could no longer bring himself to feel anger towards the man from West Virginia.

"I can't believe all this. Who was this guy?" Tony gasped as he wandered about the hangar and poked and picked at the assorted weapons.

"I don't know what this is all about, how, or why Mr. Smith decided to amass enough firepower to destroy a small country, and frankly, I don't care," Mathew said as he hefted a fifty-caliber armor-piercing sniper rifle in his hands. "This kind of thing is exactly what we needed for the cause. It's going to go a long way in seeing us properly restore democracy for our great nation." He was already rehearsing the lines he was preparing to serenade his followers with once he returned to the rest of the group. He saw that his sugared words had their desired effect. Travis was positively beaming at the Congressman's declaration.

"Sir, this is not all. Not all by far," Travis said as he pulled back the tarp and exposed what had been hidden underneath.

"That is a motherfucking tank!" Tony shouted, gazing at the steel-plated war machine. "Mr. Smith was one crazy son of a bitch. I can't even…" He trailed off, shaking his head in utter disbelief while he took in the spectacle of the massive weapon before him.

"I can't even," Mathew added, echoing Tony's disbelief. The Congressman's mind raced with all the potential implications that came with securing such a potent tool of negotiation.

"Congressman Haze?" Travis broke Mathew's introspective reprieve as he softly called the other man's name.

"Yes, Travis, what is it?" Mathew responded. The Congressman was all smiles and congratulations now that the weather had turned fair for him.

"Sir, there's more good news." Travis proudly placed his hands on his hips the way a child would in front of a parent they had just impressed.

"More good news. Travis, my boy, after a haul like this, I find that very hard to believe. Very hard, indeed," Mathew scoffed.

Travis licked his lips and clicked his tongue before he responded. "Congressman Haze, when we were out here this morning, we had a bigger look around." He paused to build some anticipation. "And there are at least eight more hangars scattered around the property just like this one."

"Just like this one." Mathew sputtered his words and nodded at the tank.

"Yes, sir, just like this one." Travis patted the tank like a hunter would pet their birddog who retrieved a fallen quarry.

"Mr. Smith, wherever you are, on behalf of the United States Congress, I would like to thank you for your service to your country," Mathew Haze called out at the top of his voice. *I guess being stuck out here in the middle of nowhere won't be so bad after all. It's the best place I can think of to figure out how to blow some shit up,* the Congressman thought gleefully.

"I've seen you do a mile in under seven. You can choke out men with height and weight on you. Your accuracy with any weapon we put in your hands is at least ninety percent up to twenty yards. You are the kind of Templar we all want to be. But for some reason, you still walk and talk like a kid who needs to sleep with a nightlight on. I don't get it, Leon. I've seen you in a challenge gone lethal. When the Arbiter says go, you are fearless, but when it's just us, you're just so... ah... timid. Can you tell me what you're afraid of?"

Sir James O'neil

Chapter 8

"Your hands are all wrong," said the Templar with a roll of his eyes and a shake of his head. "You're right-handed, so your right hand goes on top near the quillions, and your left goes on the bottom at the pommel." He moved Daniel's hands into the appropriate position on the longsword.

"But, Sir Leon, that don't make any sense. When you showed me last time, my right foot went in front. Now my right hand goes on top, but my right foot is farthest from my enemy..." Daniel said to Leon. The Templar squinted his eyes and tilted his head to the side disapprovingly. "Sorry. My opponent, my opponent," the younger man corrected.

"Yes, opponent. Those we fight are not always our enemies—" Sir Leon started.

"Most of the time they are just the guy on the other side," Daniel interrupted. He bobbed his head from side to side with each word. It was clear that this saying had been driven into the man time and time again.

"Well, it's good to see that you've remembered something since my last appointment here in the village," Leon said sarcastically. "Now, your top hand is where all your control and blade manipulation comes in. Your bottom hand is just a guide that follows your dominant hand. Your right foot is in back, because it's your dominant side, and that's where you generate all your power from. You'll be able to hit a lot harder like this, which is what longsword is all about."

Daniel winced and scratched his head. "But last time…"

"Last time I was showing you saber. That is a totally different beast from longsword. Saber is also hack and slash more than piercing, true, but at its core, the weapon is about finesse, distance, and speed. That's why your dominant hand and foot go in front with that kind of blade. You follow?" the Templar asked his pupil.

"I think so," Daniel said, uncertainty riddling his words. "But really, Sir Leon, why do Templars need to train with all these old-school weapons? You have plenty of guns and better gear at the ready."

Leon gave a heavy breath before responding. It was not out of frustration, though Daniel often tried the Templar's patience with his eager, puppy-dog ways. It was just a question that Sir Leon had been asked many times over the years. He never enjoyed having to repeat himself, even if it was to a different audience. "Templars need to be familiar with any kind of weapon which might be chosen for a challenge. Most challenges that get as far as combat end up being fought to the yield, or maybe first blood. It's rare that a challenge gets as far as a fight to the death," the Templar said softly and put his hands on his hips, reflecting on several of the bloodier conflicts where he had served as a personal champion. "That being said, guns are unpredictable. More often than not, when guns come into play, someone gets killed, whether that was the intent or not. People generally want to solve their differences without having to kill someone else, and a firearm doesn't suit that purpose very well." Leon tapped the flat of the blade Daniel was holding, then balled up his hands. "There are few things you can depend on better than three feet of steel or a quick left jab."

"Yes, I get it, Sir Leon," Daniel said as he met the Templar's eyes. "Have you ever had to fight a challenge to the death?"

Leon was legitimately surprised by the brazen lack of tact the younger man displayed with his question. It took the Templar a few moments to gather himself and keep calm. It was not easy for Leon to resist the urge to give Daniel a good tongue lashing. "I don't like that question. Please don't ever ask me that again."

Daniel was obviously thrown by the Templar's response. "Sorry, I didn't mean to upset you, Sir Leon."

"Just please don't bring it up," Leon said. A brief moment of silence passed, then he shook his head with a flash of realization. "And I've told you before, you don't have to call me sir. Leon is just fine."

"It just seems respectful to call you Sir Leon," Daniel quickly said. "You're a Templar Sebastian, after all."

"That's just what we call ourselves. We just needed a name. We're not anything special," Sir Leon said modestly.

"Not anything special. That's a laugh," came Lea's melodic voice from across the memorial park green. Leon saw the young woman exuberantly bound across the field towards him and Daniel. "You have always been a modest one, and it's never suited you well."

"Hello, Lea. It's fantastic to see you," Leon said as Lea approached him. He offered her a handshake, but she pushed it aside and firmly wrapped her arms around the Templar. Leon felt her slight and delicate frame pressed next to his. Tentatively, he put his arms around her. It was quite pleasant to feel her so close, but before Leon allowed any improper feeling to take root, he ended the embrace. It was not easy for him to push the woman away, but he forced himself to return to a suitable distance.

"You didn't think you were going to come anywhere near Northeastern Connecticut without me seeing you, did you?" Lea grinned.

"No, of course not. Would never even dream of it," Sir Leon said, trying not to smile as widely as he ended up smiling. Lea always made him smile more than he cared to.

"Hi, Lea," Daniel interjected, making his presence known. He seemed slightly awkward as an observer to the exchange between the Templar and Lea, apparently wanting to be part of the conversation.

"Hi, Danny," Lea said with a light inflection and sway of her hips. Her greeting garnered a very pleased look from the man Leon had been instructing.

"Sir Leon—" Lea started, and the Templar huffed, shook his head, and raised a silencing finger to Daniel at the mention of his title by another. "Do you think I could talk to you for a while?" Lea continued.

"Absolutely." Leon looked at Daniel and scratched his chin as he thought. Lea clearly wanted to speak with him without an audience, even though she had not said as much. "Um, Daniel, why don't you work on the five guard positions we went over with that longsword for a while. I'll check back on you in a bit, and you can show me what you remember."

"Okay," Daniel said glumly with all the enthusiasm of a child who had just watched their brand new balloon float off into the sky.

The Templar noted his student's crestfallen tone. "When I come back, if you have the guard positions down well enough, I'll show you a couple chokeholds and a few new submissions," Sir Leon said, knowing the offer of a reward like that was a sure way to restore Daniel's spirits.

"Oh, great. Thank you," Daniel said excitedly and returned to the series of defensive motions Leon had been teaching him.

Sir Leon and Lea walked away together. "Bye, Danny," Lea said with the same playfulness as her greeting.

"Bye, Lea," Daniel said with a wave of his hand and a slight stumble, as the distraction caused him to trip over his own feet while he practiced.

"That one doesn't leave you much time for yourself, does he?" Lea asked jokingly once they were out of Daniel's earshot.

"No, he doesn't," Leon stated. "I learned early on in my visits here that it's best if I give him a little attention and some titbit of knowledge to keep himself occupied while I stay in the village. Otherwise, I would spend all my time running and hiding from the guy whenever I visited."

"It must be nice to have someone who looks up to you that way."

"I won't lie, it can be flattering, but mostly it's exhausting. I'll say this. He might not be the best or brightest student I've ever instructed, but he is by far the most passionate."

"You sure he doesn't just like you for you?"

"I said it before. I'm nothing special."

"And I said it before. I disagree," Lea stated with admiration. "What do you think Danny would do if you actually squired him?"

Sir Leon's eyes grew to the size of grapefruits as the horrific fantasy of instructing Daniel full-time raced in his imagination. "I would really rather not think about that notion…and please, don't you go and plant that seed in his head."

"Oh, I would never," Lea said, placing a hand over her heart and innocently batting her eyes.

The Templar felt a growing unease with Lea. It was ironic, in a way. What made him uncomfortable with the woman was just precisely how comfortable he felt in her company. He decided to change the subject; perhaps there was some crisis that would offer distractions from more complicated feelings. "I would venture to think that there was more you wanted to speak about with me than my relationship with Daniel?"

"Yes. Yes there is," Lea said. Her eyes lost their playful glint and grew troubled. "You were at the Blinding. You know Mark is an Arbiter now."

"Yes, I saw it. I didn't want to announce myself beforehand and jeopardize Mark's concentration. I've seen a few Blindings. They're not easy to watch. I can't begin to think what it was like for you up there, let alone what it was like for Mark," Leon started. The Templar saw that his recounting of the ceremony caused Lea some distress. "I have no doubt whatsoever that Mark will be the best Arbiter this community could ask for," he added, quickly changing topic from the harsh events of yesterday to the promise of a hopeful tomorrow. His tactic had the desired effect, and he saw Lea breathe a little easier after his endorsement of Northeastern Connecticut's new Arbiter.

"I know he'll be great. It's just…Henry," Lea said, obviously finding difficulty in speaking the man's name.

"What about him? Is Henry ok?" Sir Leon asked.

"Oh, he's fine, but I'm sure you know that he's been called to serve in New Boston."

"Yes, I heard it from a couple people here and there that Henry would be headed north. In fact, I'd thought he would have already relocated by now."

"Ah, no, he's still here. At least for the very near future," Lea said. She sheepishly scratched behind her ear as she fought to overcome her obvious anxiety. "The thing is, Henry will be going to New Boston as soon as Mark is back on his feet and settled into his position as Arbiter here. Henry was…is…such a huge part of the community here, and so many people, including Mark, look up to him. We're going to feel his loss in a big way." She rambled on with a roundabout list of qualifiers and other preparatory statements.

Leon could plainly see that she struggled with finding a way to ask him something. "Lea, you can just come out and say it. It's okay," the Templar interrupted.

She stopped, seeming to ready herself, choosing her words as best she could before blurting them out. "It would be a greater help than any of us could say if you would stay in the village longer than your usual couple weeks."

Leon gave the matter only a moment's thought. He would happily stay in the village as long as he was needed. He knew that more people in Northeastern Connecticut than just Daniel viewed him as a role model, and he would make sure that Mark had a good sounding board for his early days as an Arbiter. Leon's only scruple with extending his stay would be the fact that he would be seeing much more of Lea. The Templar resolved to put whatever complicated feelings for the woman that arose during his visit to the side, like he always did. "I would be glad to spend some extra time here while Mark takes the reins," Leon said to the woman at his side.

"Oh, thank you so much. This is huge. Thank you."

"You're welcome," Sir Leon said happily. "Now, perhaps you might be able to help me out with something?"

"Anything you need. It's yours."

"I was hoping you could take a look at my tricycle."

"Is it the chain again?"

"Sure is."

"Lead the way," Lea said.

"They say it doesn't hurt, but that's a lie. Once we started running low on morphine, the ones who were in the final stages all went out loud and screaming. It was ugly. I don't want us to go like that. We're both symptomatic. We have three weeks at the most, and it's going to get real bad real fast. There is no cure. This is it for us. I'm not saying it has to be right now. We have a little good time left, but once it turns for the worst... I took some pills from the pharmacy on my way out today. We could...we could just go to sleep together. I love you too."

Dr. Morris Lambert

Chapter 9

M athew Haze was euphoric. He could not sing the benevolent Mr. Smith's praises loud enough. In one single day, the Congressman had secured enough arms and ammunition to equip every last one of his soldiers in the Patriot movement. Mathew Haze was ever the meticulous plotter and schemer. He had laid out a carefully detailed plan for moving throughout the northeast and collecting enough weapons, one score at a time, to slowly build the army he needed to confront any who might oppose his Patriots. He had begun to get upset, as the lack of progress his men made with their stockpiling efforts meant he might have to push back his move on Sebastian and his Templars. Now, thanks to Mr. Smith, the Patriots had more gear than they could have ever hoped to acquire in six months of salvaging, and Mathew Haze was ahead of schedule for the first time in a long time. It occurred to him that he was genuinely grateful to the mysterious Mr. Smith; he didn't remember the last time he felt grateful to another man.

The Congressman rooted through the hodgepodge junk of the log cabin, looking for any other treasures yet to be discovered when approaching footsteps caught his attention.

"You weren't kidding. There are enough weapons out there to build an army," Aaron said. "And the men are still finding more."

"Wonderful. What's the count now?" the Congressman asked his younger brother as he shut a pair of kitchen cabinets with nothing in them but dust and cans of baked beans.

"Eleven of those hangars so far. Tony and a couple dozen are still out and searching the grounds for more," Aaron stated happily. He traced a finger across the countertop and left a large streak in the dust settled there. "Looks like he's been gone for quite some time. I wonder why?"

"I'm not about to look a gift horse in the mouth, here. It's pretty evident that whoever Mr. Smith is—or was—he's not coming back. I won't see all this equipment go to waste, not when we can put it to very good use for the cause," Mathew stated in his best diplomatic voice. He always made sure that he spoke about the Patriots' cause with some exaggerated degree of deference. It helped reign in the true believers, like his brother. "Eleven, huh. That's good, very good. We can finally stand up to those Templar renegades."

"I can't tell you how good it'll feel to get some proper stars and stripes flying over our cities. I have to say, I was beginning to think this might have been the blow to knock our country down for good," Aaron stated with renewed hope.

These were the kind of moments Mathew relished—the chance to play the part of the supportive big brother without any real expenditure of effort or sacrifice on his behalf. "Oh, now this is not the red, white, and blue Aaron Haze I've come to know. You've never been a quitter. I can't believe for a second that you of all people would lose faith in the cause or in this great nation of ours," Mathew said as he patted his younger brother on the arm.

"Yeah, you're right about that. I never could stop until we saw democracy properly back in its place or I was dead," Aaron said after a brief moment's reflection.

"You and me both," Mathew said with a Cheshire-Cat grin. "And we have a lot of loyal men and women who will be with us when we take the fight to Sebastian and his treasonous followers."

Again, Aaron thought for a moment before speaking. "Mathew, do you think that maybe Sebastian, his Templars, the Arbiters, and all of them—do you think they might step down peacefully? They might want to see America returned to a real government as much as we do. It's possible, isn't it?"

Aaron's older brother gave a puzzled look, as the question caught him off guard. The initial shock on Matthew's face gave way to a scowl. True to his form as a politician, he hated when a question surprised him. "No, I don't. I'm sorry to say it, little brother, but if anybody really wanted to see a return to democracy, it would have happened by now. Those who swooped in and seized power *after* are not likely to just give it up." He tried to sound convincing, and he did a good job of it, but he realized that perhaps his brother was correct. He hoped Sebastian and his Templars wouldn't have the sense to play him at his own game. Mathew knew he had the firepower now to wage a war against any foe, but he was well aware that he didn't have the support base to beat a popular man like Sebastian in a general election. "I think any dream of a peaceful restoration is just that. A dream. We're headed for a fight, and it's a fight that real Patriots like you and me are going to win."

"It's just that maybe nobody else thought it could be like it was, like America was *before*. It's been hell since, and folks have just been trying to do the best they can. I don't think we have to start a war. People are not beyond talking out their differences and will agree to reason if we show them," Aaron rebutted.

Mathew hated arguing with his brother. He decided to use an approach that had served him well in the past. "Oh, Aaron, ever the optimist. It's one of the things I love about you. You know, I hope you're right and we can do this without blood being spilled. We'll just have to see," said the Congressman with all the skill and poise of a trained liar and sycophant.

"Yeah, I hope so," Aaron mused. He looked over the kitchen and its clear state of abandonment. "Have you looked anywhere else in here yet?"

"No, not yet. I was going to check the living room next. Do you want to help me search in there?" Mathew asked. It was one of the rare times that his question meant precisely what was asked and did not carry any ulterior motive.

"Sure. Tony and his guys have things well in hand outside. What are we looking for?" Aaron asked with a high inflection to illustrate his quandary.

"Honestly, I'm not totally sure what we're looking for. After seeing what was inside those hangars, I'd say we should be prepared for anything. I think that if there's anything worthwhile in here, we'll know it once we find it," Mathew said as he walked slowly with his brother into the living room at the back of the cabin. It was a spartan and nearly barren room, with some furniture for a small sitting area in front of an inviting-looking fireplace and one lone book shelf. The Congressman imagined that Mr. Smith probably ate his meals in here while warming himself in front of the hearth and enjoying an obscure piece of literature.

He had nearly given up on the room before fully setting foot inside, but in an instant, his interest was captured. A large throw rug had been folded over on itself, and underneath it looked to be what could have been a floor safe. The sturdy-looking metal door set into the living room floorboards.

"Well, I would venture to say that I think we found it," Aaron said with a good-natured chuckle.

"I would agree with that," Mathew said as he took a knee beside the metal door. Whatever was concealed within must have been quite large, because the door was of a good size. Mathew did find it odd that there was no combination lock, keypad, or any evident form of security device on the safe. There was just a simple deadbolt lever and handle to pull the door open. "Well, let's see what Mr. Smith was hiding," Mathew continued as he released the deadbolt and opened the safe door.

They had been wrong. There was nothing inside the safe; in fact, it was not a safe at all. Beyond the heavy six-inch-thick metal door was a ladder leading down into pitch-black darkness. The brothers exchanged curious looks; this demanded further investigation.

"I'll go first and make sure it's safe for you to come down," Aaron said as he pulled a heavy-duty LED light from its nylon pouch on his utility belt.

Mathew was so pleased. You couldn't buy loyalty like Aaron's. The Congressman's younger brother was a fine testament to the Patriots' movement. Mathew still needed to play the part of the fearless leader, so he had to make a show of things. "No, no. I'll go first. I couldn't let anything happen to you," he said, knowing that Aaron would immediately reassert his desire to be the first to descend into the unknown.

"This is not up for debate. You're the ranking government official and the best chance this country has. I'm going first," Aaron said with unwavering resolve.

"But…" Mathew started, deliberately slow with his speech so he could give his younger brother enough time to interrupt him.

"I said this is not up for debate!" Aaron cut his brother off as Mathew had expected.

Mathew stayed quit for a few moments to give the impression that he was under emotional distress for his brother's safety. "Just be careful down there and get out the second you even think something is wrong," Mathew said with the conviction a master thespian would envy. The Congressman pulled out a flashlight of his own and shined it down into the passageway while Aaron started the climb. There wasn't much to be seen down the hole, just what looked like a big slab of concreate at the bottom.

Mathew saw his brother reach the bottom of the shaft and briefly disappear out of sight. He felt a few fleeting moments of actual concern and admitted that he had not expected to feel such a way. "What can you see down there?" the Congressman called out. For a few fretful moments, his call went unanswered, and Mathew felt a slight pang of panic, wondering if something really had happened to Aaron.

"I can't see much. It's dark and very cluttered, but it looks like there's a lot of room down here." Aaron's voice came echoing back up the shaft.

Mathew felt some measure of relief now that he knew his brother was okay and that the area below the cabin seemed relatively safe. "You think this is some kind of bunker or fallout shelter?"

Again, Mathew was kept waiting for a response for several seconds. "Yeah, a bomb shelter or something like would be my guess as well. I think that—" Aaron's words halted abruptly.

"Aaron, what's going on down there? Are you okay?" Mathew called, alarmed by the sudden silence.

"Yeah, I'm fine. Everything's good. I just saw something. Wait one second," Aaron called back up to his brother.

Mathew was riveted with anticipation. He heard some scuffling and banging around drifting up from below. "What's happening, Aaron? Talk to me."

"I said wait a second." There was more shuffling, and then a loud pop and flash. "I got it," Aaron exclaimed as lights flickered on in the space below the cabin. "It looks like the same battery setup as the hangars outside… Mathew!" Aaron shouted.

"What's wrong?" the Congressman called down.

"I think I located Mr. Smith," Aaron said.

"You know, I always wanted to play Carnegie Hall. If you're a classical musician, that's the dream. You can ask any one of us, and they'll tell you the same. For a long time...after...after it stopped and things became like they are now, I didn't think about it. I was like everyone else. I just thought about getting to the next day. Then one morning, I woke up, and Diana was humming the opening movement to In the Hall of the Mountain King. *I tried to think of the last time I'd heard music before that day, and it wasn't easy. That made me wake up and realize that just because the world is different now, we don't have to give up on our dreams. I'll admit that I'd hoped to be playing for an audience of more the six the first time I made it to this hallowed stage, but I'm honored to be preforming for each of you. You got the best seats in the house, that's for sure. So thank you again. I can't fully put what I'm feeling right now into words, so I'm going to stop talking before I further embarrass myself. I'm going to start tonight's selection with Beethoven's* Moonlight Sonata in C-sharp minor."*

Tonya Emmerson

Chapter 10

The Labor Day Celebration was upon the village of Northeastern Connecticut. The memorial park green had been made into a bright and festive spectacle. A couple spare generators had been wheeled out in an effort to power the lights and sound system. Doctor Michael and Henry, along with a handful of other volunteers, had spent the vast majority of the morning stringing the gazebo with Christmas lights and other colorful decorations. Mark had attempted to lend assistance, but that had proven folly for him. Lea had asserted that he was to do nothing but enjoy the festivities. Mark was still recovering from the Blinding, and she refused to let him do anything that might jeopardize his healing process.

Lea had been able to gather a few helpers of her own, and she set about preparing a copious sandwich tray with other items for the buffet. Across from the green in the faded white building of the First Baptist Church, Lea and a pair of her sous-chefs prepared some trays of lasagna for the main course of the evening. Lea had spent a decent part of the previous night rooting through the village deep-freezer stockpile in an effort to locate the least freezer-burned packages of meat. For special occasions like this, the community liked to break out the good food.

Lea paced back and forth in the church's kitchen, constantly checking the tinfoil-covered trays inside the ovens. Every now and then, she pulled out one of the trays and peeled back the corner of the tinfoil to see if the cheese on top of the lasagna had turned that telltale, delectable golden-brown color.

She had just returned the lasagna back into the oven for the umpteenth time when she saw Sir Leon and his doting follower approaching her post by the oven. "Happy Labor Day, gentlemen," she said with a friendly smile and greeting waive of her hand.

"Hello, Lea," the Templar responded with a subtle waive of his own.

"Hi," Daniel said from his spot at Leon's side in a much louder and jubilant fashion than either of the others.

"Are there some carrots that require some personal championing against some oppressive onions, or did the two of you just feel like stopping by for a visit?" Lea joked as she playfully pushed Leon in the shoulder.

"If the vegetables in your kitchen have begun to issue challenges, you best get that sleepy man of yours in here to adjudicate before I decide if I'll stand for challenged or challenger," Leon said as he gently brushed aside Lea's hand from his shoulder. He didn't think of it before it happened, but his fingers touched hers. Even with traces of tomato sauce staining her hands, Leon was taken by how inhumanly soft and warm the feel of her skin was. The Templar struck that thought from his mind and forced a smile. "Has Mark done anything besides sleep since I've been here?" he asked with a chuckle.

"Only when I haven't been there to keep him in bed. He's been very anxious to rejoin the rest of the community, but he forgets he's still mending from the Blinding. He's a handful," Lea said with a well-mannered pout and roll of her eyes.

"I feel terrible that I haven't been able to give him proper congratulations on his appointment, let alone see him since I got into the village."

"I know. He'll be at the celebration tonight. That's for sure. I can only do so much to keep him in bed."

"I'm glad he'll be able to enjoy the festivities," Leon said with a nod. He looked away from her when their eyes met, fighting the call to get pulled in by her gaze every time he happened to glance at that enchanting feature of hers. Leon's diversion of his vision caused him to look at Daniel at his side, and he was suddenly reminded of the cause for his visit. "I thought that perhaps you might need some help here in the kitchen, and Daniel wanted to offer his services."

Lea batted her striking eyes and gave the Templar a tight-lipped smile. She could obviously see through his game, but apparently, she would no less delight in playing along. "Oh, did he? Daniel, that is very thoughtful, and thank you. There's some punch we need to get started on. Why don't you go to the pantry and get some cans of pineapple juice out and ready," Lea said to the Templar's companion as she pointed to the walk-in food storage area down the hallway.

"Okay. You're welcome, Lea," Daniel said as he started off for the pantry.

Once Daniel was behind the closed door, Lea spoke to Sir Leon. "I assume you're going to make your escape now."

"You know me too well. I hope it's not too horrible of me to pass him off on you for a while. I've just had my quota of Daniel for a while."

"I understand, and it's no trouble at all. What are you planning to do with yourself?"

"I actually have yet to say hello to Henry. I realize that today is as much about him as it is about Mark."

"That's very true. Henry would love to get a chance to talk with you for a bit. You just came from New Boston, so I think he would like it if you could give him a feel for the pulse of things up there."

"That was my thinking. I saw him and Michael stringing up lights and setting up some speakers for tonight. I think I'll go give them a hand."

"That would be good," Lea said, and the Templar walked out the door. "And you'd better save a dance for me tonight," she called after him. The Templar bit his lip and curled his hands into fists at the woman's last statement. Lea never realized how hard she made it for him.

Leon left the church, stepped outside, and walked across the street to the memorial park green. He saw Henry valiantly attempting to untangle a seriously twisted knot of twinkle lights. "Wasn't it you who told me to be smarter than the inanimate object?" Leon beamed as he walked up to the Arbiter.

"Leon, you wonderful ass, come here!" Henry said, throwing down the tangle of lights and giving the Templar a hug that lifted the man from his feet. "There are exceptions to every rule, and I think I've found the one here," Henry continued as he kicked the entwined length of wire with his boot.

"It's good to see you, Arbiter Rauls. It's been far too long since our paths have crossed," Leon said as they broke from the brotherly embrace and clasped hands in a more formal greeting.

"Likewise, Templar Scott. I'm sorry to say I don't remember the last time we saw each other," Henry said sheepishly.

"Oh, I'm sure you do. There's no way any person on earth could have forgotten that," Leon said as he rubbed his chin.

The Arbiter thought for a moment, then Leon saw the dawn of realization hit Henry like a falling tree. "Danny... in the firehouse..." Henry started.

"With the moose!" they both exclaimed in unison. The two men shared several minutes of pure, jubilant laughter as they recounted the memory of Leon's disciple tormented by an eleven-hundred-pound wild animal.

"Ah, I can't believe that wasn't the first thing I thought of when I saw you. I still don't know how Danny managed to get himself into that mess," Henry said, popping himself in the head with the palm of his hand. "Leon, I don't know how you put up with that boy, I really don't. You have a tolerance and patience I've never seen in another human being."

"To be fair, Daniel really doesn't give me much choice. I was able to buy myself some time and pawn him off on Lea for a while," Leon said with a glance over his shoulder at the church.

"She's a good one, that girl," Henry said. He then looked down at the plethora of lights strewn about before he continued. "We're starting to run short on time. The Labor Day party is only a few hours off. I know there's a lot we have to discuss. We're going to have to talk and work at the same time."

"That's how I prefer things," Leon said.

***

The time until the holiday celebration ticked down quickly. Lea and her group had conjured up a veritable feast for the village. Henry, Leon, and Doctor Michael had completed the decoration of the green amid the friendly banter of the Templar and Arbiter. As the sun set, the villagers of Northeastern Connecticut slowly trickled in to congregate. It was a warm and joyous time. The lights were bright and colorful. There was good food to be had, and plenty of it, plus music and dancing. All the people were in high spirits as they said goodbye to the summer and greeted the coming autumn.

The event was at its pinnacle when everything but the CD-player stopped to address the final arrival to the party. Mark stood at the edge of the park green, dressed in a warm grey sweater and some freshly ironed black slacks. He had fresh gauze over his left eye and a smile on his face in spite of the lingering ache from the Blinding.

Henry stood tall in the gazebo of the green and raised his red solo cup. "Ladies and gentlemen of Northeastern Connecticut, Arbiter Mark Fishers."

Henry's greeting was followed by a host of raised beverages, then a loud symphony of applause and cheers in honor of the new Arbiter. Lea ran to her man from her station behind the buffet and threw her arms around him, assaulting him with a flurry of kisses.

"I love you. I'm sick of lying in bed all day. Now please, let's have some food and enjoy the party," Mark said.

"You got it, Arbiter." Lea said the last word with a clear measure of admiration.

The festivities continued. The villagers paid Mark an unending string of complements. They were kind enough to allow him to intermittently come up for air and a bit of something hot to eat during the endless outpouring of support. Mark and Lea swayed closely to the music coming over the speakers when the Arbiter felt a hand tap him on the shoulder. He sighed, as he had begun to tire of the string of praise he'd been receiving, but when he turned around, the face that greeted him took him by surprise.

"Arbiter Fishers," said Sir Leon as he extended his hand.

"Leon," Mark said happily, taking the other man's hand.

"Congratulations. You'll be a real credit to the village."

"Thank you for the vote of confidence. I hope I can do everything that's needed."

"You'll be fine. I wanted to greet you properly. I'll let you get back to the party," the Templar said as he tried to leave.

"You're going so soon?" Mark asked with a puzzled look.

"Not at all. We'll have plenty of time to catch up," Leon said. The Templar gave Mark's dance partner a nod as he spoke next. "Your lady convinced me to take an extended stay here in the village. I'll be around for a good amount of time."

"Did she?" Mark said as he looked lovingly at Lea. She gave her man the most insincerely innocent look in her repertoire.

"I'll leave you two alone. Enjoy the party," Leon said.

"Oh, no. You don't get off that easy. Now you get over here and you give me that dance I was promised," Lea said to the Templar.

Leon looked to Mark anxiously. The Arbiter gave Leon a friendly smile. "Lea says you need to do something, you need to do it," Mark said as he stood to the side.

Lea leaned in and spoke quietly to Mark. "I think you should find Henry. You need to say goodbye. He'll be heading out in the morning."

"I know, I know. I..." Mark drifted off as he rubbed at the edge of the gauze over his left eye. "I love you, Lea."

"I love you back," she replied. They kissed once more before Mark went in search of his mentor to say farewell. Once he was gone, Lea looked at Leon. "Now, you get over here," she said with a grin.

Leon had a difficult time hiding his reluctance to dance with Lea. He was not good with lies, even tiny white ones, so he had no choice but to take Lea in his arms and dance with her. He hated how good it felt to hold her close.

"I knew it. I knew it. The CDC has covered up everything. It's all a lie. They know exactly what started the sickness. I have the proof that it was their fault. This is what they get for playing god. There are things that should not be meddled with. Now, here comes the government, trying to wipe out everyone who won't submit to their fascist regime. No, I won't let them get me like that. When they come for me, I'll be ready. I'll live through this thing. I have the provisions and firepower to survive anything these tyrants throw at me. I'll live. I'll live and tell everyone the truth. They should have believed me from the start. They won't call me crazy anymore once I show them."

Mr. J. Smith

Chapter 11

*G*od bless Mr. Smith, thought Mathew Haze while he rooted through the box of papers he had transported from the fallout shelter to his field tent. The Congressman had quickly deduced that Mr. Smith was totally insane. Or rather, had been totally insane. Mathew was in the midst of the third file box of papers containing Mr. Smith's manifesto, laughing quietly as he educated himself on subjects like the United States Government training wild animals to attack illegal immigrants; the United Nations' conspiracy to build a self-sufficient city for the world's richest one percent at the bottom of the Atlantic Ocean; the irrefutable proof of extra-terrestrial life controlling the minds of over half of all world leaders; and a bevy of other essays and thesis papers that put all tabloid magazines in the history of journalism to shame and disgrace.

Mathew had to give it to the old man—he was devout in his beliefs and not too far off the mark with his apocalypse theory. Although, in fairness, the Congressman had counted no less than a dozen distinctly different end-of-the-world scenarios vividly depicted in the ramblings of Mr. Smith. From what Mathew could glean from the papers, Mr. Smith had come from money but largely squandered the family fortune preparing for the end, grossly fattening the bank accounts of a couple Army Cornels and a handful of Sergeants-at-Arms during the first half of the 2030's. It was amazing how a few signatures here and there and adding or dropping an odd digit on an armory inventory manifest could easily make all sorts of items disappear into thin air. Mathew reflected on the fact that, had Mr. Smith not been so clearly out of his mind, he likely would have had a strong aptitude for political office.

It was ironic that Mr. Smith had been so obsessed with the impending fall of the word *before*. Here it was that the man had made every effort to survive through whatever might have come for him, and in the end, it had been his own paranoia that killed him. He had ended up amassing an armory that would have turned back most hostel invaders, but it was not men that had come for him; it had been the sickness. Mr. Smith had died just like the other seven billion victims of the affliction. His efforts were commendable, even if they had proved insufficient means of survival.

Mathew Haze found it so peculiar that in this world *after,* one of the people he liked the most had been a dead man. Mr. Smith had given the Congressman all the weapons he could have hoped for and more, he had provided the Patriots a figurehead that the Congressman could paint as a martyr to the cause, and most importantly, the crazy old fool had been dead long enough in the bottom of his fallout shelter that any stench of rot and decay had long since subsided. *God bless Mr. Smith*, Mathew thought again, delving into the writings produced by a deranged mind.

Tony entered the Congressman's field tent and drew Mathew's attention from the boxes of papers in which he'd been so engrossed. "Tony, did you know that a Pitbull's sense of smell can determine if a person is less than seventy-five percent Caucasian? And the reason that ships and planes cannot successfully negotiate the Bermuda Triangle is because they're destroyed by the United Nations secret, sub-aquatic city's missile defense system?" Mathew asked with as straight a face as he could manage. The Congressman was unable to hold his composure for more than a few seconds before he and Tony burst into mocking laughter.

"What the hell? Who is this guy?" Tony got out between fits of laughter.

"I don't know, and I really don't care. These papers are some of the most fun I've had in a long time. Mr. Smith was absolutely bat-shit out of his head. You have to read some of this crap," Mathew said as he managed to calm himself down enough to speak at regular intervals. "So what's the word outside? How are the men doing with the new gear?"

"It's been going real nice. We're done cataloguing and inventorying ten of the twelve hangars. We've set up a few shooting ranges and have started field-testing the weapons. So far, everything our guys have touched has been in proper working order. There's enough ammo up here that everybody should be able to shoot plenty and still have tons left over," Tony said as he took a seat in the folding chair next to the Congressman. "I got together a couple dozen of the guys I feel the best about with past military and law enforcement experience to start handing the specialty weapons like the heavy sniper rifles and explosives. They say it's all coming back to them pretty fast."

"That's great. And what about the tanks?" Mathew asked in eager anticipation.

"Well, none of our guys have ever driven one, but we do have a former reservist. Walter, I think his name is. He worked in the motor pool and did maintenance on transports and armored vehicles. So far, he's been doing a good job of figuring out the big bastards. He's good with the driving, and he can almost hit what he's aiming at with the big gun," Tony said with a satisfied nod. It drew a similar gesture from the Congressman.

"Good. Good. And how is this ammo fixed for the tanks?"

"Same as everything else. We have more than enough."

"Excellent. Once Walter has a feel for them one-hundred percent, I want you to pick twelve guys to train with him as primary drivers, then another twelve guys to train as backup drivers."

"Got it. Each tank will need a crew of three, though. One driver and two gunners."

"Okay. Once our guys can pilot their assigned vehicles well enough, have them pick a couple men to shoot for them," Mathew said. He poured himself a glass of brandy from the near-empty bottle on the table next to him. He offered the bottle to Tony, who took it and finished it off with a few sips. "How are we set for provisions and supplies?"

"We have about six weeks' worth on hand. We also might be able to come up with something more from in town after some scavenging."

"Perfect. I figure we can stay put here for about three weeks, maybe a month, and get accustomed to the new equipment before we take it on the road. It'll also give us a bit of time to plan the best approach to take towards the Templars' stronghold in Manhattan," said the Congressman while he finished the drink. "For tonight, though, I want to make a big deal about Mr. Smith, give him a hero's funeral, praise him as a friend of democracy. Ya know, give the men something nice to hear. I need to get to writing a speech for that."

"I completely understand," Tony said as he tugged on his right earlobe. "There's something else, though."

"What are you talking about?" Mathew asked. His tone was even enough that Tony couldn't decipher if the Congressman was intrigued or cross.

"Some of the men scavenging in town found a couple people in hiding. They have some pretty nice equipment and traces of plastic explosives on them. They're Templar Sebastian and look like they were the guys who took out the National Guard armory. Probably laying low and looking for a chance to slip out of town when we weren't looking," Tony said, bracing himself for one of the Congressman's trademark emotional outbursts.

"What the fuck? Why didn't you lead with that!"

"Saving the best for last. Anyway, it's not like they're going anywhere. How do you want to handle it?"

"I assume we have them restrained and in custody."

"Yes, we do."

Mathew Haze thought for a moment and considered the numerous options at his disposal before speaking. "Have them gagged and brought up to the camp. I want to put on a display for of the guys."

"You got it." Tony got up to leave but turned back to Mathew first. "Oh, the Templars did kill three of ours while we were taking them in."

"Whatever. We didn't lose anyone that mattered, did we?"

"No. Nobody worthwhile."

***

"And here they are, the enemies of democracy and cowardly terrorists. The so-called Templar Sebastian!" the Congressman shouted as he pointed an accusatory finger at the two men bound and gagged on their knees. Hostile shouts and insults were flung from the circle of Patriots surrounding the Congressman and his captives as he laid a verbal assault on the Templars. "They are the worst kind of terrorists. Those who commit treason against this great nation of America. They would see this country of ours overthrown and install their own dictatorship in place of the greatest form of government the world has ever known," Mathew continued. It was an ugly display for those who observed the spectacle with an objective eye. Sadly, there were no such spectators to be found. The Congressman had whipped up his mob of followers into a violent frenzy with all the skill of a master cult of personality. Those who listened to Mathew Haze had either high praise and adulation to shout for the man and the country he espoused, or the vilest curses and names to spit at the branded enemies of freedom.

Only three voices fell silent during the horrendous event. Two belonged to the Templars, who were unable to speak. One of the men had defiant eyes beneath the layers of dirt and grime turning his sandy-blond hair a nasty brown. His gag was soaked through with spit and sweat, as he had tired himself while issuing a long string of muffled objections to the Congressman's lies. The second Templar had fearful eyes and was equally as filthy as his brother-in-arms. His voice would have been silent even if his mouth had been restrained from speech. The third man with neither praise nor vitriol to dispense was the Congressman's younger brother, Aaron. The Patriot was eerily silent and wore a face of chiseled stone, though if anyone had looked close enough, they would have seen a measure of shame, guilt, and even protest within Aaron's eyes.

"These dogs—under orders from public enemy number one, Sebastian Clarke—have taken violent paramilitary action against the armed forces of our beloved nation. That's textbook treason. These vicious men have made no claim to hide what they have done. They even considered it an act of pride." Mathew spoke loudly and with heavy bravado. This was the kind of debate the Congressman favored—one where his opponents were unable to speak in their own defense or offer rebuttal. Mathew found grave difficulty in playing the part of the morally wounded leader and keeping himself from beaming with joy. "It makes me ill to think that I—that we all—share the proud mantle of Americans with such insidious men."

Mathew paused for a few moments to allow his words of hatred to simmer and boil within the hearts of those who listened. All eyes were fixed on the Congressman, the shining beacon of freedom, and the American way he represented among the Patriots. Nobody noticed Aaron leaving the gathering. The Congressman's younger brother often went unnoticed next to the eloquent behemoth that was Mathew. Aaron had had his fill of wrathful speech and knew what his brother intended to do. The Patriot had no stomach for what was coming next and did not care to be a witness even if he knew that refraining from objecting made him complicit.

"Treason is a crime punishable by death. We the people must call for the greatest punishment for those who would rise up against this country. Traitors to America must die a traitor's death," Mathew roared. His words were met with a thunderous applause from the surrounding Patriots. He bathed in the glory showered upon him by his followers, holding onto that moment for as long as he could before moving on to the next part of his act. "But…" The Congressman raised a hand to silence the mob's rage. "But we must remember that our country is built on values like mercy and compassion just as much as freedom and liberty. We cannot forget these bedrock principles of this great nation, lest we become like those who would seek to destroy it." Mathew paused amid awed murmurs from the gathered crowd. "We are a people of law and order. Justice tempered by mercy is the essence of law. So it will be like this. One of these men shall receive a piece of mercy they do not deserve for their crimes against this nation. We Patriots will show that we can be more generous to our enemies than they are to us. That is what makes us a great people. These treasonous men praise blood sport and sanctioned murder without deliberation by a party of a man's peers. For tonight, I will demonstrate the folly of the Templars' values by a practical exhibition."

Tony came through the crowd of Patriots, carrying a pair of hunting knives. The Congressman's most trusted aide took his place at Mathew's right hand and drew the knives from their sheaths, brandishing them for all to see. Both Templars lowered their heads in premature grief when the realization of what was about to happen dawned on them.

"My fellow Americans, Patriots, one of these traitors will live and be free to go. The other will die as an example of what fate lies in store for any who oppose the rightful restoration of democracy," Mathew said in a loud, booming voice. The Congressman then pointed a finger in turn at each of the Templars before he continued his proclamation. "You both follow a code that says it is okay to kill each other as long as it is revered and ritualized. Now you are going to put that belief to the test and fight each other until one of you is dead. The winner will be free to send a message to that bastard Sebastian Clarke that his days usurping this country are numbered!"

The crowd erupted in thunderous applause after Mathew Haze finished speaking. Tony approached the most spirited Templar of the pair first, then spoke quietly into the man's ear. "We hear anything harsher than, 'Thank you, sir, may I have another?' from you and we shoot you both in the head. Nod if you understand me." The man stared a burning look of hate at Tony before nodding in confirmation. Tony removed the Templar's gag and cut his bonds before tossing one of the hunting knives on the ground next to the prisoner. He repeated this exchange with the other Templar, who also reluctantly agreed to check his words. The Congressman's aide returned to his post at the Patriot leader's side.

Both Templars stood and transferred their attention between themselves, the weapons they had been given, and the man who had commanded them to fight to the death. The Templar with defiant eyes spoke first. "If we don't want to fight each other, I suppose you kill us both?"

Without missing a beat, the Congressman retorted, "You don't want to accept the terms of clemency? I can respect men who would rather die than abandon their principals, even if their values are deplorable," Mathew said with a noxious smirk. "But you are Templar Sebastian. Killing is what you do, is it not?" he continued in a mocking tone. "I should think you both would have leapt at—"

"Whoever lives, you let them go free. You promise?" interjected the Templar with the silent disposition and sorrowful eyes.

"Yes. On my word as a Patriot, an elected official of the United States Congress, and my honor as an American. Whoever wins this fight will be granted mercy in spite of their treason. They will be free to go," Mathew Haze said, placing a hand over his heart.

The Templar who had requested this promise looked at his brother-in-arms before he spoke next. "Sir Kenneth, I'm sorry," the man said. He then took the hunting knife he'd been given and rammed it straight through the side of his own neck. With a final tug, he ripped the blade through the front of his throat and fell to the ground, where he bled out in moments.

"David! No!" the surviving Templar screamed in an animalistic rage. In a breath, three Patriots had restrained the man and bore him to the ground.

There were gasps of shock and horror as the onlookers processed what had just happened over the span of the last few seconds. As soon as the Templar had opened up his own jugular, the Congressman had spun his back to the crowd. He could not let anyone see his natural reaction to the man's sacrifice, which was to laugh. Regaining his character, he set his face into one of disbelief and revolt before he turned back to address his followers. "You see? You see? This kind of madness and barbarism is exactly what we're fighting against. America!"

The crowd echoed the chant, "America!" over and over. The word drowned out the grief-stricken sobs of Sir Kenneth as he looked at Sir David's lifeless body.

***

The following morning was chilly. The Jeep sped down the road to the town line shortly after the sun had come up. Tony and Mathew laughed and joked the way they had since their college days. Sir Kenneth lay motionless in the back seat. His normally piercing and resolute eyes were now cloudy and broken with anguish.

The Templar had resolved to deliver the news of Sir David's heroism and sacrifice to Sebastian himself. Sir Kenneth contemplated his options. He figured that he could likely find a working car by nightfall at the latest, and with any luck, he could be in Manhattan within two days' time. He would also need to find a functional CB radio so he could broadcast a warning to the other Templars and initiate a rally against the so-called Patriots.

Sir Kenneth's plotting was cut short when the Jeep came to a sudden stop. Tony got out of the driver's seat and went to the back, where he unlocked the handcuffs binding Sir Kenneth to the Jeep's back door. The Templar got out of the Jeep while Mathew held a gun on him. Tony went to the back of the vehicle and removed a backpack, then threw it at the Templar, who caught it.

Sir Kenneth looked inside the bundle the Patriot had just tossed him. It contained some bottled water, some mixed nuts and snack food, a flashlight, compass, and some other survival gear. "You're really going to let me go free?" the Templar said.

"I'm a man of my word. I said whoever won the fight would walk away unharmed," Mathew said with a pleasant expression plastered on his face.

"You know I'm going to warn everyone about you. There will be retaliation for this. You get that, right?" Sir Kenneth said angrily. Mathew and Tony just looked and grinned at the Templar. Sir Kenneth turned and began to walk away.

"It just sucks for you that that bullshit that happened back there couldn't really be called a fight, now could it?" said Mathew. The Templar turned just in time to see the muzzle flash of the men's guns.

***

Matthew and Tony stood over the motionless heap that had been Sir Kenneth. They exchanged maniacal glances before laughing and emptying the rest of their clips into the Templar's dead body at their feet.

"Well, I say that about does it for adjudication. It's pretty clear that you both are good with the terms. Tomorrow at midday, first guy to pin the other's arm to the table best two out of three times wins the challenge. Jack, if you get it, you get to keep your moonshine still intact, drink as much as you like, and Bill moves out of the house. Bill, you win, Jack quits drinking cold turkey and scraps the shine still. Oh, there's one last little thing. Jack, let me introduce you to a good friend of mine. This is Sir Gregory, but most people call him Tree. He will be Bill's personal champion in the challenge tomorrow. Jack, I'm not supposed to do this at this stage, but I do have some discretion with the law. You want to reconsider yielding now? Yeah, that's what I thought. Tree and I will do you a favor and help you break down the still tonight."

Arbiter Paul Harrison

Chapter 12

"State your name," Henry said.

"My name is Jonathan Tiler," said the man. He was angry, that was plain to see, though the man had calmed himself down considerably since his earlier tirade.

"Declare your challenge to your intended opponent," Henry said somberly.

"I challenge Ryan Frankin," said Jonathan. He spoke the other man's name through tightly clenched teeth.

"State the cause for your challenge," said the Arbiter.

Henry was getting used to saying that phrase since his move to New Boston. He spent more days out of the week adjudicating than not since leaving the peaceful village of Northeastern Connecticut. In the

short time he had resided in New Boston, he had overseen more challenges than he had in the rest of the time he had served as an Arbiter.
*Cities are toxic. People are not meant to live one top of each other. This
is what happens*, Henry thought. He knew full well that New Boston was
hardly a real city like its predecessor *before,* but still, it was dense with
a diverse population.

"He went behind my back and had an affair with my wife," Jonathan seethed. It was evident that he wanted to say far more, but Henry
had managed to impress upon the offended man the import of decorum
and the need to be tactful during adjudication. In fact, the Arbiter had
refused to even speak to Jonathan until he was able to get out a sentence
that didn't contain a slew of vulgarity.

"And what measure do you seek to find peace?" Henry said, loud
enough for all to hear.

"I want that bastard gone. I never want to see his face in New Boston again," Jonathan yelled as he pointed a finger at Ryan.

Judgmental murmurs and whispers arose from the crowd as those
who had assembled to witness the challenge reacted to Jonathan's accu-
sation. Henry's good eye fell to the frightened man who stood in the
doorway of his home. Beyond Ryan, the Arbiter could see traces of
movement inside his house. It must have been Jonathan's wife hiding
form the proverbial stones to be cast by her neighbors.

"Ryan Frankin, you stand challenged by Jonathan Tiler. How do
you answer this challenge?" Henry recited the practiced words.

Ryan was slow to respond. It was unclear what was most unnerv-
ing to him—whether it was the fact that he had been caught in the act,
the level of anger Jonathan displayed, or the sizable gathering of onlookers that had shown up on his doorstep. For several moments, it looked
as though Ryan might have up and bolted. He wouldn't have been the
first man to run from a challenge. In any event, the accused finally sum-
moned the resolve to speak. "I will not leave New Boston. This is my
home," Ryan said, gaining confidence as he finished speaking. Even
louder words passed between those who had come out to see the happening.

Henry gave a slight look around and considered how this drama might play out before speaking next. "The challenge will move on to adjudication. I will set time for adjudication for tomorrow at ten o'clock in the morning. Ryan Franklin, as the challenged, is this acceptable to you?" the Arbiter asked the man who remained frozen in the doorway of his home.

"Yes, this is acceptable," Ryan said in a guilty voice.

"Jonathan Tiler, as the challenger, is this time for adjudication acceptable to you?" Henry asked, though he already knew the man's answer and at the very least how the next few seconds would progress.

"No, tomorrow morning is not acceptable to me," Jonathan said angrily. It was a predictable response from a man who had just found out he'd been cuckolded. While Henry had never adjudicated a challenge like this, he knew they were more common in number than the serious variety. The offended party in situations like this nearly always wanted blood and always wanted it fast.

"Jonathan Tiler, you have declined the proposed time and date of adjudication. State a time and date to adjudicate this challenge that is satisfactory," Henry said. It was a formality to speak the words. The Arbiter knew that this was going to be a quickly-fought challenge. Henry contemplated exerting his discretion and citing that Jonathan's emotional state prohibited him from a mindset engendering mature and rational thought. He decided against such a course of action. As much as the Arbiter wished to see cooler heads prevail, he could not justify a perversion of the law. Jonathan might have been furious, but he was a long way from insane or mentally unsound.

"I wish to adjudicate terms immediately," Jonathan blurted.

Henry shifted his eye to the challenged before he spoke next. "Ryan Franklin, do you have sound cause to delay the adjudication of this challenge?" He hoped that perhaps Ryan could think of something to buy some time and allow Jonathan's temper to calm.

Ryan shifted his weight form foot to foot and wiped his face with his hands before anxiously running his fingers through his hair. Henry could tell the man was racing to find something that might serve as a stay of execution. "I would—" Ryan started, then abruptly cut his words short. "I can't. It would be hard to…I…" The man struggled with his words as his mind whirred for a source of escape that was nowhere to be found. Finally, Ryan spoke the answer they all knew he would speak. "No, I have no sound cause to delay adjudication."

"The challenged and challenger have agreed to terms for an adjudication. It shall begin immediately." Henry looked about the area and longed to remove this fiasco from public exhibition. The Arbiter knew that Jonathan coming face to face with his adulterous wife would likely be volatile, but Ryan's home seemed like the best avenue for privacy. Henry hoped that perhaps someone other than Jonathan's wife skulked inside. "Ryan, are you amenable to talking indoors?"

Ryan's eyes widened fearfully. He shot a glance back inside, then exchanged some words back and forth with the person lurking within his home before returning his attention to the Arbiter. "Yes, come in, but only if he stays calm," Ryan said as he gestured to Jonathan.

"You think you can keep it together?" Henry asked the emotionally wounded man.

"Yeah, I'm good," Jonathan growled.

The Arbiter looked around at the crowd once more and noted the trio of Templar Sebastian in attendance. Henry couldn't fathom either of the men involved in this challenge requesting a personal champion, and it was even more unlikely that any Templar would agree to represent one of the parties. It was virtually unheard of for a Templar to become entangled in any sort of domestic or personal tiff. The three men were the first of the gathered crowd to leave, and others quickly followed the Templars' lead. "Let's go inside," Henry said to Jonathan. The two men made for the doorway of Ryan's home.

Henry made sure to keep himself positioned between the challenged and challenger. The Arbiter kept himself on high alert in the event that Jonathan abandoned any measure of reason or civility and charged the man who had insulted his honor. Henry's sense of danger grew when he saw the woman standing inside Ryan's home, and that sense grew even more when he saw Jonathan's reaction to her presence. She was unmistakably Jonathan's wife.

"Stacy…" Jonathan started, then faded while he shook his head and balled his hands into fists.

Henry fixed his eye on the challenger and raised a hand to signal restraint. "Maybe it's best if you leave us be," he said to the woman.

"I'm not going anywhere, and I'm certainly not going to listen when someone tells me to leave my own home," Stacy shot back bitterly.

"This is not your home...you...you..."

"Keep it level, Jonathan!" Henry spoke over the man before his heated emotions reignited into a full-on blaze. "Fine, you may stay, but the second you interfere with my ability to adjudicate this challenge, you're gone. I don't care if you live here or not, you understand me?" Henry told Stacy firmly. She did not speak, but she nodded in understanding. "Take a seat," Henry said to both men. Challenged and challenger found chairs on either end of Ryan's living room. Stacy took a seat next to her lover. Henry continued to stand and hold his post between the two men. "Either of you may request a witness to observe the adjudication process at this time," he said, but both men remained silent and shook their heads. "We will now begin adjudication and set terms of the challenge. Jonathan, do you wish to speak before we begin?" Henry asked.

Jonathan looked as though he contemplated some kind of statement, but he answered with a simple, "No."

"Ryan, do you have anything you wish to say before we begin adjudication?" Henry asked, looking at the man sitting nervously at the other end of the room.

"No," Ryan said quickly.

Henry took a brief moment to recall the formal words because he was still getting used to speaking them. "I, Arbiter Henry Rauls, herby commence adjudication of the challenged issued by Jonathan Tiler to Ryan Frankin. Ryan Frankin, as the challenged party, you have the first option to select principle terms of the weapons that will be used in the challenge or the time and location that the challenge will take place. What say you?" Henry said it all in one breath. He looked at the nervous man who had taken Stacy's hand in his and wondered what might be going through this man's head at the moment. He did not have the look of a fighter about him, but he did have a small physical advantage in height and weight over Jonathan.

Ryan took very little time to respond. The speed of his decision actually surprised the Arbiter. "I will choose weapons, and I say unarmed."

It made sense to Henry. It was unlikely that Ryan would have been eager to put any lethal weapon into the hands of the man whose wife he was bedding. "It is so noted that this will be challenge by combat, and combat will be unarmed. Ryan, you may seek to establish specific parameters of arms at this time," said Henry.

It took Ryan a few moments to speak, but once he did, Henry heard a note of confidence in his voice. "I want this challenge to be fought under classic boxing rules. Gloves and headgear."

"Oh, hell no! I want to be able to hurt this—" Jonathan was cut off by a wave of Henry's arm and a sharp glare of his eye.

"Jonathan, you may seek to negotiate terms of arms at this time," Henry said.

"I want bare knuckle and no holds barred," said Jonathan.

Henry shifted his eye to Ryan, who shook his head. It was not too hard for Henry to postulate a proper middle ground to the challenge. The men were not so far at odds. "Requests are noted. Will either party submit to the proposed request of their opponent?" Henry said. Unsurprisingly, neither man indicted acquiescence. "Very well. Then allow me to propose the following parameters. Traditional professional mixed martial arts rules…" Henry said. He noted a savage glint in Jonathan's eyes at the prospect and consequently a defeated fall in Ryan's gaze, so he quickly followed up the brief pause in his words. "And seven-ounce gloves," the Arbiter finished. He noted that small caveat evoked the smallest tilt of the head from Ryan. "Ryan, are these acceptable terms of arms to you?"

"Yes, they are," Ryan answered.

"Jonathan, are these acceptable terms of arms to you?" Henry asked the challenger.

"Yes," Jonathan responded.

"Very well. The terms of arms have been mutually agreed upon. Now, Jonathan, you may dictate the time and location of the challenge," Henry said as he looked back to the man who had started this endeavor.

Jonathan sat impatiently in his chair while his knee rapidly bounced up and down. "I want this done today and right here in town," said the Challenger. This declaration came as a shock to no one.

"Ryan, do you understand the terms of time and location?" Henry asked the challenged. Ryan nodded. "Next is the matter of boundaries and starting position," said the Arbiter. "Jonathan, as the party responsible for determining time and location of the challenge, you may propose initial terms of boundaries and starting position for adjudication."

Jonathan stared across the room at Ryan and Stacy. Silence hung for a moment as he judged the pair. "A suitable ring, cage, or other confined space in town, and we start at natural corners," Jonathan said.

"Is this agreeable to you, Ryan?" Henry asked.

"It is, provided we can agree on the specific site before the challenge begins," Ryan said as he crossed his arms.

Henry looked to Jonathan, who nodded in agreement. "With that settled, the final matter is degree of severity and terms of victory. Ryan, as the party responsible for selection of weapons, you may lay starting terms for adjudication," Henry said.

"Fight to the knock-down," Ryan said with an air of hopefulness.

Henry looked to Jonathan, who had a displeased look cast on his face. The Arbiter gestured to the challenger to state his rebuttal. "Fight to bloodshed," Johnathan stated.

"Ryan, is this agreeable to you?" Henry asked.

Ryan considered for a moment before speaking next. "We fight to the yield," he said with a cool element in his words.

"Jonathan, as challenger, you cannot call for greater severity than combat to the yield. Gentlemen, the terms of this challenge are set. Ryan Frankin, should you fail to answer this challenge, you must vacate the city of New Boston, never to return. Do you understand these terms?" Henry gazed at the challenged and his newfound love interest.

"I do," said Ryan.

"Jonathan, do you understand the terms of this challenge?" Henry asked the challenger.

"I do," Johnathan said.

"Terms are set. Follow me, and we'll secure the needed items for the challenge and have you both checked out by the doctor and cleared to proceed," Henry said. Everyone in the room stood and followed the Arbiter out the front door of Ryan's home. Henry let out a long, depressing sigh as he set foot into the streets of New Boston.

"I loved this city. You know, I always thought of her like a daughter. I think that's why you all sent me to the Mayor's office for over a decade. I was like a father to every one of my constituents, and that is not rhetoric. You all know it's true. I knew I would never climb any higher than the Mayor's office, because I was one of those fools who got into politics for all the right reasons. I was okay with only ever presiding over Boston, it is...it was my home. I won't ever leave her, and I hope that none of you do either. But after what's happened—the sickness—we're a different people, and she's a different city. She's a New Boston."

Mayor David Tanner

Chapter 13

It had been a long but productive month. Mathew was thoroughly satisfied with the progress his Patriots had made with the new weapons. All his capable, fighting men demonstrated some measure of proficiency with at least one the tools of warcraft in the arsenal. Soon, it would be time to leave. Training was nearly finished, stores of food and consumables would soon need to be replenished, winter was fast approaching, and the Congressmen did not want to get stranded in Maine by snowfall. But these were not the greatest things prompting Mathew's desire to move on.

He knew that the pair of Templars would be missed if they hadn't been already. It was unlikely that Sebastian Clarke and his higher-ups would have any idea of exactly what had happened to their men. Still, when it was discovered that the duo were unreachable, that could very well put the rest of the Templar Sebastian on guard. The Congressman did not care to encounter that situation.

Mathew and his Patriots had been lurking beneath notice for some time; most who might have encountered them would have taken them for a nondescript band of raiders. The Congressman wanted to keep the information reaching the Templars' war room about his Patriots to a bare minimum. Mathew wanted to hold onto the element of surprise as long as possible. Once that resource was spent, it could never be reclaimed.

Mathew looked at the empty glass in his hand, then to the empty bottle on the table beside him. The brandy he had been sipping was long gone, and the ice cubes in the glass had almost melted completely. His took a sip of melted ice and was wholly unsatisfied with the experience. *Three more days*, Mathew though—the amount of time it would take to break camp. When he met with Tony later than afternoon, he would get the latest report of the men's progress and give the order to be ready to head out. Mathew returned his focus to the maps on the table, but there was little to be done with them. The Congressman had already gotten with his ranking men and planned the best path to take once the Patriots began the move south.

Waiting was the worst. Mathew had never been a patient man, but at this point, all he could do was bide his time until the convoy was ready to leave this town. He scratched his head and wondered about making a trip into the village. There had to be at least one bottle of booze he could scrounge up to pass the time. At this point, he would take whatever swill he could get his hands on. He didn't care about the taste or quality; he just needed to get foggy. The thought of spending the next three days in the middle of nowhere, Maine, dead-sober made Mathew cringe.

While he thought of where he might go to locate some libations, the Congressman's fingers scratched his chin, and the feel of stubble caught him off guard. His last disposable razor had given up on him the day before last. He normally kept himself clean-shaven and hated the feeling of being scruffy and unkempt. Mathew added a new set of razors to his mental shopping list.

The main tent flap opened, and Aaron stepped inside. The Congressman's younger brother wore an unhappy look, and Aaron's sudden and unexpected arrival put Mathew on edge. He also quickly realized that he had scarcely exchanged more than a handful of words with Aaron over the last month. Whatever was about to happen next, he knew he would not like it.

Aaron stood in the field tent silently. Mathew attempted to gauge his brother's metal state. The Congressman could not tell if Aaron was confused and lost for words or if he was afraid to say what was on his mind. Either way, Mathew found the silence between them to be more than he cared to endure, so he ended it. "Hello, Aaron. Why don't you come sit down? Can I get you a drink? Sorry to say, but at this point, all I have to offer is water."

"No thanks, I'm good," Aaron said, raising a palm to stop his brother from getting up. "We need to… I need to talk to you." He broke into nervous pacing back and forth. Aaron had developed the habit in his preteen years, and it had never left him.

The pacing signaled to Mathew that this was definitely going to be a conversation he could have done without. "Sure. Of course, I can make time for my little brother," Mathew said. He didn't add the caveat that the time he would make would only last as long as the fading buzz of the brandy he had finished off earlier. "Now tell me, what is it you have on your mind? Something seems to be troubling you."

Aaron's pacing stopped, and he looked at his brother. "The two men, the Templars—" He looked down and rubbed his hands together, as if that motion would somehow conjure the will to continue. "They should have had a trial," he finished in a flurry.

Mathew had to forcibly stop his hand from smacking himself in the head after hearing the statement. The Congressman had learned to expect his brother's idealism, but sometimes Aaron could still shock him with his naivety. "What? Um, a trial. Aaron, a trial," Mathew stammered. He hated how undignified and unrefined his response had been. The fact that only his brother had heard his uncharacteristic lack of eloquence helped to take the sting out of it. Mathew hated it when he was hard pressed to find the right words.

"Yes, a trial. They broke the law and should have answered to a jury of their peers…" Aaron started, pausing with a frown. "Not forced to do whatever you call that thing that happened."

"Aaron, those men were guilty of treason, no question."

"I'm not saying they weren't. Honestly, I don't think there was any testimony or evidence on the face of the planet that could have exonerated them."

"Then what's the big fuss about a trial?"

"*The big fuss*," Aaron said with anger and disdain for his brother's trivialization. "Just because a verdict is all but assured doesn't mean we get to deny people due process. Hell, they probably would have even pled guilty and been proud to do so, but they still get presumption of innocence."

Mathew wanted to punch his little brother in the face and go find something hard to drink, but he wouldn't—he couldn't. Right now, he needed to play the part of a caring older brother. "Okay, I hear you. I understand your point, but I had a point that needed to be made as well."

"Oh, and what was that?"

"I put every Patriot face to face with the doctrine of the perversity that has taken the place of Democracy. People need to see what we're fighting against."

"Maybe, maybe. Just so long as we don't forget what we're fighting for."

"You really think there's a man or woman in this camp who needs to be reminded of our cause?"

Aaron's fire had died down some, and he was calmer now that he'd said what he had come to say. "No, I don't. These are good and principled people here. They make me proud to call myself an American."

"Ain't that the truth. Look, I made my point, and I hear you. We will not forget what it is to be an American," Mathew said with one of his well-rehearsed smiles. "I promise you." He stood and patted his brother on the shoulder.

"I just didn't like how that all played out is all. It just… it just wasn't right." Aaron looked down, bit his lip, and rubbed his neck in an embarrassed manor.

Mathew was so happy at Arron's last statement. His younger brother had finally given him the avenue needed to finish this inane conversation. "You're absolutely correct, it wasn't right. It wasn't right at all, and our good people needed to see it. It had to be more than some story we told them or some faceless propaganda. They needed to *see* how wrong this thing that took over our country is. Now it's certain that we're in the right."

Aaron gave a long sigh of acceptance. "You're right. I get it. I just needed to say what I felt."

"And I'm glad you did," Mathew said while he put an arm around his brother. "Now come on. I'm going in search of a good drink, and you're coming with me. You look like you could use one far more than me."

"Thanks, Matt. That sounds nice."

"Pneumonia. Pneumonia! If it was the sickness, cancer, or something like that, I could have understood. But Pneumonia? People are not supposed to die from that. This is an illness that we've had a cure for for decades. I had it twice when I was a kid. I spent all of one night in the hospital between both times. If it had been just five years ago, I could have just gotten in the car and taken him to the walk-in clinic. Now, there are no more doctors or new medicine being produced, and because of that, my son is dead. For the first time since it ended, I regret living through the sickness. I hate the way the world is now."

Martin Adams

Chapter 14

S now in October. It was awful. Debbie refused to accept what she had seen. She told herself that this was a simple trick played by her eyes and the poor light of the early morning. There was no way that what she had seen drifting on the wind were snowflakes. It was not unheard of for Nashua or other parts of New Hampshire to get snow this time of year, but it was far from the normal course of the weather. Debbie shuddered as she entertained even the slightest possibility of a white Halloween.

"What are you doing out here so early?" said Evan as he came up next to Debbie. He looked at her with a flirty, lopsided grin and moved to put his hands on her waist.

"Oh, I was just waiting for my boyfriend," Debbie said with an equally flirtatious measure. She backed away from the man before he could draw her close.

"Oh, I should have figured that a pretty young woman like you would have a boyfriend," Evan said, continuing the charade. "Do you normally meet him out here at the river bridge before the sun comes up?"

"You know, I do, come to think of it. We like to go for walks."

"Walks. If I had a girlfriend who looked like you, I don't think that going for walks would be the first thing I wanted to do to you in the morning."

"I think you better get going before my boyfriend shows up and hears you talking like that."

"Is he the jealous type?"

"Only if I give him a reason to be."

"Do you want to give him a reason?"

"Well, you do look a whole lot like him, and I'm not the type to be kept waiting when I want something..." Debbie untucked her shirt.

"Come here, you," Evan said, ending all pretense. Debbie immediately went to her boyfriend, and the two embraced each other before kissing wildly. "I think I saw some snow this morning on my way here."

"Shut up and don't say that word. That thing isn't allowed until after Thanksgiving," Debbie said in protest. She stopped kissing him and backed away as soon as he mentioned the white menace.

"Woah, I'm sorry. I didn't realize I was about to go and kill the mood."

Debbie looked at him with an enticing and cheeky smile before she responded. "Really didn't think you *would* kill the mood. You have a woman with her hands down your pants, and you want to talk about the weather."

"I guess you're right. I brought some of the dark roast with me today," Evan said as he pulled a thermos from out of his backpack. "And *real* sugar this time."

Debbie turned and pranced away in a fashion she knew would make her legs and butt look wonderful. "That's a good start. I think I'll let you keep trying to make it up to me," she said, beckoning him to follow her with a gesture of her finger.

"Just let me, and I'll give you something to smile about all day long," Evan said, then chased after her and gave her a gentle pinch on the bottom.

Debbie turned and threw her arms back around Evan. They kissed again, groping each other underneath the creaky covered bridge. Debbie had to force herself to pull her mouth from Evan's before they fell to the wood beneath and stripped off all their clothes. "Wait, not here," she said more bashfully than she meant to sound.

"What, you getting shy all of a sudden? Nobody's going to see. Everybody else in Nashua is still fast asleep."

"You don't know that," Debbie said as she pushed him back. "Now follow me and let me cash in on that promise of an all-day smile."

They slowly walked across the bridge, pressing their bodies close together and allowing their hands to roam unrestrained. The pair knew they would not be able to hold off their intentions much longer. Fortunately, one of the secluded places they liked to utilize for their little trysts was only minutes away. Debbie pulled her neck away from Evan's probing tongue as a rumbling sound grasped her attention. "Do you hear that?" she asked.

He made no effort to detect any kind of sound and only continued trying to return his longing mouth back to Debbie's neck. "No, didn't hear a thing at all," Evan mumbled.

"Shut up. No, I mean it. Listen, don't you hear it?" Debbie persisted, forcibly pushing Evan off of her. Her genuine sense of alarm had managed to quell Evan's lechery.

"Hey, what is it? What's the matter?" Evan said.

"That sound, like a low humming. You hear it?" She had honed in on the sound and knew for certain that it was not a trick of her ears.

Evan strained for several moments to hear the mystery sound that had taken Debbie out of her amorous state. It took him several moments to pick out the noise over the quiet gurgling of the brook running under the covered bridge, but eventually, he heard the sound as well. Evan didn't have long to ponder the exact cause of the noise; he had a hard time believing his eyes when he saw what was coming down the road towards the town. "Debbie, run and get Thomas and Mariel, now," he said once he gathered enough sense to form a plan of response. He tugged on her jacket sleeve to make sure he had her full and undivided attention before he continued his instruction. "And get Arbiter Randal as well."

"Oh my god. Oh my god," Debbie said in a way that managed to sound like a gasp of surprise and a shriek of terror all at the same time. She turned around and ran back towards the town center of Nashua. Evan quickly followed behind her after taking one final, awestruck glance at the intimidating advance of red, white, and blue.

***

Thomas was terrified. He had not expected to ever see anything like the scene before him in what remained of his life, and he certainly did not expect to be woken to it this morning. This was more than a band of raiders; this was an army. He only hoped that the men who had descended on his peaceful town of Nashua realized the modest population of sixty-three possessed little worth taking. He didn't know what to make of the convoy of armored vehicles that had rolled right up into the center of town or the heavily armed men and women marching in the street. Thomas grasped his cousin Mariel's hand for support as the parade of war machines ground to a halt.

A man more clean-cut and well-kempt stepped out of the passenger seat in a Jeep at the vanguard of the approaching group. He had a confident smile about him and a trustworthy face. He was calm and assured in his moments and seemed to glide rather than walk. Before he had even said a single word, Thomas wanted to like the man—trust him, even. It was impossible to be at peace though, because the plethora of weapons at the man's back put a primal fear into the hearts of the Nashua populace.

"Good Morning, my fellow Americans," said the man who had just gotten out of the Jeep. His voice was loud enough for all sixty-three of Nashua's citizens to hear him clearly. The man had a voice that befit his confident outward appearance. "My name is Mathew Haze, and I am a representative of the United States Congress for the Great State of Rhode Island's Second District," he said. Mathew paused for just the right length of time to let his words sink in and resonate with his audience. There were some murmurs of deference and respect, mixed with

88

and odd sneer or mocking comment. "I would like the privilege and opportunity of speaking with you today as an equal, as a citizen of this good country, and as a patriot. May I ask who is your presiding elected official in this fair town of Nashua, New Hampshire?"

After a long silence, Thomas and Mariel reluctantly stepped forward. "My name is Thomas Pat, and this is my cousin Mariel Hardy. Nashua doesn't have any formal leader, but most people here look to us for guidance when it's needed," Thomas said as he took off his cap to reveal short-cut white hair surrounding the bald crown of his head.

"We would like to know what business you have here in our town with all your guns," Mariel said curtly. Thomas gave his cousin a harsh sideways glance as she adjusted her thread-bear, purple knit scarf.

Mr. Haze smiled. "Miss Hardy, your cousin actually cuts to the heart of the matter here. We have all survived a horrible tragedy. In the face of the greatest epidemic the world has ever endured, we have survived, but the same cannot be said for our country." The Congressman paused once again for dramatic effect. He let the unsaid question of his previous statements worm its way into the minds of his listeners. "And as such, it pains me. It truly pains me. This is not the America that once was, but we're here to help our great nation heal and return to all her former splendor. And we do that by ensuring that we restore a proper democracy and elected government of the people, for the people."

The Congressman's soliloquy sank in and garnered a wide range of reactions. His words drew applause and cheers from his Patriots. Several of the Nashua gentry joined in with their own expressions of approval. Mathew maintained his approachable and relatable demeanor, though something insidious shimmered in his eyes.

"That's a lot to take in there," Thomas started after the cheers had faded and normal conversation could resume. "I don't think many of us have given much thought to the notion of democracy or government since...well, since it all happened." He was reminded of what it was like to have lived through the sickness. Not many people in Nashua spoke of it, and the sudden reminder of the lives lost so quickly made Thomas a little forlorn. Mariel patted her cousin on the back with a loving hand when she saw the effect the mention of the sickness had on him.

"I know, I know. In those dark days, most of us probably thought that this was it. This was the end of all of it. But we lived, we made it, and now it's time to see America put back together," Mathew said. As usual, his words were greeted with an explosion of applause from the Patriots.

"Hang on a moment. You're talking about things better left in the past, here," came a voice from the gathered people of Nashua. A man wearing the telltale eyepatch of an Arbiter stepped from the ranks of his New Hampshire brethren. Arbiter Randal walked right up to Mathew. He would have gotten eye to eye with the Congressman were it not for the pair of assault-rifle-toting Patriots who placed themselves between the Arbiter and their leader.

"And who are you, my friend? What should we be leaving in the past?" Mathew said. He parted the pair of Patriots and stood face to face with the man.

"My name is Arbiter Randal Durr, and I think you're talking about a world that no longer exists," the Arbiter said. His words also drew some mixed reactions from the crowd, though far fewer people seemed in favor of what he was suggesting than in the lofty promises of the Congressman. Several people from the Nashua Township supported the Arbiter; more held a fearful silence, and every Patriot who heard the man responded with jeers and boos.

Mathew seemed shocked, even emotionally injured at the Arbiter's comment. "Are you saying that you don't feel America exists anymore? Because I assure you that the earth we are standing on is the very sovereign soil of the United States," Mathew said, gesturing theatrically.

"Look, I don't care how many guns you have, how may red, white, and blue flags you paint on your vehicles, whatever kind of title you want to call yourself. Hell, you could say you're the damn President for all I care, and it doesn't matter," the Arbiter said with a huff. He adjusted the musty leather band covering his left eye.

"Randal…you can't…you!" Thomas interjected quickly. He surged to try and think of something to follow up his exclamation but was at a distinct loss for words. He prayed the Arbiter was not about to instigate a bloody exchange.

90

"No, no, it's okay. Let the man exercise his right to free speech," Mathew said. A hint of smugness crept into his voice.

"The sickness changed everything. The world is a different place now, with different rules. The law of the challenge is a good way, and it serves all people well in this time *after*," Randal said fervently.

"Look, I hear what you're saying, and you're welcome to run a candidate in an open election for whatever party and whatever cause you feel would best serve this country. But make no mistake, it is still *this* country. America has survived oppression by a crowned tyrant, a civil war, two world wars, three total economic collapses, countless terrorist attacks, the assassination of more than one president, and now the sickness. We are still one nation indivisible under God, and nothing will change that," Mathew said. He words ended in a seemingly calculated crescendo of zeal and well-honed righteous indignation.

"We have a new way here. It works for us. We all are happy here, and we're not going to let you come in and tell us how to run our town. We do not recognize you as any kind of authority or power that we need to answer to, and we will do whatever is needed to keep our way," said the Arbiter, crossing his arms defiantly. Many of Randal's townsfolk supported him with vigorous nods and shows of agreement.

Mathew was slow to respond. "I have a hard time listening to such words. What you're saying could pass for treason." His hand fell to the gun holstered at his side. "Would you like to find out what we do to traitors?"

"I swear, our little girl asked for a ratchet set. No joke. It's what she wants for her birthday. What thirteen-year-old wants a ratchet set? I guess we should be happy that she's not asking for makeup and cloths that show off way too much, like all her friends. I know, I wish she was more ladylike at times too. But Lea...well, she's something special. You know, I caught her in the garage the other day. I thought she was trying to sneak some beer from the fridge. No, she was trying to change the oil on the pickup."

Peter Vanderbelt

Chapter 15

It was so different without Henry. Mark had known it would not be the same once his mentor left the village of Northeastern Connecticut, but he had not expected his reaction to Henry's departure. Mark was experiencing what could only be described as the grieving process. Sometimes, the Arbiter would be in the middle of a simple, everyday ritual, like sipping a mug of morning coffee or taking out a full trash bag, and the next thing he knew, he was fighting a tearful breakdown.

Mark was not alone in his grief. He had seen Lea in similar straits. Only the night before, he had walked into the kitchen after dinner, expecting her to be cleaning the dishes like she normally did. Instead, he found her sobbing over the sink. The pair were each other's greatest source of strength for dealing with the loss. Nether Mark or Lea knew what they would do to cope with Henry's absence if they had to go it alone.

Strangely, Henry's departure had strengthened their relationship. Mark was frightened in a way, because he was not sure it was possible for him to feel any more deeply for Lea. The Arbiter could not deny that his love for his woman had grown stronger. He was coming to realize that he would not be able to take on this cold new world *after* without her.

He sat at his dining table in the time between morning and noon. Lea had left a little less than an hour before to spend some time at the garage, where she maintained the village's small motor pool. With the weather turning cold, it was time for her to prepare the vehicles for impending snow and freezing nights. Mark was still trying to get a feel for what his days were supposed to look like. He stared at the bottom of his long, empty coffee mug and scratched at his nose. He had almost broken in his eyepatch, but the leather still chafed his skin sometimes. Prior to taking the mantel of Arbiter, Mark would spend his time doing whatever needed to be done around the village—the quintessential jack of all trades. He wondered if he should just return to playing the part of the dependable handyman.

Mark had a case of something like buyer's remorse. He was starting to question why he had ever upset the happy balance of his role in the village and his blissful life with Lea. *What am I going to be able to do now that makes it so different?* Mark thought as he ran his fingers over his eyepatch.

A knocking at the front door snapped the Arbiter from his ruminations. Mark was glad for the interruption; left to his own devices, he knew he wouldn't enjoy his wandering mood. He cleared his thoughts and checked his reflection in the windowpane so he could quickly tidy his hair before he received company. "Come in. The door's open," Mark said in a calm voice that juxtaposed his inner emotional circus. The front door of Mark and Lea's quiet little country home creaked open. The sound reminded him that the hinges could use a fresh treatment of WD-40. Now he knew what task he would undertake after he met with his visitor.

"Good morning, Arbiter Fishers," said Sir Leon as he entered the house. "Daniel said you asked to see me today."

Mark looked through the dining room French doors and across the living room at the Templar as he stood in the landing. Sir Leon was nearly standing at attention. Mark would have sworn the Templar was nervous. He realized that when he had asked Danny to go summon the Templar, he had not specified the reason. More often than not, when a Templar was called for, it was to play a part in the bloody business of a challenge. Mark was also privy to the fact that, despite Sir Leon's masterful aptitude for all things martial in nature, the Templar had little stomach for violence. His reason for seeking Sir Leon that morning, though, was more personal in nature. In hindsight, Mark admitted to himself that, while he couldn't fully disclose his purpose to ask for Sir Leon's presence, he probably should have made it clear that this was a matter of peaceful discourse.

"Good morning, Sir Leon," Mark responded with a friendly smile after his moment of thought. He waived the Templar to join him at the dining table. "And to you, it's always Mark, not Arbiter Fishers."

"As long as you return the favor and manage to keep it to just Leon," the Templar humored. As Leon sat, he appeared to relax his guard. The Arbiter's welcoming hospitality was clearly soothing.

"Can I get you anything, something to drink?" Mark asked as the other man scooted his chair up to the table.

Sir Leon seemed about to reflexively decline the offer before he caught himself. "Thank you, some water would be great, please," he said quietly.

"Sure thing," Mark said as he rose from the dining table. He went to the cupboard and got a pair of drinking glasses. "Would you like ice?"

"Yes, please," Leon said quickly.

The Arbiter opened his generator-powered deep freezer and chipped off a couple chunks of ice for the beverages. Mark returned to the dining table with two tall, cold drinks of water. He sat and took a small sip before talking next. "Did Danny tell you anything other than I was looking for you?"

"No, he just told me that you wanted to see me and that was it," Leon said after taking a drink. The Templar kept both his hands clasped on the icy glass.

"It's okay. You don't need to worry. This is not about a challenge. This is about a personal matter, and I could use your help with it," Mark said. He noticed that his statement seemed to further relax the Templar.

"Absolutely. What can I do to help?" Sir Leon inquired before he raised his water to his lips.

"It's about Lea," Mark said. He halted his words when the Templar coughed and gagged on his mouthful of water. "Are you okay, there?" he asked, leaning forward.

"Yeah, I'm good. I'm good…it was just… I'm good," Leon said.

"Okay. Lea…everyone knows that we love each other—" Mark said before he stopped suddenly.

"Yes…" Leon followed up, taking his time saying the word and trying to coax Mark to continue his thought.

"We have been together for quite a while now."

"Yeah, pretty much since she showed up in Northeastern Connecticut."

"Um, this is hard for me to say."

"What is it? I don't see a problem with two people loving each other."

"Heh. It's… it's… I want to ask her to marry me," Mark blurted out. His confession drew a few stunned moments of silence from the Templar.

Sir Leon regained his composure. "Is that it? I mean, it's wonderful that you want to do that. I just don't see what's difficult, here… I know she would say yes before you even finish asking."

"It doesn't seem silly to you, asking her to marry me?"

The Templar took a moment to think. "Not in the least. It's what people did *before*. There isn't any reason to stop a custom just because the world flipped upside-down. Besides, everybody loves a party. A story like you and…and her…it should be celebrated."

"It makes me feel better that someone with a level head like you doesn't think I'm being sentimentally foolish."

"I wouldn't say you aren't being sentimentally foolish…" Sir Leon said and playfully trailed off, pausing long enough to make Mark start to doubt himself once more. "But I also wouldn't say that's a bad thing."

"I guess you're right. It's been so easy to be consumed by practicality and necessity. I think I have to remind myself a lot of the time that we're capable of doing more than finding food, keeping warm, and surviving to the next day."

"I think it's great. But...where do I play into all of this?"

"This is really kind of what embarrasses me...but, uh, I need a ring. Well, I want her to have a really nice one," Mark said sheepishly. He rubbed his chin and was grateful for the stubble that he had yet to shave off that morning. He was sure it would help to obfuscate the shade of red that must have been taking over his face.

"Okay, I'm still a little lost, here."

"Well, I can't really leave the village for long, and even if I could, I certainly couldn't get away without Lea knowing what I was up to. The pickings around here are pretty slim in terms of fine jewelry, even down around the old capital, New Haven, and any of the bigger cities in the state."

"I think I see what you're getting at," Sir Leon interjected as Mark took a drink from his water glass.

"You are in and out of the village pretty regularly, and you know how to get to Manhattan and back better than anyone else here..." Mark raised the inflection in his voice and spread his hands open.

"And Fifth Avenue really hasn't been scoured when it comes to engagement rings," the Templar finished Mark's statement, nodding in understanding.

"Precisely," said Mark with a relieved sigh.

"I think I can arrange some time to go look for you. Is this something you need me to do right away?"

"No, you don't need to head out first thing...but I would like to ask her sooner rather than later."

"I understand fully. Truth be told, it'll be nice to get away from here for a little while."

"What? Is there something upsetting you here in the village?" Mark asked his friend with a measure of concern.

"No...well, not really upsetting, but it would be nice to escape from Daniel's clutches for a couple days," Leon said with a fleeting note of shame. He furrowed his brow as he thought for a moment. "I could also stop in at Templar Sebastian Proper, check in face to face and reequip some of my gear."

"I can't blame you at all, but you do know that you're Danny's hero."

Leon's eyes went wide, and he nearly shouted his next statement. "Oh, I know, I know…yeah. Is there a kind of ring you want me to look for?"

"I hadn't even started to think about that. I want something really nice and pretty for her," Mark started. He scratched his head behind his ear as it dawned on him just how unprepared he was for something like picking out an engagement ring. The Arbiter's fingers found their way onto the strap connected to his eyepatch, reminded of how Lea adored his emerald eyes. "Maybe something with green in it. Yes, definitely green. I think she would love that."

"What size ring does she wear?"

"Um…I don't know. How do you figure that out?"

Leon had no answer for his friend, only a blank stare and a shrug.

The Thirtieth Law
All Challenges must be withdrawn or resolved within a year and a day from the time they are issued.

Chapter 16

"This looks like a good place to stop and rest up for the night," Tony said to Mathew. The Patriot looked at the Jeep's fuel warning light that had just come on. They had plenty of portable gas cans in the convoy, but the forgotten city along the northern border of Massachusetts would likely offer the Patriots a way to refuel without digging into their own stores.

"My thinking exactly. Take the next exit ramp and we'll see what we can salvage from the city before turning in," Mathew said as he adjusted in the passenger seat. The long ride had reminded the Congressman that his lower back was not as young as it used to be.

"There aren't any signs of life here. I don't think we're going to have to contend with any locals who need...convincing," Tony remarked. "We should be able to roll up and get right to it."

"Probably, but I want to have a cautionary sweep of the area just for peace of mind," Mathew responded as he rubbed his hands. The weather had turned cold enough that it dried out the Congressman's skin, and he was battling split knuckles. After the moment of discomfort passed, Mathew grabbed the walkie-talkie on the dashboard and keyed it. "This is Haze. We're going to pull off here and break for the night. Come back."

One by one, the drivers from the rest of the convoy acknowledged the order. The Jeep slowed and pulled into the rightmost lane of the highway. Mathew looked in the rearview and side mirrors. Then he turned and glanced back over his shoulder to make sure that the rest of the convoy was close on his tail. He marveled at the impressive sight of the armaments he had in tow. Mathew called over the radio again. "Stay on the lead Jeep, and once we stop, I want the teams on tanks one, two, and three to spread out and secure the area. We expect this city to be empty, but we want to be sure that we're alone before we get comfortable. Understood?"

The drivers of the first three Patriot tanks responded to the Congressman's command in the affirmative. The Jeep slowed as it made its way down the exit ramp. Tony had to take some slight evasive action to avid clipping a long-abandoned, stalled-out car that had not been pulled off the road completely. Both the men in the Jeep looked up at the buildings lining the sides of the main street on which they found themselves. The buildings were multistory but a far cry from skyscrapers. The city was burnt-out and looked like it had not been touched by man for ages. Still, Mathew and Tony were both well aware that the urban environment was large enough to conceal the movements of small groups of onlookers very easily. There were also ample spots for snipers to set up shop and wait for passersby. Both men in the lead Jeep sat lower in their seats as they drove through the silent collection of buildings.

"We should be able to gas up pretty easy, here. I saw a couple of stations from the highway," said Tony while he maneuvered the Jeep around sporadic fields of debris.

"Sure. The first place we find is good with me," Mathew responded as he shifted his view from vacant window to vacant window. "Maybe we can get lucky enough to find a place with fuel and booze," Mathew continued with an inward chuckle.

"Vodka. Yeah, some Vodka would do me good. I don't care what kind it is, but I need to get some Vodka," Tony said. He smacked his lips and swallowed hard.

"Really, Tony. You know, I love you, but I can't stand you and your pussy drink," Mathew jokingly provoked his compatriot.

"Fuck you," Tony laughed. "I'm sorry that I haven't burned out my mouth on that soot in a bottle you chug."

"You never complain about my brandy when I offer you a drink," Mathew said while he prodded Tony with an elbow.

"Well if it's a choice between a shot of your nastyass brandy or staying sober, I'll put up with your shitty booze," Tony said as he deflected Mathew's elbow.

"More for me, then, and I'm good with that," Mathew said with a shrug and a grin.

The Jeep rolled into the heart of town and pulled up to a surprisingly clean-looking gas station. All the glass in the station was still intact; unbroken glass was a rarity in larger cities. It was rather curious to find such an untouched oasis in the midst of the shattered and damaged urban sprawl. Such a finding tended to indicate that someone was using this location as a hideaway.

The Patriots poured over the gas station, and the teams assigned to securing the outer perimeter began their sweep of the area. Black combat boots pounded over the cracked and chipped asphalt of the city streets as Mathew's men looked for anyone who might have been observing the convoy.

Mathew and Tony kept their distance, as they normally did, remaining close to the safety of their armored vehicles. The Congressman looked on while his subordinates potentially put themselves at risk. Mathew was certainly not the sort who would put himself in harm's way if he could avoid it. He drew a long sip of unpleasantly warm water from the canteen he had stowed in the Jeep's cup holder. The Patriots searched the ruins for several minutes and found no signs that anyone had been there for quite some time.

"Looks like we're the first visitors this place has had in a while," Tony remarked casually. The Patriot wiped the oily smudges of his aviator sunglasses on the front tail of his shirt. "I think it's safe to go inside."

"Yeah, I would say so," said the Congressman. "Okay, people. Looks like it's just us here. Let's re-up," Mathew called out for all his men to hear. "You know the drill. Food and fuel, then anything else that might be useful."

Mathew and Tony headed inside the gas station. The front doors to the store stuck a little bit when Tony first pulled on the handle, but a short, strong tug opened them. The world had played a cruel joke on the two men; while the outside of the gas station was seemingly untouched, the inside had been nearly picked clean.

"Fuck!" Mathew exclaimed, looking at the sparsely stocked shelves and coolers.

"Damnit. Looks like this was too good to be true," Tony responded in disappointment. "At least we didn't strike out on the gas." He glanced at the Patriots outside who had set up their fuel-syphoning equipment.

"That's a plus, so we'll be able to get away from this big waste of time. Maybe there's something here that got missed. Let's have a look around," Mathew said. He poked and shook the assortment of empty boxes and bottles strewn about the inside of the gas station.

Tony followed suit and gave it several minutes of unrewarded searching before talking again. "You think that everywhere we hit before Manhattan will go down as easy as Nashua?" the Patriot asked as he pulled the racking out from one of the beverage coolers.

"That's hard to say. I honestly don't know. Nashua was such a small town, I wonder if it even counts. I mean, they had what? Not even seventy-five people and maybe two dozen guns between them," Mathew said, scratching his head while he recalled the fall of the New Hampshire town.

"I know it was a small sample size, but it looked like most people there didn't need much convincing to see things our way. What, there were maybe ten holdouts at the start?" Tony called across the store while investigating the floor of the gutted cooler.

"We do present a convincing argument for people to fall in line," Mathew said mockingly, gesturing to a pair of tanks parked outside. "Still, it would be nice if that kind of ratio holds up for us as we stop in at other populated areas. I'll admit it would have been fun to see what our new toys were capable of, but for Aaron's sake, I'm glad Nashua was a peaceful surrender. Well, mostly peaceful, anyway."

"Yeah, I don't see us convincing too many of those one-eyed psychos to come with us. For a second back there, I thought that Arbiter guy was going to start some shit and get everyone fired up and ready to get stupid." Tony laughed as he stepped out of the cooler he had been investigating.

"Well you know, I had to put in some work on that guy. I knew he was never coming with us, and as much as I would have liked to make an example of him and string him up with some stars and striped carved into his forehead, doing that would have set Aaron off. After the show I put on with those two Templars we caught up in Maine, I need to be a little more sensitive to what I show my kid brother. So when I shot that dumbass in his one good eye, I needed it to look like a heat-of-the-moment self-defense kind of thing," Mathew said, feeling very proud of himself for the performance he had put on in Nashua.

"Well it worked. You made yourself look real good for our guys and the rest of Nashua. I couldn't' even tell that you'd been trying to provoke that guy to jump you," Tony said with admiration.

"What can I say? I'm good. I'm really fucking good," Mathew said with an evil smirk. "Even the way it did play out, it took me a good two hours to get Aaron to calm down off the warpath," Mathew said while he kicked some empty soda cans.

"You put a lot of care into that kid, don't you?" Tony asked.

"Damn right, I do! He's my brother. He's one of the only people I really give a shit about in all this fucked-up mess of a world we're stuck in. We don't have many people who are actually worth a damn nowadays, but Aaron's valuable. His idealism inspires most of the men we have with us. I'm not about to lose an icon like him if I can avoid it," Mathew said fiercely. It stung his pride a bit when he thought of the kind of loyalty and respect that Aaron commanded among the Patriots. The Congressman knew that, while he could talk, convince, and persuade people into following him, his younger brother commanded a following of his own by genuinely living the ideal the Patriots espoused.

"I get it, and you aren't wrong. Aaron's a force to be reckoned with," Tony said slowly. He thought long and hard before continuing. "You don't think the respect he has from the rank and file might be a problem for us later on? You know, if you two ever disagree and you can't rein him in?"

"And I can't reign him in? Do you forget who the fuck you're talking to?" Mathew joked. The Congressman's face grew more serious before he continued. "You know, I have thought about that issue once or twice, and I don't worry about it for a couple of reasons. First, my little brother ultimately does what I tell him. He may be fearless, but he doesn't have the balls to stand up to me. Most important, though, is the fact that Aaron has no idea how to be a leader. He doesn't even think of himself as one. I'm not going to have to worry about him stepping out of line."

"And if that ever changes? Say, one day, Aaron gets the wild notion to think for himself, just for hypothetical shits and giggles?" Tony asked with a tilt of his head, rubbing the tip of his nose.

Mathew took his time with the question, letting it roll around in his head. The Congressman did not like where his imagination took the idea. He let his eyes fall to the floor where he stood behind the cash register while he tried to stop his train of thought. Mathew's eyes suddenly grew wide with excitement. "Like I said before, I'm really fucking good."

"What... what is it?" Tony said in a moment of confusion.

Mathew disappeared from Tony's view as he knelt behind the counter. He pulled back a towel covering a broken milk crate and revealed several bottles of alcohol. Some were even still factory-sealed. Mathew gave a sigh and chuckle as he stood, holding a pair of blue glass bottles in each hand. "The good news is it's Vodka. The bad news is you get to choose from peach or pineapple." Mathew chortled.

"Fuck, I don't know how to feel about this, exactly." Tony made his way up to the counter and took the bottle of peach Vodka from the Congressman.

"It's okay. I was just pulling your leg a little," Mathew said as he disappeared back below the counter. "There's a bottle and a half of straight silver label in here as well," he said, standing and plopping the broken crate down on the countertop.

Tony gave a quick scan of the crate's contents. "Whisky, rum and bourbon. Not a bad haul. I think it's going to be a good night tonight, Mr. Haze," Tony said happily.

"A good fucking night indeed. I was getting worried. It hasn't been easy to ration that flask of gin I've been nursing since Nashua," Mathew said.

"I know. A full town, and the only drink they got was a few drops of grandpa's backwash. You would think they'd have had something nice between the lot of them," Tony responded as he held the blue bottle up to the light.

A sly expression came over Mathew's face before he spoke. "I don't know if I would say all that," he said.

"What are you talking about?" Tony twisted off the cap of the half-empty bottle of silver label vodka.

"That Debbie girl. I'd say she was something nice. At least to look at, anyway," Mathew said with a chuckle. He pointed out the gas station window to the woman loading some scavenged canned goods into one of the Patriot box trucks.

"I'll drink to that. She's a prettier face than we normally get to see," Tony said as he took a long drink from the bottle.

"You know, I had our quartermaster give her a uniform that was at least a size too small. Makes her nearly spill out," Mathew said, leering at her body. "She's some fucking kind of trailer-trash hot. Big old floppy tits and day-old makeup."

"Fuck yeah. After we rolled up in Nashua and got to talking, I thought to myself that I'd like to feel the back of her throat with my dick," Tony said, voice more of a predatory growl.

"Heh. It'd be nice to cum in a mouth that still has all its teeth. Most of the bitches we have on the regular aren't much more than a wet hole. It gets the job done, but I'd like to be able to fuck with the lights on every once and a while." Mathew groaned and scratched his crotch.

"Well, there's Chrissy. She's hot, but I get it. I don't like to gamble with my dick," Tony remarked.

"I been there a couple times, but I know what you mean. I'm not in the mood to get herpes, and she's broken out more than not. That, and if you can't bareback a bitch, I don't see much point to fucking them.

Feels like a waste of time," Mathew said as he took a sip from the open bottle of vodka Tony handed to him. He grimaced with displeasure. He had hoped that the beverage was not as unpleasant as he remembered, but it was. Mathew broke the seal on a bottle of whisky to chase away the taste.

"So you gonna fuck Debbie?" Tony asked, grinning in seeing Mathew turn up his nose at the vodka.

"Shit yeah, I'm gonna fuck her! I'm not about to let a piece of ass like that go to waste," Mathew exclaimed after taking a shot of whiskey from the newly opened bottle. "I'm not about to sit by while that limp-dick Evan guy she hangs around with gets to hit that every night."

"So then, what's the plan to get her to give it up? Or you want to do her the hard way?" Tony asked. His brow furrowed in genuine curiosity.

The Congressman pulled out a corked and sealed bottle of wine from the milk crate. "Well, she looks like a red kind of a girl to me. I give her something special and stoke her ego, saying that she's really helping the cause and that she can go far, all kinds of potential and a bunch of horseshit like that. Then, once she's good and wasted, talk about how stressful and lonely it is to be the leader and champion of democracy. She'll get the idea of how best to serve her country."

"You are really fucking good. No lie about that," Tony said with an approving nod and mock bow to the Congressman.

Mathew took the compliment graciously and thought for a moment. "When I'm done with her for tonight, you want seconds?"

"As long as you don't break her too bad, that would be cool," said Tony.

"I want to keep this one around for a while. I'm not going to be rough with her yet," Mathew said before taking another sip of whiskey. "Unless she makes me, of course."

"It'll be nice to get off with someone I haven't fucked yet before we head to New Boston tomorrow," said Tony.

"You lost the challenge that was agreed upon in adjudication. You were supposed to stop hitting her. You didn't. I came to tell you that you had to go. You failed to abide by the terms agreed upon. Then, like a damn fool, you don't leave town. Not only that, you still kept hitting her. I hate you for this. In all my time serving as an Arbiter, I have never once had to perform this duty. Damnit, you could have just gone and lived. Stop it! Stop begging! You had your chances. Just close your eyes. It won't hurt."

Arbiter Bruce Caulder

Chapter 17

This was the second time in a row that Sir Leon had meant to leave from his current station first thing in the morning but was delayed. When he had meant to leave from New Boston and make the trip to the Village of Northeastern Connecticut, a challenge had prevented his timely departure. Now, the Templar had intended to make for Manhattan before dawn broke in Northeastern Connecticut, where he had been residing since the autumn, but that had not happened either. It was not a challenge that had stopped him from leaving this time. It was something far more difficult for Sir Leon to endure. Lea wanted to say goodbye to him.

The Templar wanted to be on his way to the big city, where he would make good on his promise to his friend. He knew exactly where he would look for an engagement ring Mark could give to Lea. He had passed by the jewelers on a few occasions and knew it had a wide stock to choose from. Leon was certain he could find something appropriate in that store.

It was a bit ironic that Mark was ultimately to blame for the Templar's delay in leaving the village. Mark had let it slip to Lea that Leon was leaving. The Arbiter was at least able to keep the purpose of the Templar's mission concealed. Once Lea had gotten wind that one of her friends would be leaving the village, she refused to let him go without first cooking him a proper breakfast and saying goodbye. Ever since Henry's reassignment to New Boston, Lea had become even more attached to those she cared for.

"Are you sure you got enough to eat? It looks like you barely touched your eggs. Was something wrong with them?" Lea said to Sir Leon with concern.

"No, not at all. They're great, thank you," Leon said reflexively. It wasn't a lie; the food was prepared very well. The Templar's mind was just miles away, so he had spent most of breakfast moving the scrambled eggs around with a fork while Lea and Mark ate. "It's just that I don't want to fill up too much before I ride out. I hate the feel of biking on a full stomach," the Templar continued. He wanted to find some way to excuse himself from the meal without offending his hostess.

"Well, you could just not go today, you know," Lea said with a beaming smile. "More coffee?"

The Templar held up his hand. "No thank you. I appreciate the offer, but I really need to get on the road soon," Leon said.

"Yeah, I got that part. I'm still not too happy that you were planning to slip out of here without letting me know. That wasn't very nice of you," Lea said in a sassy tone.

"Hey, keep it civil, you," Mark said to his beloved playfully. The Arbiter took a long sip of coffee from the chipped porcelain mug that was his favorite.

"Oh, and don't think that I've totally forgiven you, Arbiter Fishers. You know I hate it when I have to drag information out of you," Lea chided.

"I know, but I do love your interrogation methods," Mark said in a flirty manor, copping a feel of Lea's breast.

Lea gently slapped her man's offending hand away after the shock of his brazen impropriety passed. "Mark, really. In front of company?" Lea gasped, seemingly disgusted but far more flattered. Then her face blushed a bright red.

"Sorry, I just can't help myself. You're just so irresistible," Mark said. "I apologize if I made you uncomfortable, Leon."

"No, it's fine," Leon lied. He felt enraged at himself. The tender and jovial intimacy he witnessed between his two friends was something he treasured. What made the Templar so angry was the fact that he envied and even longed for it. Leon concealed his deception behind a mouthful of scrambled eggs.

The moment between Lea and Mark passed, and the couple returned to breakfast with their guest. "You could just take one of the village cars. I don't see it as a big problem. Especially if you're only going to be checking in and re-upping your gear," Lea said to the Templar.

Sir Leon poked at his eggs while he thought a little about Lea's suggestion. "I really feel more comfortable on my trike, and I don't want to put the village out the fuel," Leon started. He saw Lea immediately form an objection, but before she voiced it, he continued. "But we can part with some fuel at Sebastian Proper, and a vehicle will get me there and back faster than peddling will. So I'll take you up on the offer."

"Wise man, you. It's good that you learned it's best to say yes to this one," Mark interjected. "One way or another, she always gets what she wants." His comment was met with a light punch in the shoulder from Lea. Mark burst out laughing.

"Do you have a reliable vehicle in mind?" Leon asked.

"There are a few options I can think of off the top of my head. After breakfast, I'll take you down to the garage, and I'll get you something that works. I'll make sure to give it a quick double-check and tune-up before you take off," Lea said after a moment's consideration. "Now that that's settled, quit playing with your food and finish your eggs before they get cold." She topped off Sir Leon's coffee.

The three friends finished the meal and made short work of the dirty dishes left behind. Leon was relieved when Mark decided to join the trip to the garage. He was grateful for any opportunity to prevent himself from being alone with Lea; Leon dreaded any sort of remotely intimate moment that might pass between them. For all his discipline as a warrior and man of principle, keeping his feelings for Lea quelled had been a losing battle. He wanted to blame it on the close proximity he had shared with her since extending his stay in the village, but the Templar knew that, even were she to be far from his sight, she would still take up a large portion of his thoughts. He did his best to remain disengaged and let Lea and Mark carry most of the small talk.

It was a fast trip to the garage, still early enough in the morning that the streets had yet to come to life with villagers tending to the orders of the day. Leon was grateful for the short time it took to get to the building housing Northeastern Connecticut's working vehicles. The garage was close to the main street. There were a few suitable automotive service stations within the borders of the village, but for practicality's sake, the villagers made an effort to consolidate any actively used buildings. There were almost two dozen various cars, trucks, and smaller vehicles parked and covered with tarps in the pharmacy parking lot adjacent to that garage. The chain-link fence behind the garage held some of the specialty vehicles the village kept on hand. A semi-truck, a bulldozer, and a camper were a few of the assorted eccentric pieces in the assembly behind the garage. Virtually all the village's vehicles were unused, but Lea kept them all serviced and in fine working order just in case a need arose.

She jingled the garage keys in her hand and took the two men in through the side door of the building. She then opened the large pair of rolling doors separating the two service bays. There were no clouds in the sky, so the open rolling doors let in enough natural light that Lea didn't need to fire up the generator and turn on the overhead lamps.

"Jeep, Truck, SUV?" Lea asked the Templar in her usual perky and upbeat voice.

"Whatever you think is best. I don't need too much storage room, and I'd like to make as few stops to fill up between here and Sebastian Proper as possible," said the Templar.

"Okay. I have just the thing. Sit tight for a few," Lea said. After perusing a large selection of car keys hanging on a pegboard fixed to the wall, she selected a key ring and briskly walked out the leftmost bay door.

After Lea had been gone for a few moments and Mark was sure she was far out of earshot, he spoke quietly to Leon. "Thanks for doing this for me. It means a lot."

"It's no trouble. I'm happy to do this for a friend. I just hope I find you a ring that she'll love," Leon said.

"I'm sure that whatever you pick out will be great. I trust you and your judgment completely," the Arbiter replied.

Leon felt like he had been hit in the chest by Mark's last statement. The Templar felt so vile, that the Arbiter would profess such a profound level of trust while he secretly betrayed Mark with his feelings towards Lea. "Thanks," was the only response Leon could manage to drum up. The rumble of an engine coming to life and the slam of a car door saved him from the uncomfortable silence.

Lea drove a Jeep up into the garage. It was a utilitarian vehicle, and the top had been removed to allow for easy access. Lea pulled the Jeep up onto the service lift and cut the engine. "She sounds pretty good to me, but I'll give her a fast once-over before you take off," Lea said with a smile that nearly killed Leon when he saw it.

"This is perfect. Thank you," he said.

"There's a doughnut tire and jack over in the corner that I want you to take. Hopefully you won't need them," Lea said, pointing and directing Leon's attention to the items. "Would you please top off a couple of the five-gallon gas cans and load them up?" she asked Mark.

The Arbiter was about to respond when a cry of alarm broke the silence. "Help! Help!" All three people in the garage instantly whipped their heads around to see who had shouted. Peter came barreling into the garage, all out of breath.

"Peter, what's wrong? Is Danny hurt? Raiders?" Mark asked with alarm.

"No. Danny's okay, and he's still on lookout. No raiders," Peter gasped as he leaned over and put a hand on the back bumper of the Jeep to support himself. "There's a woman walking down the road. She looks hurt."

"She's on 395 North?" asked Sir Leon. Peter only nodded.

"Lea, take the Jeep. Go grab Doctor Michael and head out to her. Leon, would you go with them? I'll head over to the fire station and grab a radio. Have Mike call me with what he needs me to set up for medical," Mark said commandingly.

Nobody said anything; they simply did as the Arbiter had instructed. The doctor was ready to go with first-aid bag in hand before the Jeep pulled up to his door. Lea, the Templar, and Doctor Michael speed down the interstate in the Jeep. They saw the woman stumbling down the road, and she didn't move out of the way of the oncoming Jeep. She just shuffled her way forward. Lea slammed on the breaks and leapt out of the Jeep with the doctor. Leon stayed in his seat and carefully surveyed the surrounding tree line, holding the cocked revolver at his side.

The woman was covered in black soot and blood. Lea was aghast at the sight, but as they ran towards her, it was plain to see that the woman only had some superficial cuts and scrapes. Most of the blood soaking her must have belonged to someone else.

Michael gave Lea a sign to slow down as not to startle the woman. "Ma'am, I'm a doctor. My name is Michael, and I want to help you. Can you tell me your name?"

The woman did not respond, just continued forward.

"Ma'am, can you hear me?" asked the Doctor. The woman still didn't indicate any kind of understanding.

Lea couldn't stand by any longer and went to the woman. Michael tried to stop her from pushing past him, but his efforts were null and void. Lea gently touched the woman on her shoulder. At first, the woman instinctively recoiled, but the sensation of Lea's touch looked like it ended the woman's state of shock.

She looked at Lea with tearful eyes and spoke as she wept. "It's gone…it's gone…they killed them all…it's gone."

Lea's eyes went wide, and she gave a mortified glance back to Michael. Registering the terrified look on the doctor's face, she wanted to make sure that someone else had heard the same words. "What's gone?" Lea asked with all the empathy in the world.

The woman cried hard for a long time before she was able to

speak. "New Boston."

"Don't cry... Don't cry. I'm not in any pain. I will... I will be with your father soon. I miss him so much. When I'm gone, I'm going to... I need you... I need you to look after your brother. The people who live through this will need leaders. Mathew can do some amazing things, but he doesn't have... He is... he is a great man, but you are... you are a good man. Of everything I've done in life... I am most proud of the man you grew up... grew up to be. Could you get me another blanket? I am... so... so cold."

Shelby Haze

Chapter 18

"My girls. How are my girls?" the wounded man spattered through bloody teeth. He kept trying to open his eyes and lift his head, but Aaron stopped him each time. The man's neck was likely broken, and if he moved his head, it was apt to cause more damage. Ultimately, it didn't matter; the man was going to die soon anyway. A broken neck might actually have been a blessing. It would have meant that the man wouldn't be able to feel the bullets lodged in his ribs and spine.

"Shh, stay still. It's going to be okay," Aaron comforted the dying man. The Patriot cradled the other man's head in his hands and restrained him.

"My girls, Sara and Rachel...I need to...I need to find them," said the man as Aaron held supportively but tenderly. The wounded man's skin was bluer than its normal, healthy tan color, the ground around him drenched in red.

"Hey there, just stay still. Listen to me. It's okay, it's okay," Aaron said. The Patriot exhibited fine resolve as he managed to keep himself from sobbing. Aaron was glad that the man's eyes were closed and that he couldn't see how broken his body was, the tears Aaron fought in his own eyes, or most importantly, the bodies of Sara and Rachel lying coved in white sheets nearby. "Your girls are fine, just fine," Aaron lied.

"Good... good... I... need to..." The man moved his arms and tried to lift himself up into a sitting position.

Again, Aaron stopped him. "Hey, hey now. Just be still. I know where your girls are. I'll get them for you. I'll go bring Sara and Rachel right to you," Aaron said softly. "Are they your daughters? What's your name? I want to tell them that their dad is waiting for them," he continued in a calm and even tone. His voice came out like a soothing lullaby and helped the man to be still.

"Paul... my... my name..."

"Shh, it's okay. It's nice to meet you Paul. My name is Aaron."

"Aaron."

"Yes, that's it. I'm going to sit with you for just a few moments longer before I go get Sara and Rachel for you."

"I need them... Sara..."

"I know. I know. You're doing really well, Paul. You're a good father. Your daughters told me that. Sara and Rachel, they love you very much."

"That's nice...you're a good man, Aaron... I... I love..."

"It wasn't supposed to be like this. I'm sorry."

"It's... it's okay... my girls..." Paul said, barely louder than a whisper, before he went limp and stopped moving completely. He wasn't gone yet. The man's chest still rose and fell with shallow breaths.

"Shh," Aaron whispered. He held Paul and waited. The Patriot stayed with the man until his breathing stopped. Once Paul had died, Aaron stood and got a white blanket for him as well. He covered the body after moving it next to the corpses of Sara and Rachel.

Aaron looked around at the shattered glass, chipped concrete, and warped steel that had started the day as New Boston and was now a compilation of carnage and war. The state of the city was of little significance when measured next to the staggering death toll the Patriots had wrought on its inhabitants. Nearly ten thousand lives gone in a matter of a few hours. It couldn't have been called a fight. While New Boston boasted far superior numbers over the Patriots, outside of the Templars assigned to the city, few people there were of strong fighting quality. None of those who stood in defense of New Boston were a match for the heavy arms and armor that Mathew Haze had brought to bear.

Aaron tried to remember how it all had started. They came into the city in their usual fashion. Mathew had met and talked with the people considered the most important. It had begun peacefully but quickly degraded like it had in Nashua. Diplomacy turned into insults, then into threats. Finally, it all came down to violence.

New Boston struck first—or that was what Aaron seemed too recall in his foggy memory of the incident's onset. What he did remember clearly was the bloodlust that overtook the Patriots. The battle only lasted a few moments. Nobody called for surrender: it was all just a lot of screaming, gunfire, and dying. What happened after the paltry resistance of the city could only be called a slaughter. Aaron had seen some people escape the madness, but they were a precious few. Mathew's approach of the city had been well-conceived, and there were practically no clear avenues of escape for any who tried to flee the chaos.

Aaron tried to process his feelings; he had never been in shock before, but he had to believe that this was what it was. He wanted to cry and yell at the same time. He wanted to punch a wall and rip off his own skin. He wanted to crawl into a hole and never come out again. Aaron started laughing and didn't know why. Most of all, he wanted to make this massacre unhappen.

The Patriot stayed by himself in what could be described as the eye of a storm. It was not as loud as it had been earlier, but gunshots still sounded out in the city. There were still the screams of people being killed—or worse. Aaron covered his ears and forced those sounds and the guilt they produced out of his world. He looked at the three white blankets on the ground and the red stains underneath them. Aaron shut his eyes, unable to look at the destroyed family any longer. He felt like he was going to be sick. Aaron lay down next to Paul, Sara, and Rachel and stayed there for a long time.

"Are you okay?"

The sound of Mathew's voice made Aaron open his eyes. He didn't realize that he had actually dozed off for a while. He would have liked to stay asleep for the rest of his life if he could have managed it. Aaron looked up from his brother's scuffed black boots and met his eyes. "I'm not hurt," he said coldly.

"I've been looking for you for nearly an hour. You scared me," Mathew said with something that sounded like a mix of relief and concern rolled into one.

"You found me. I said I'm fine."

"Are you sure about that? Because you don't look fine."

"Well, it's hard for me to say. I really have no clue what *fine* looks like after…" Aaron gestured widely with his arms, "…after all of this."

"Hey, calm down. Everyone's okay, and we're going to move on tomorrow."

"What? What the fuck? Everyone is *not* okay! They're not okay," Aaron shouted, pointing to the three bodies at their feet. "All this is not okay!"

"Calm the hell down. You think I wanted any of this? You think I wanted dead children? What kind of man do you think I am? Call me a fucking baby-killer if that's how you feel." Mathew shoved his little brother in the chest.

"That's not fair. I didn't say it was your fault. It's just…" Aaron tried to sort out his feelings and put them into words. "I didn't want any of this. I have a hard time seeing this as the right thing."

"That's because it's not the right thing. It's just what happened. Remember, they shot first. I tried to talk it out. *They* shot first. I didn't want any of this, either."

"I know they did." Aaron fell silent for several moments as he retreated into his conscience. "I really don't want to be around you right now."

"Fine. Have it your fucking way. We're gone first thing in the morning," Mathew said over his shoulder. The Congressman stormed off and left his brother to sulk in his own guilt and self-loathing.

***

Mathew was proud of himself. He was perfectly happy with how the whole thing had played out. He knew there would be better armed men waiting for him in Manhattan, but New Boston had been an excellent trial of how his Patriots would perform in combat. *Sebastian Clarke doesn't stand a chance*, he thought as he swaggered through the ruined streets.

The Congressman made his way back to his base of command and looked for Tony. He saw his confidant leaning up against one of the tanks and smoking a fat cigar. Tony waived the Congressman over.

"To victory in New Boston, Congressman Haze," Tony said as he handed Mathew a cigar from his shirt pocket.

"You asshole. You been holding out on me," Mathew said. He took the cigar and put it to his nose. It was a far cry from a Cuban, but it still smelled wonderful.

"I was saving them for a special occasion. I felt that today seemed appropriate." Tony pulled out a cigarette lighter and held it up for Mathew to ignite his cigar.

Mathew took in a long and heavy drag. He held the smoke in his lungs for several moments before exhaling a noxious black cloud, followed by a slight cough. "That is real nice. It's better than I thought it would be. Age doesn't seem to have hurt them at all," Mathew remarked as he admired the cigar in his hand.

"You know me. I only deliver the best," Tony gloated.

"Don't go too far. The smokes are good, I'll give you that much," Mathew said before taking another puff on his cigar. "They hit us back at all?"

"About forty guys. Not too bad. About fifteen more with cuts, bruises, and broken bones. All the big guns are still in top shape," Tony responded as he pated the tread of the tank he rested up against.

"Not too bad a day's work at all."

"That what I say. You find Aaron?"

"Yeah, he's fine. Well, he's not hurt, but he's off whining like a little bitch. Apparently, a few kids as collateral damage is too much for his fragile sensibilities."

"That sounds like Aaron, all right. You think he's going to be able to stick this thing out all the way?"

"Yeah, I'm sure. He's going to keep on doing just like he's told."

"I hope so," Tony said cryptically. He stubbed out the end of his cigar on the side of the tank and threw it to the ground, where he crushed it under his heel. "So what's the next move?"

"We'll head out in the morning. I want to keep it pretty quick. There's no way a radio call didn't make it to Manhattan. If Sebastian didn't know about us before, he sure does now."

"Who knows? There's a chance he might just write it off as raiders. He doesn't necessarily know that we're gunning for him."

"True, and that would be nice if it's the case. We'll take the rest of the day to resupply and get ready to hit it bright and early in the morning," Mathew said. Then a thought took him. "For right this moment, though, I want to do a little more celebrating. I think I want to get my dick wet."

"Debbie again?"

"Well yeah, of course. But since it's a special occasion, I think I want her to bring a friend to join in the fun," Mathew said with a sleazy smirk. "I do have a small project for you. Nothing for right now. You should find a good time for yourself tonight too."

"What are you thinking?"

"Tomorrow, I want you and a few guys to stay back while the rest of the convoy moves out. Those Templars and Arbiters from today, I want to make an example of them."

"Okay. What about the ones that are still alive?"

"Oh, them too."

"If I haven't contracted it by now, I'm not going to. You need to stop wasting your breath telling me to go. I'm not going anywhere. I'm going to stay right here with you. As long as you're alive, I'm going to be with you. I said in sickness and in health until death do us part, and I meant it. I hoped I would never have to prove it, but then, does anyone? I love you. I love you. I love you. Just sleep for now. You look so tired. I'll be here when you wake up. I promise."

Anna Rogers

Chapter 19

"She's out cold now. Some rest will do her a world of good," said Doctor Michael as he came down the stairs of the firehouse. The conversation among those gathered on the ground floor ceased with the doctor's arrival.

"Was she hurt bad?" asked Danny.

"No, not too bad. Actually, the biggest thing that was wrong was some moderate dehydration. She's got plenty of fluids going on now, and she'll bounce back," Michael responded in a positive and hopeful tenor before his face darkened. "Well, physically, at the very least," he concluded with an air of foreboding. From what he had been able to see, she showed signs of Post-Traumatic Stress Disorder. The woman from New Boston would likely heal in body, but her mind was bound to carry psychological scars for the rest of her life.

"Are we in danger?" one of the villagers called out.

"I heard that New Boston was destroyed. Is that true?"

"She's just some crazy person," declared another voice.

"Who's responsible for what happened to this woman?"

The sudden outcry from the gathered villagers overwhelmed Michael. He could handle blood and gore and keep cool during emergency makeshift surgery like a world-class practitioner of medicine. When it came to managing a crowd or public speaking, he reverted from a confident and capable man into a fearful child. His mind reeled, and his nerves jumped into overdrive as he was peppered with questions. Michael felt the handrail of the staircase grow slick against his sweaty skin.

"Hey, calm down, everyone!" Mark said with abundant authority. The Arbiter's words restored silence and order within the firehouse. "We are not in any imminent danger. The truth is, we don't know what's happened."

"How do you know we're safe? How can you be so certain that we have nothing to worry about?" said a silver-haired woman standing at Mark's right. Her words rekindled the alarm the Arbiter had just settled.

"I can promise you this much. For right now, we are safe, and I will do everything within my ability to keep everyone in Northeastern Connecticut that way. We will find out exactly what's going on, and as soon as I know what happened in New Boston, so will everyone here. We're all going to be okay," Mark said, reestablishing control over the crowded room. "Now, calmly, are there any questions?"

"What's her name?" Lea piped up.

"Stacy," Michael responded as he wiped his moistened palms on his pants. Strangely, speaking the woman's name deepened the sense of clam Mark had managed to engender in the room. Giving the woman an identity helped steady some nerves. Michael noted the telling look Mark shot him with his one emerald eye. The doctor was intuitive enough to understand that Mark wanted to speak privately. "I think it would be best if we could move along and leave her to rest for a while," Michael said to the crowd.

Mark and Lea adeptly managed to usher most of the villagers out of the firehouse. The pair did a remarkable job of offering confidence and answers to all the uncertainty plaguing their friends and neighbors. It was a marvel to see how reassuring they could be with so few facts in their possession. It didn't take long to escort the bulk of the villagers out of the room and send them on their way. At the very least, Mark and Lea were able to buy a night without widespread panic taking hold of the village.

By the end of it all, only Mark, Lea, Michael, and Sir Leon remained in the quieted firehouse. The Arbiter shut the door after seeing the last of the villagers out, finally able to let the mask of bravado fall away from his face. His brow creased with a heavy burden of worry.

"What's the story? How credible is she?" Sir Leon asked the doctor while he filled a plastic cup from a water jug sitting on a nearby desk.

"It's hard to say. I didn't get much from her. She was borderline unresponsive most of the time I treated her. Though I will say that her symptoms point me towards shock and PTSD rather than dementia and mental illness. I wasn't able to give her a full physical, let alone get her into clean cloths, but from what I could see, her wounds are consistent with a recent traumatic event," said Michael. He took the water jug from the Templar and used it to fill the reservoir on the countertop coffee-maker. The doctor rooted through the cupboards overhead for some instant coffee and condiments.

"She wouldn't be the first person found wandering outside civilization. I think it's more likely that she's a little unhinged than all of New Boston being wiped out," said Leon after a sip of water.

"I agree with you. At least, I would like to think that we happened across someone who suffers from something isolated," Mark said. He licked his lips apprehensively.

"I don't want to discount Stacy's recollection of what she experienced, but I have to believe that if there was some crisis in New Boston, we would have heard something on the radio." Michael shook a near-empty container of powdered creamer.

"And on that note, don't you think it's alarming that we can't reach anyone in New Boston? Nearly two hours on the radio and no response. I don't like it," Lea said.

"We've lost radio contact with New Boston before, and it's been okay after a day or two," Michael replied, spooning a second heap of sweetener into his hot mug of coffee.

"So what? What are you all saying? There's no chance that something happened in New Boston?" Lea broke in passionately. "If there's a chance that something happened up there, we have to do something."

"I'm not saying that we sit on our hands at all. I just want to think about what this could be before we get all worked up. I just want to consider our options." Mark supportively put a hand around Lea's waist and drew her close. She resisted at first but quickly allowed herself to be pulled in tight.

"Options?" asked the Templar while he pulled out a chair to sit.

"Do you think this could be some kind of setup? Raiders trying to get us out of the village or something like that?" Mark asked. His question was not directed to anyone in particular, but everyone knew Sir Leon was the only one of them who had seen any violence after the initial craze of the sickness had subsided.

"That is a sort of tactic raiders have employed in the past. It's a tried and true method, actually," Sir Leon said, realization spreading across his features.

"You think that's what we have, here? If that's the case, she makes for one convincing decoy," Michael said before blowing on the steaming cup of coffee he had just prepared for himself.

"No, I don't," Sir Leon said after a moment. "If I wanted to draw people out of safety, I would have a better cover story than disaster in New Boston. Something smaller in scale and easier to sell. Not to mention the fact that raiders don't come this far north with any regularity." He frowned, studying the staircase in thought. "Still, she had to get those injuries somewhere. About the only thing I can say with any certainty is that somebody hurt Stacy."

"Are there any other options you can think of to explain her showing up in the village that don't lead back to something happening in New Boston?" Michael asked. The doctor looked at the Arbiter, who seemed to delve even deeper into concentration. "Mark?" Michael asked, slightly louder, after a moment of silence.

The sound of his name got his attention, and Mark snapped his head up. "Huh? Oh. No, not anything feasible, at least…" Mark drifted off as he returned to his thoughts.

"What were you able to get out of her?" Lea asked Michael as she pulled away from Mark and hopped up to sit on the counter next to the coffeemaker.

"Well, not much more than when we first found her on 395. Just a lot of 'It's gone,' and 'They killed them all.' Otherwise, it was a whole lot of nothing I could pick up on," the doctor said to Lea.

"Henry…" Lea started but stopped. Her eyes welled with tears and her lips trembled. Defensively, she aimed her gaze at the floor.

"Is it possible that it could…do you think…could it be the sickness returning?" Mark finally blurted out fearfully.

It was like he had just accused someone of murder. The three other people in the room were stunned at the mention of the epidemic that had brought the world to the edge of apocalypse. Clearly, nobody else had even slightly entertained the possibility that the sickness might have reared its head again. The anxiety charged the room like static electricity. Everyone in the firehouse found themselves remembering the early days *after*.

"I don't want to think about that. There's no way. Just no. It has to be something else," Lea said, bringing the deathly silence to a conclusion.

"Well then, what could it be? Ten thousand people and fifty Templars are not a soft target. Ten thousand…" said Sir Leon before mumbling the rest of his words into his cup of water.

"I don't want to get too caught up on conjecture and possibility. I think we need to stay calm and keep from overthinking this," Mark said, returning to his more confident form. "There are still a lot of things in play and much that needs to be answered. I can't say it enough—we don't have all the facts."

"Not knowing what happened doesn't make me feel any better," Lea said glumly, poking at the coffeemaker beside her.

"Maybe, but at least not knowing is a step up from knowing for sure that something horrible has happened," Mark said in an effort to console his partner.

"Ha, that's debatable," Lea said with an air of defeat. It was rare for her mood to be anything less than a ray of sunshine, but it did happen from time to time.

Mark seemed about to speak but was interrupted by a sound from the second floor of the firehouse that only lessened the already down-trodden morale of those gathered below. It was the sound of Stacy sobbing uncontrollably.

"Lea, you think you could help me out? It might help Stacy rest easier to have another woman around," Michael asked.

"Sure, if I can," Lea responded.

"Thanks, you two. I know you'll take care of her," Mark said reverently.

Michael turned briefly on the stairs and saw Mark kiss Lea warmly on the cheek. The faintest hint of a smile graced her lips. Then she nodded at Michael and followed him to the second floor.

"And you guys should try and get some sleep yourselves," Mark called after them. "About the only thing I know right now is we're going to have to send some people to New Boston... and soon."

"Please let me out. Please. I can't die in here. Just open the door. Everyone else in here is dead or in the late stages of the sickness. Most of the guards have stopped showing up. Even the Warden has run off. I get it, nobody cares about us. They were just planning for anyone in a cell to just up and die like everyone else. There's no point in saving us. But I'm not dying. I don't have it. They checked my blood twice and it's been clean both times. Please let me out. They didn't send me to death row or put me away for life. I was sentenced to five to seven, and now I have less than two to go. But if you don't help me, I'll die in here. Please. Please. I'm begging you, open the door. Let me out of this cage. Please. I don't want to die. I don't want to die. I'll do anything, just please..."

Harold Moor

Chapter 20

They didn't know what they would find in New Boston. Mark had spent the rest of the night and most of the predawn time hovering over the shortwave radio in the firehouse. He had hoped that everything that had happened up until this point would be undone with a transmission from the big city to cut the silence and explain it all. That message never came. Mark had met the morning exhausted and mentally drained. The Arbiter wished he was able to go with the group to New Boston, but he knew that was not a realistic desire. Someone had to stay and lead in Northeastern Connecticut. As difficult as it was to stand idle in this matter, Mark knew that the villagers—his friends, neighbors, and family—were ultimately his greatest priority.

The decision of who should go and who should stay behind was not an easy one. The leadership of Northeastern Connecticut knew that mobilizing a large expedition could start a panic in the village as well as leave the rest of the villagers open to attack. Sending a smaller group meant they ran the risk of being ineffective rescuers once they got to New Boston. In the end, it was decided that it would be best if a discrete but skilled party made the trip. If all that was required in New Boston were able bodies to help rebuild in the aftermath of some tragedy, then time was not of the essence, but anyone who was capable of rendering emergency aid was dispatched on the mission. A group of ten headed out on the northbound Interstate. Lea, Sir Leon, Doctor Michael, and Danny were among them.

Mark had watched the vans speed away up the asphalt and fought to hold his resolve while Lea vanished out of sight. He knew she would be as safe as she could be with the Templar at her side. Sir Leon would not let any harm come to her while he still had a heartbeat. That thought gave the Arbiter peace of mind. What unsettled him was the fact that he couldn't help but picture a situation where Lea would need a trained warrior's protection. At the very least, Mark knew that the group headed to New Boston was as far away for him as the other end of the radio. He went to speak into the microphone but stopped himself. They had not been gone even ten minutes, and he already wanted to check in with them. Mark told himself he needed to be stronger than that. It wouldn't send a good message if he let his fear infect those on the road.

Mark stood from his chair by the firehouse radio and paced back and forth several times over the creaky wood floors. He calmed himself as he reflected on the reality that nothing tragic had been confirmed. There was still the hope of a happy ending. The Arbiter resolved to keep that hope alive until reality said otherwise.

He couldn't take the mocking of the silent radio any longer and went down the stairs to the ground floor. He made his way to the coffee-maker and filled the water reservoir before turning it on to heat up. The simple ritual of making a hot beverage would provide the man with a few moments of distraction. At least that would be something other than the unbearable quiet of the early morning.

After several more moments of silence, the firehouse was filled with the bold aroma of freshly brewed coffee. The machine hummed and bubbled, and the Arbiter intently watched the coffee drip down into the pot waiting on the burner. The sounds and smells served their purpose to get his mind off what was happening on the road. He went to the cupboard above the countertop and plucked out a mug for himself. Mark was reaching for the powdered creamer when he heard the sound of someone moving in the room above. Stacy must have finally woken. The Arbiter reached for a second mug.

***

The interstate was clear and the vans made good time. Lea had seen them all well cared for and properly maintained. She had not made the trip to New Boston in years, but she still knew the way by heart. It was not a hard path to remember—just a straight shot north. She looked at the handheld radio sitting on the dashboard and hoped it would light up with the sound of Mark's voice—or even better, Henry's. It didn't. The black little device only stayed there silently. She went to reach for it, but Sir Leon's hand jutted out from the passenger seat beside her and stopped her from picking up the radio.

"I don't think that's such a good idea," Leon said. The speed of his hands and the abruptness of his speech caught Lea off guard.

"What do you mean?" she asked, wondering as to the cause of the Templar's wariness. Her eyes lingered on the man next to her for a moment too long, and she felt the rumble of grooved pavement shake the frame of the van. Lea corrected the course of the vehicle and brought it back into the lane.

"I know. I want to check in with Mark too. It's just that you can never be quite sure who's listening out there," said the Templar with a nod at the radio.

"Really? You think somebody's eavesdropping on us?" Lea said in a tone, one part sarcastic and one part genuine. She appreciated the Templar's sense of security and tactical acumen, but she felt that his hesitation to open radio contact with Mark back home could pass for paranoia.

"Probably not. I certainly wouldn't bet on it, but I don't want to

127

take any chances, all things considered," Leon said.

"I don't like this. I just want to let Mark know we're okay and not to worry," Lea said. She knew Leon's intentions were pure and sound, even if the possibility of a threat was highly unlikely. Still, it was hard for her to keep from sounding like a teenage girl whose father had just taken away her cell phone and car keys.

"I tell you what. In about another three exits, we'll only be another fifteen minutes out. We can check in then," said Leon.

"I think I can live with that," Lea responded, a measure of her usual cheer returning to her voice.

Only a few minutes passed before the radio clicked and a buzz of static filled the van. Lea and Leon sat up in their seats, startled by the sudden interruption. "Hey, it's Mark. I haven't heard anything from you guys since you left. How are you doing on the road?" The Arbiter's voice crackled over the radio.

"Well, so much for waiting," Leon said with a partial grin.

Lea's hand shot out like a bolt of lightning and snatched up the radio as soon as she heard the sound of Mark's voice. Her enthusiasm made the van run up on the grooved pavement of the side of the road once more. She corrected the course of the vehicle, then keyed the radio. But before she spoke, she looked to Leon beside her. The Templar offered a nod and a blink, silently giving her his blessing to respond.

"Things are going well out here. We should be there soon." She took Sir Leon's caution into account when forming her response, choosing her words carefully. She wanted to let Mark know that everything was fine and they were safe, but she didn't want to give up any details, just in case there were in fact unwanted people listening into the conversation.

"It's good to hear your voice. I'm glad the trip is going smoothly so far," Mark responded.

"We'll let you know what we see once we get to our destination," Lea said quickly. She tried not to get drawn into a conversation—or drain the radio battery—but she couldn't help her curiosity. "How are things back home? Is our guest doing all right?"

"Stacy's okay. She was up for a little, talking over coffee. I was going to take her to the pantry and get her something to eat. She's pretty hungry," Mark's replied over the radio.

"I think that sounds like a good idea. It's been at least a whole day since she's had any food. There are some..." Lea trailed off as her fingers left the radio key button. She stared, dumbstruck, at what lay before them.

"You're breaking up. I lost your last message," Mark said

Sir Leon grabbed the radio from Lea. "Just drive," he told her. "We don't know what that's all about yet. It could be a lot of things."

The determination in his voice gave Lea some focus—something to think about other than her knuckles turning white as she griped the steering wheel of the van like a vise.

"Mark, this is Leon," the Templar said, his voice flat and even.

"Leon, what's happening? Is Lea okay?"

"Lea's fine. She's driving right now. We're a little concerned by something we're seeing."

"Don't scare me like this. Just tell me what's going on," said Mark. His voice was still at speaking volume, but he was clearly on the verge of shouting.

"We can see smoke above the tree line. A lot of smoke," sir Leon said grimly.

There was a pause, and silence filled the van before Lea and Leon heard the radio click. "Can you tell what's burning?"

"No. We can only see smoke at this point. We'll let you know what we find when we find it. We'll be in New Boston in minutes now," Leon said.

"Thanks. The second you guys even suspect that you're in danger, I want you to get out of there at once. Understand?" Mark commanded.

"I understand. I'll make sure everybody stays safe," the Templar said, glancing intently at Lea.

They were tense moments in the van as Lea accelerated down the home stretch. The two vehicles following her struggled to keep pace. The frame of Lea's van shook as the speedometer crested over ninety miles an hour, and the sensation returned Lea from the inner tempest of horrid possibilities to the present. She let her foot off the gas and gently tapped on the break. The deceleration drew out a sigh of relief from the Templar, who clutched his armrest with a grip that could have broken bones.

"I'm sorry," Lea said quietly as the van returned to a more reasonable speed.

"I want to get there as much as anyone else. I understand how you feel. This is not an easy trip for me, either," said the Templar, cracking his knuckles.

"No," Lea said softly.

The tree line thinned out and parted as the trio of vans came up on the exit for New Boston. "No," she said again, this time louder; she saw now the origin of several trails of smoke reaching into the sky.

"Hold on. We'll see what we see," Leon said, apparently trying to be as soothing as he could but failing miserably. The tension in the van only grew as the smoke in the sky thickened the closer they got to New Boston. "It will all be okay."

It was not okay. Stacy had not been exaggerating when she said that New Boston was gone. There was not a living person to be found. Massive, fiery holes had been blown through the buildings. The streets of the city were littered with broken glass, fragmented steel, and concrete. Then there were the bodies strewn everywhere. It was heartbreaking.

The expedition from Northeastern Connecticut had to slow the procession of vans to a crawl as they searched the city. Eventually, the wreckage and debris was too dense that they had to leave their vehicles and proceed on foot. They were not sure exactly what they were searching for, just something other than smoke, fire, and the dead. It was hard for Lea to report what she was seeing to Mark over the radio. She fought valiantly to keep her composure, but the surrounding carnage had the greatest impact on her. The Templar relived her of that burden. It seemed easier for him, somehow, to verbalize the destructive aftermath.

The group fanned out while they looked for any survivors. Some of the dead had been covered with blankets or sheets, but the vast majority had just been left to rot in the streets where they lay. Those who searched through the rubble of New Boston shared in a unified sense of sadness mixed with rage.

***

Doctor Michael covered back up the body of a teenage boy who had been hit in the chest with a burst form a small-caliber automatic weapon. The doctor felt the taste of bile in his mouth. He turned to look at Sir Leon and Danny when he felt the presence of someone approaching.

"Nobody's alive. Not one..." Danny said meekly.

Michael stood and looked past the Templar and his doting acolyte to where Lea wiped tears from her face as she covered up a mother and daughter who had died in each other's arms. He leaned in to the two men and spoke low enough that Lea would not be able to hear. "Something I've noticed. Nearly every one of the bodies had a single bullet wound to the head. Many of them were inflicted post mortem as well."

"Why would anyone do that?" Danny asked hopelessly.

"Why would anyone do any of this?" Michael said as he gestured around at the smoldering ruins of New Boston.

"They were dead-checking them," Sir Leon said grimly.

"What?" Danny and Michal said in unison.

"Dead-check. It's something soldiers do after a battle. It's to make sure that nobody's playing dead or survives their wounds. They go and shoot anyone they can find, even if they don't look alive," Sir Leon responded.

"That's sick," said Michael. It was hard for him to get the words out as he felt the burn of acid in his esophagus.

"Yeah, but it's tactically sound. It stops any warning or information about the enemy getting to the other side," Leon said flatly. He looked like the act of sharing this information in itself was making him sick.

***

The group plodded through the wastes of the city. All they found was more of the same. Each step further into the killing field only demoralized them more and more. Sir Leon was in the front when the group rounded a corner that opened up into what had been the central junction of New Boston. He nearly fell to the ground once he processed what he saw, and the entire party stopped dead in their tracks.

"What? What is it?" Lea called from the back of the group.

The Templar's eyes widened with the realization of what seeing the gruesome display might do to the woman. "Do not come up here," he ordered.

Lea ignored him and ran quickly toward him. "Tell me," she yelled.

"Lea, stop." He put up a hand like it might help dissuade her from approaching the scene. He wanted to forcibly restrain her and spare her the sight, but he couldn't bring himself to lay his hands on her.

"No, no. No!" Lea sobbed after she rounded the corner and took in the horror awaiting her. The woman dropped to the ground, overtaken with the morbid energy plaguing the streets of New Boston. She lay there, tearful and grief-stricken.

No one else could take their eyes from the sight. There was the great stone arch with the words "Boston Strong" carved into it. It had served as an icon of the city's spirit and a testament to the resolve of its people to endure even the most profound hardships. New Boston's arch was one of the greatest sources of pride in the northeast; it was truly the first great landmark born in the world after the sickness had come to call.

Over the words on the arch hung a great white banner with a single word scrawled on it in crimson—"Traitors". Below the banner, hung by their wrists, were the corpses of fifty Templar Sebastian, forty Arbiters, and Henry.

It was a long time before anyone could do anything beyond stare at the grotesque theater before them. Sir Leon was the first to act. He keyed the radio and spoke. "Mark, are you still on?"

"Yes, I'm here. What's going on?"

"Lea's... We're all in rough shape. We're coming back now," said the Templar.

"What happened up there? Is anyone hurt?" Mark asked, a clear level of distress in his voice.

"No… no, uh… No, there's nobody we can help," Leon said, feeling an intense emptiness.

"Forgive me, Father, for I have sinned. This is my first confession. I don't even know where to start. I didn't believe in God before. I can't tell you if I do now. Isn't that the most foolish and prideful thing you've ever heard? All that's happened—what could it be but an act of God? And here I am, still a faithless nonbeliever. I've lied, cheated, stolen, hurt people and not given a second thought, but...but...this is so stupid... I never cared what others felt as long...as long as I got what I wanted. God or not, I don't want this to be who I am anymore. I mean, I had to live through it for a reason. There has to be a reason I lived and others didn't. Please tell me."

Unknown

Chapter 21

The van was quiet as a grave on the way back to the village. Sir Leon drove this time. Lea had curled up in the passenger seat, her cheeks still wet from the tears, but she had at least stopped sobbing for now. It had taken a great deal of coaxing from the Templar and several of the villagers to get her to her feet, let alone back to the van. The radio had been silent the whole trip thus far.

"I don't like that we just left him there," Lea said.

It partially relieved the Templar that she had broken the silence, but it also terrified him; he had little idea what he could say to console her. "We'll go back and make sure we take care of him. I promise," Leon said. He hoped he could find some way to pull Lea out of the emotional depths in which she now floundered.

"He belongs at home. He...he was one of us. We should have brought Henry back to the village," Lea said, cold and unfeeling.

Not much could be done for the men who had been strung up under the New Boston Arch. The people from Northeastern Connecticut were not about to leave them hanging for the crows. With the exception of Lea, the group had spent some time cutting them down and finding blankets to cover the dead. The plan was to get back to the village and figure out the best way to bury the countless dead in New Boston.

"Once we make sure that everyone in Northeastern Connecticut is safe, we'll have a proper memorial for him. I know many Templars who will come up form Sebastian Proper for this. Sebastian Clarke himself will want to be here," Sir Leon said with an impressive resolve.

Lea shifted and squirmed in the seat. For a moment, the Templar thought she was about to explode on him. She clearly seethed with rage and grief. "I don't think I want to talk about this anymore," she said quietly.

"Okay," Sir Leon responded in an even tone. He was glad for the return to silence. Lea was going to have to work through the sea of emotions filling her heart.

The convoy of vans sped along the interstate back towards Northeastern Connecticut. The findings in New Boston had taken a heavy toll on everyone who had taken part in the expedition. They couldn't get home fast enough. Each knew that the things that they had seen that day would stay with them for the rest of their lives, but the return to something familiar would help aid in their mental reconciliation. They were about half an hour from the boundaries of the village when the radio keyed on.

"Hey, did you guys have to detour over to I-95 to get back to I-395?" came the sound of Mark's voice over the radio on the dashboard. It was the first time he had broken the radio silence after learning of Henry's death.

Sir Leon's brow furrowed as he wondered what Mark could be getting at. He noted Lea sit up and come to attention in response to her lover's latest transmission. The Templar picked up the radio from the dashboard and keyed the microphone. "No, Mark. We're coming back the way we came. We're still on I-395 and southbound," Leon said warily.

"We have signs of movement coming up on I-395 northbound," Mark transmitted.

Leon felt his heart skip a beat. He could only imaging what Lea was feeling. He saw the woman's hands shoot to her temples, like she was on the verge of shutting down from all the emotional stimulation assaulting her. "Mark, that is not us on the road. We're still far from visual contact. That's not us coming northbound," Leon said with all the bravery he could muster.

"I don't like the way this looks. There are a lot of vehicles in-bound," Mark said over the radio. His transmission was quick but choppy and slightly garbled.

"What can you see? Can you tell us anything about them?" Leon said. Out of the corner of his eye, he saw Lea shaking her head as if from some horrible dream.

"There are a lot of vehicles. They're uniform in appearance... I... can see... distance..." Mark said through a wave of crackling static.

Lea came out of her fog and grabbed the radio from the Templar's hands. "Mark, baby? Mark? Can you hear me? Mark?" There was only silence. She tried to reach him again and again, but her efforts provided no results.

"Lea, we're going to get there—" Sir Leon started in an effort to calm the woman whose world was rapidly falling to pieces.

"Just drive, drive, drive... Please, drive..." Lea interrupted, on the cusp of rambling incoherently.

The Templar pressed his foot down on the accelerator. He knew that blindly charging into a potentially dangerous situation was ill-advised, but he couldn't let Lea dwell within the dark inner pit down which she was obviously spiraling. More than that, the Templar could not in good conscience allow the people of Northeastern Connecticut to come into harm's way. He also had to consider that maybe the inbound forces were friendly. Mentally preparing for the worst, Leon still held out a small flicker of hope that fortunes were about to change.

The two following vans matched pace with Leon's vehicle. He sped back to the village as fast as he could manage—a terribly nerve-wracking thirty minutes. The village water tower came into view, and soon thereafter, Leon fixed his eyes on the outermost buildings of North-eastern Connecticut.

"Mark? Mark? Please pick up. Mark, baby?" Lea spoke into the radio, nearing hysterics.

The Templar slowed his van to a much less reckless speed. "Things look okay from what I can see," he said, feeling hopeful. The village looked much like it had when the team had departed for New Boston earlier in the day. Things certainly did not appear anything like the horrid field they had uncovered in the city to the north. Even with the innocuously calm state of the village, things did not sit well with Sir Leon.

"I don't like this. Just get us home," Lea said.

"I will get us there. It'll be okay. Just a few more minutes." Leon strained to catch any details which might give some insight into the alarming news Mark had sent during the return trip home. His eyes wandered the buildings of the town. The Templar scanned each window and rooftop, trying to pick up anything out of the ordinary.

In a moment, the tense atmosphere erupted into total mayhem. It was too late when Sir Leon spotted the shooter. A rocket-propelled grenade blazed a trail through the air and slammed into the rear van. The vehicle exploded into a ball of flame and shrapnel, flipping end over end and landing on its roof. It was a quick death for the men inside. They never felt a thing.

Leon processed the event with lightning speed, instantly formulating a plan of evasion. It was not a moment too soon, because the Templar managed to swerve his van out of the path of a second rocket-propelled grenade. The projectile would have smacked into the windshield of Leon's van and blown it to scrap, but instead it detonated on the asphalt behind them. The explosion caused both remaining vans to lose control. Leon's van tipped and rolled side over side, while the other slammed into a couple of abandoned cars pushed off to the side of the road.

He couldn't tell if it had been seconds, minutes, or hours since the explosion and the car crash. The next thing Leon could tell for sure was that he had lost consciousness for some period of time. He found a high-pitched ringing in his ears and a partially deflated airbag stuffed in his face. His shoulder was sore where the seatbelt had restrained him, and his head pounded from the concussive force of the blast and the following series of impacts. Warm blood ran down the left side of his face; fragments of the driver's side window were still imbedded in his cheek and scalp.

We need to move, now. If we stay here, we're dead, Leon thought. He was terrified to look over at the passenger seat, dreading what might have happened to Lea. For all his courage and resolve, he didn't know if he could stand seeing that fantastic woman seriously injured...or worse. Necessity and survival instinct moved the Templar's body, and he looked over—which was now up, as the van lay on its side—at the seat where Lea had been.

"We need to move, now. If we stay here, we're dead!" Lea shouted from the passenger seat. "Can't you hear me? We need to go now!" She reached out to pull the Templar free from the driver seat.

Leon tried to blink the inner mental fog away, and Lea screaming at him helped to refocus his mind once he began moving again. "Out. Out the back," he rasped as he unbuckled his seatbelt and took her hand. She helped the Templar extricate himself, and they clamored into the back of the vehicle.

The smell of burning rubber, leaking motor oil, and gasoline hit the pair as they maneuvered past the sideways seats of the van. Automatic weapons fired somewhere outside. Leon risked a quick glance out of the cracked rear windows. He could not see the village from that angle, but he could make out the second van, mangled among the wrecked cars lining the interstate.

"Once we get out of the van, we need to stay close to cover and make for the trees when we have a clear avenue of escape," Leon said, opening his jaw wide and wiggling a finger in his ear. The high-pitched ringing in his head still affected him. He could see Lea's face set in a hollow and empty expression, but her fingers shook like she had just stepped into the bitter winter cold without anything more than a t-shirt. "Lea? You still with me?" asked the Templar.

It took the woman a moment to acknowledge the question, but she turned to Leon like he had just snuck up on her while she was enthralled in the pages of her favorite book. "Yeah, yeah. I'm good," she said unconvincingly.

The Templar looked about the jumbled contents of the items tossed all over the rear of the van. He identified the travel pack he had worn in New Boston under a pair of torn emergency blankets and a broken seat headrest. It carried survival essentials—food, water, antibiotics, and some hand tools. It would be enough for Leon and Lea to remain self-sufficient for several days.

"Lea, help me with this seat," Leon said as he tried to move the broken middle passenger bench seat. It had come off its brackets and pinned the pair of rifles he had brought against the wall of the van. He was just about to urge her to move quicker when she came to his aid. After a couple coordinated pushes, the seat finally moved and freed the weapons. "Are you okay with the AR?" the Templar asked.

"What?" Lea responded, still not fully present in the moment. She clearly still battled with all the mental endurance she had to keep herself from shutting down.

"The automatic rifle. Are you good to operate that weapon while I take the bolt-action rifle? I'll need you to lay down cover fire if I have to take a shot," Leon said hurriedly. Time was running short, and he could hear the sound of approaching vehicles on the road outside.

"Yeah, I can handle it," Lea said in one of her more mentally solvent moments.

"Okay, good." Leon gave the weapon a quick check before handing it to Lea. "It's all loaded and safety is off."

The Templar checked and secured the bolt-action rifle. He uttered a curse under his breath as he noted a hairline crack in the scope. It was most likely a cosmetic issue and would not interfere with the weapons accuracy, but Leon hoped he didn't have to find out the hard way. The Templar rubbed his hands and fingertips to get the blood flowing and feeling back into his extremities before grabbing as much ammunition as he could readily find in the messy van's interior. They wouldn't be able to last in any prolonged firefights, but they had enough bullets to make it hard for anyone else with designs on causing them harm.

"I'm going to open the rear doors now, and when that happens, we need to make for those three trucks stranded on the median," Leon said. He pointed to a collection of broken vehicles that looked like they would provide sound cover and a better vantage point to assess an escape route. Leon suspected they would have to work their way back along the winding path of wrecked cars before they made a break for the tree line. There was just too much open ground between the road and the woods on either side; it would be too easy for even a novice sniper to hit someone trying to disappear into the forest.

"Just follow me," Leon added and put his hand on the latch to open the back doors of the van. He was just about to breach out when he stopped himself. "If anything happens to me, stay close to the wreckage. Move along the interstate from car to car until you can't see the village anymore, then head into the woods. Okay?" he said morbidly. Lea said nothing. She just looked at him, like she silently accused him of prematurely accepting death. "Okay?" Leon repeated, an increased fire in his words.

"Okay," Lea responded with an underlying anger.

"Here we go." The Templar flung the doors open.

Light hit them both in the face, the sun of the bright day blinding them for a moment. Leon moved out of the smoking van with Lea close in pursuit. The sound of gunfire came from the town, and bullets cracked and clanged against the metal of the derelict cars scattered about the interstate. The pair made it to the three trucks Leon had indicated and took cover. They were well protected from the long-range shots coming from the rooftops and windows of Northeastern Connecticut, but the pressing concern were the four rapidly approaching Jeeps.

The next car that would shield them from the gunfire was only a short distance away, maybe ten feet. Leon had plotted out a course and knew the next five abandoned vehicles to which he would escort Lea. The Templar looked at the broken hull of the second van, where it had lodged itself between a pair of long forgotten cars. He waited for a few moments, trying to detect any signs of movement from the second van. He hoped the villagers had survived the crash and managed to escape. "Can you see anyone moving in the other van?" Leon asked amid the hail of bullets striking their shelter.

"No, nothing," Lea said.

Leon was just about to move on to the next car when the back doors of the second van opened and revealed Doctor Michael, Danny, and two other Northeastern Connecticut residents. They all sported cuts and bruises, but at least they were alive. Leon made eye contact with Michael and raised a hand to signal for him to stay put. The doctor understood the gesture's implications and held his position inside the van. Time for escape had nearly run out. The Jeeps pulled up, and over a dozen well-armed men got out and took firing positons.

"Mike, come to us. We'll cover you while you move," Leon called. "Once we start—" He stopped when he saw the front driver's side door of the van fly open, and the two men who had survived the crash stepped out to make a break for the tree line, followed by Danny and Michael. "Wait! Don't go for the woods! Stop!"

The two villagers got about twenty feet from the interstate when a blazing trail lanced from one of the windows in the village. The first man ran for several more steps despite three quarters of his skull being blown off by the sniper's tracer round. In one moment, the other man had been on his feet and only heartbeats away from the safety of the tree line. Then, two more sniper rounds hit the man in the torso. He fell to his knees, covered in his own blood, screaming in pain and terror while he held the majority of his intestines in his hands.

An onslaught of gunfire followed, but somehow, the sound of the dying man's cries rose above everything else. A human was not supposed to make that sound. Leon turned from the sight to see Michael standing by the van. It was plastered on the man's face; his duty as a healer overrode any sense of fear or self-preservation. Michael was too compassionate to turn his back on one of his own, even if they only clung to life by the slimmest of margins. The doctor grabbed his bag from the van and was on the asphalt with Danny close behind.

"Don't do it, Mike!" Leon shouted to no avail. "Lea, cover fire, now!" He hoped they could at least draw some of the aggression off of Michael and Danny, and they opened fire on the attackers. The rounds from Lea's automatic rifle struck the Jeeps nearby and made several men take defensive posture. Leon was pleased to see the damage to the scope of his rifle was in fact only cosmetic. The Templar took five shots with impressive speed, slaying three of the aggressors.

Michael was nearly to the wounded man when three more shots came from the village and ended his comrade's suffering. The realization that he was in open ground and totally unprotected hit the doctor hard, and he froze. "Danny, get out of here now," he yelled, frantically turning around.

"Mike, Danny, on me! On me!" yelled the Templar as he loaded a fresh magazine and shot wildly, partially exposing himself in an effort to bait return fire from the enemy.

Michael and Danny ran toward the three trucks where Lea and Leon hid. Lea and the doctor exchanged a glance just as a bullet ripped through his throat. "No!" she screamed.

One of Michael's hands went to his neck as it opened a fount of blood from his jugular. The other pushed Danny away and toward cover.

Leon notice Lea rush to the dying doctor's aid—a fool's errand. He would not see her killed for her love of family. The Templar's hand caught her collar just in time, and he drew her close. She was a petite woman, but the Templar felt as though he had just locked his arms around a lioness whose cubs had been threatened. He managed to bear her to the ground behind the trucks before she exposed herself to enemy fire. Then he met her gaze and pressed his body close to hers. She tried desperately to get out from under him to go to her friend, but Leon used his well-conditioned muscles to pin her to the asphalt.

Men were trying to kill them, good friends had just been murdered, two communities had been destroyed in as many days, and all Leon could feel was the pulsing of Lea's body beneath his and the sublime warmth of her breath on his cheek. This woman stirred a wicked longing within him. He was disgusted with himself, but his soldier's mettle won out over his self-loathing.

"He's dead. We can't save him," Leon said through clenched teeth.

"No," Lea whimpered.

"He's gone."

"No."

"Lea, I need you with me."

"It's not right."

"I know. Right now, we need to move."

"No," she sobbed.

Leon looked her dead in the eyes, feeling like a single ship fighting against a monstrous storm on the open ocean. He had to be calm and deadly, show her a peaceful heart and a warrior's spirit. "They killed Henry. They killed Michael and our friends and family. Do you want to make it easy for these bastards to kill us too?" Leon asked with ironclad resolve. His words seemed to touch a place of primal anger within Lea, like a key in a lock. A floodgate opened within her, and where there had been defeat, he now saw determination.

"No," Lea said with fearsome eyes and the pride of a legion of fighting men. "I want to kill them all."

Leon let her up. He glanced out at Michael's body; the doctor had stopped moving and was nothing more than a corpse growing cold. Danny was nowhere to be found. Lea and the Templar readied their guns and began a ferocious fighting retreat.

***

"Holy fuck, do you see that shit out there?" Mathew said to Tony as he observed the running gun battle through his binoculars.

"Yeah, those two little shits have killed about eight of our guys," Tony growled, looking at the carnage on the interstate leading to Northeastern Connecticut.

"That's not what I'm talking about," said the Congressman. He put his foot up on the lip of the firehouse roof and leaned forward, resting his hands on his kneecap.

"What do you mean?" Tony asked. The Patriot lowered his binoculars and gave the Congressman at his side a quizzical look.

"Do you not see that piece of ass out there with that Templar fucker?" Mathew said with an indignant huff. He was upset that he had to spell out something so obvious to his closest confidant.

Tony returned to his binoculars. "Oh yeah. She's pretty hot," he replied with an air of comprehension.

"There's no way I'm missing an opportunity to go balls deep in that at least once. I might as well blow my dick off if I let her get splattered now."

"I understand completely," Tony agreed.

The Patriot leader unclipped his radio from his belt and broadcast a transmission. "This is Haze. I need you men on the highway to take those two alive."

"Copy that, sir. We'll force a surrender."

"Excellent," Mathew said with staunch approval.

Tony gave the Congressman a confused look. "I get her, but why do we need the guy alive?"

"Just watch me work. This is going to be a good night tonight. Just like old times," Mathew said, salivating with anticipation.

The Fifty-Second Law
An Arbiter may uphold any decision mutually agreed upon by the Challenged and Challenger, even if it violates the laws of Adjudication.

Chapter 22

Northeastern Connecticut had fallen to the Patriots. The forces of Congressman Mathew Haze were like a red, white, and blue plague of locusts. They had marched from the most secluded woods of Maine down the east coast, visiting a trail of fire and sorrow upon all standing in their way. The last hope for stopping the Patriots from breaking out of the northeastern territory and spilling west was Sebastian Clarke and his Templars in Manhattan. The Templar Sebastian might have boasted superior numbers, but by all accounts, the Patriots were armed and equipped well enough to engage a more numerous foe. Northeastern Connecticut was the final settlement between Mathew Haze's Patriots and Sebastian Clarke's Templars. Less than a day's travel was bound to end in massive bloodshed and loss of life.

Every village and city had fallen to Mathew the same way. It started with a false showing of diplomacy, followed by a subtle instigation and provocation by the Congressman. He always got them to fire the first shot. He was a truly gifted manipulator. It was as impressive to watch him speak as it was repugnant, but a strange juxtaposition was at work. While the Congressman's masterful oratory skills drew his followers ever closer in their fanatical loyalty, each time the eldest of the

Haze brothers made a show of civility, it only widened the growing rift with his younger sibling.

Now was the final night before the Patriots' push to victory in Manhattan. Mathew expected to win in glorious fashion against the Templar Sebastian, but he held no illusions that it would be a hard-fought battle and a costly engagement. In observance of this fact, he wanted to spend the last night before his great offensive creating a truly memorable experience. He wanted to celebrate the imminent demise of his only opponent with something he could always look back on with fondness.

The village of Northeastern Connecticut had very little to offer the Patriots in the way of spoils. The treasure to be plundered from the quant little community was certainly a far cry from the resources taken after the fall of New Boston. The food pantries were amply stocked, but that was of little use to Mathew Haze's considerably larger troop of men. Plenty of vehicles had been well looked after, along with all the appropriate tools to maintain them, but the Patriots already had quite the robust motorcade. The Congressman managed to scrounge up some alcoholic libations from the town, but none of it resembled anything top-shelf quality. In truth, Mathew had thought the town would be little more than a place to rest his head for the night. At least they had worthwhile beds in the village.

His harsh criticism of the sleepy northeastern keep rapidly changed when the Congressman first laid his eyes on Lea. He had not seen such an attractive woman since *before*. His latest dalliance, Debbie, had quickly lost her appeal. Even when Mathew handled Debbie roughly, she often failed to please him. Lea's timely appearance seemed like a gift from on high, in a way. She would be a fitting trophy for Mathew to commemorate his triumphant march southward. He would enjoy breaking her. The Congressman had come to realize, in his appreciation of beautiful things, that he derived the greatest pleasure from seeing them controlled, dominated, and destroyed. And Lea was beautiful indeed.

Some of the Patriots had turned in for the night, but most found ways to celebrate their conquest of another bastion opposing the noble restoration of democracy. The village of Northeastern Connecticut rang rampant with cheers of victory and proclamations of national pride. The men were drunk on Mathew Haze's proud words. The heart of the once peaceful village now overflowed with a mob of crazed warmongers, save for one relatively quiet location

It was a cold walk to the library from the pharmacy medication cage, where Leon and Lea had been detained. So close to winter, the autumn night was chilly, and Lea was without her jacket, stripped down to her t-shirt and ripped cargo pants. The cold snap in the air made her shake and tremble, but so far that remained the only reason for her quivering.

Mathew, Tony, and six other Patriots surrounded Lea and the Templar, who stood in the middle of the library lobby. Each man regarded the pair like a great white shark would stalk an unsuspecting seal before breaching on its prey, brandishing their rifles and other firearms. It was a silent show of force. The pack of men simply wanted to bury the point up to the hilt with their exhibition of dominance.

Tony had personally selected the six Patriots who accompanied him and the Congressman, each one a kindred spirit to Mathew Haze; they all shared his particular brand of morality. These were not the sort of men who followed the Congressman because they believed in the dream of an America reborn and a fresh new democracy. They followed the man because they had a thirst for power. Their breed thrived on the revolting scenario about to unfold before them.

Mathew Haze sprang up from his seat behind the book checkout station. His motion was quick and sudden. He had planned his disturbance of the uneasy silence to garner maximum effect and draw all the focus in the room to himself at once. He said nothing, only walked across the room to where Lea and Leon stood with their hands duct-taped behind their backs.

The Congressman met Lea's gaze first, lingering there. She proudly and defiantly gave him an unflinching stare. Mathew slowly moved his face towards hers, still saying nothing. Neither one broke eye contact. "You're a fighter. I see it," Mathew finally said before withdrawing his face. He wanted to say more, but he needed to exercise some

147

restraint for the next few moments. There would be plenty of time to gloat later.

Next, Mathew moved over and looked Leon in the eyes. He did not take his time falling into the Templar's stare like he had with Lea. "Huh," he grunted before turning his back to the Templar. The tension held in Leon's posture relaxed, but then Mathew spun back around and struck Leon in the solar plexus. The Templar seemed to flex his core just in time, potentially lessoning the blow, but the wind was still knocked out of him. Mathew quickly followed up his sucker punch with several blows to the staggered Templar's face.

"No! Stop it! Stop!" Lea yelled.

Mathew stayed his hand and looked Lea in the eye again, thoroughly content with what he saw there. The hard edges and armor he'd detected within the woman had been stripped away by attacking the Templar. She clearly had strong feelings for the man, and it was precisely the leverage he'd been trying to find. "Good. I'm glad we got that straight," Mathew said as he went to lean up against a long, rectangular table.

"Leon, your face," Lea said, squatting next to her friend. The Congressman's strikes had exacerbated several cuts on Leon's face from the car crash.

"I'm fine. It'll heal," Leon said reassuringly. Having been battered into a kneeling position, the Templar returned to his feet.

Mathew folded his arms and savored the moment before he launched into his performance. He always took pleasure in the time preceding one of his addresses. "It's a special night tonight, and you both get to be part of it. You do as you're told, and you might even live to remember it. Before I go any further, I need to make sure that we all understand each other," Mathew said with a vile smirk.

He approached Leon again and took a brief second to admire his handiwork on the man's face. "Listen to me, you Templar piece of shit. You do anything I don't like, you speak, you try to run or resist or even look at me in a way I don't agree with, I'll take a hacksaw to those perfect, perky tits of hers and let your girl bleed out upside down from the flagpole outside." His words seemed to cut the Templar like a hot blade.

The Congressman heard Lea stifle a gasp of horror next to him. The threat seemed to have done its job, but the Congressman was the sort to guild the lily, and he pressed the freshly subjugated man. "Do you for one second think I won't?"

Leon shook his head. The Templar's acknowledgment of submission made Mathew beam with wickedness. Having captured Leon's spirit and brought it firmly under his heel, the Congressman moved back to Lea.

Again, he savored looking into her eyes, relishing in the cracks showing through her mental fortitude. Mentally abusing this woman was going to give him as much pleasure as the physical torment he had arranged, if not more. "You. I'm sure you can figure out what's about to happen. You resist us at all, and I break his arms and set his legs on fire before I dump him in the pond down the street. Tell me you understand."

Lea couldn't put up a brave front any more, her eyes wide with emotion. She nodded.

Mathew gave the Templar an oppressive look. He waited to see the flicker of acceptance in the man before he slapped Lea across the cheek. She let out a light grunt when his palm connected. The Templar was obviously using every ounce of his considerable resolve to keep from lunging at the Congressman. "I said tell me you understand, you fucking whore," Mathew said. His comments drew several chuckles and jeers from the Patriots gathered around.

"I understand," Lea said.

"Good." Then Mathew unleashed a load of spit straight into Lea's face. "Don't you fucking wipe that off," he added, delighting in the beautiful woman's disgust. The Templar beside her averted his eyes. "We only want one thing from you." He grabbed Lea by the shoulder with one hand and slipped his other down the front of her pants. He pushed two fingers inside her, and she shouted in pain and humiliation. Mathew withdrew his hand and gave a pause to let the full realization of what was in store set in for her. "Actually, that's a lie. We want a few things from you." Then he grabbed at her breasts and cupped her mouth with his right hand.

Mathew returned to his spot leaning up against the long table, letting his prisoners stew in the expectation of immanent brutality. He further mounted the tension by temporarily removing his focus from his victims and addressing his followers. "We're on to Manhattan tomorrow, and with it, we'll be up against the greatest challenge the cause has yet to face. We'll be going head to head with Sebastian Clarke and his Templars. They're far more dangerous than any of the little country folk we've encountered thus far. Make no mistake, we will beat them, but they won't go easy. A lot of good men, true Patriots and real Americans, will die tomorrow." Mathew slowly paced around the long table. "So, for tonight, we'll be like fucking gods and take everything we want!" he shouted, punctuating his statement with a fist smashed into the table. Like always, his words caused his followers to erupt in cheers and applause.

***

It took everything Lea had to keep from breaking into tears. Leon subtly moved closer to her and brushed the back of his bound hands against hers in a gentle, peaceful motion. The calming gesture helped them both find a fraction of peace to cling to in the madness. At the very least, they knew that whatever happened, they did not have to endure it alone.

Leon's kindness and compassion helped guide Lea back to that mental armor, shielding her mind and preventing cruel men from crushing her spirit. She was every bit the warrior as the Templar at her side. She stole a look into Leon's eyes, instantly renewed in her bravery. He was like the eye of an autumn storm. Peace at the center of chaos. Her mettle had wavered before, but now she made herself an oath that whatever these men might do to her body, she would not let them own her spirit.

***

Mathew let the library fade back to its deadly, silent atmosphere before he returned to the bound pair in the middle of the room. The Congressman noted a change in Lea's demeanor. Her hands did not shake or tremble as before. Most of all, that defiant, challenging stare had been reborn in her eyes. Mathew could not abide that.

In the past, when he had taken what he wanted from a woman by force, he had seen such a look before. His victims would sort of step outside their bodies as he used them. While it rewarded him physically, that was all these experiences had done for him. He needed her to be here, present and receptive, so he could derive maximum enjoyment from the ordeal. Mathew needed to break her in a way from which she could never return. Fortunately for the Patriot leader, he had just the plan of attack in mind. Ruining this beautiful woman would be spectacular.

"One of the things I've learned to be a great truth is never to rush a good thing," Mathew said with a palpable air of malice. "Something quickly obtained is of lesser value than a thing that comes as a reward for patience and restraint. This is what we have here. If we just go and hurry to the end, none of us get to enjoy the journey." He addressed this last statement to the men gathered around, garnering several nods and looks of agreement. The Congressman moved in close to Lea and softly put one hand on the side of her face, whispering into her ear. "You think you can hate me. Good. You should try. But you can't hate me. You're too weak to hate me. I don't fucking lose to little girls."

He stepped back, then withdrew the hunting knife sheathed at his waist. Pressing the flat of the blade into the side of Lea's face, he circled around behind her. The woman never moved, her eyes shut tightly against the knife at her cheek, and then Mathew cut the tape binding her hands. He did the same with the Templar.

The Congressman returned to prowling the room as he commenced his oratory. "As much as I like taking what I want, it's nice to see things given willingly. I won't have you be so defiant when my guys here work out some of their pent-up aggression." He circled back around to face Lea, taking his time. He wanted to take a few breaths so her imagination would become her own enemy for a moment. "I want you to fuck him," Mathew said, pointing to Leon.

"What?" she gasped, blinking rapidly. The Templar blushed profusely.

Mathew thought about hitting her for her lack of comprehension but decided against it. He felt his words would be enough without the physical pain to accompany them. "I want you to fuck him, and I want you to convince us that you want it," Mathew said. He could see it in Lea's face; this was the way into her mental isolation. She was not going to be able to hide from this in a realm of desensitization.

"What? I…" Lea started.

Mathew pulled out his gun and put it to Leon's head. "I'm not going to tell you again, you stupid slut. You fuck him like a dirty fucking whore," yelled the Congressman. "Tell him you want it. Tell him you're a whore."

Lea froze in place, then drew in a sharp gasp as Mathew pulled pack the hammer on his pistol and pressed it further into Leon's forehead. She stared at the Templar, seemingly waiting for him to intervene, but the man did nothing.

"I'm a whore." Her voice came out as little more than a whimper.

"Oh, fuck. I said be convincing," Mathew snarled.

"I'm a whore. I'm a whore," Lea said, much the same way she had at first.

"Shit, you're fucking useless." Mathew stepped back and took a shooter's stance. His gun barrel was aimed right at Leon's head.

"I'm a whore! I'm a whore! I'm a fucking dirty whore!" Lea said with improved conviction. Her voice still waivered and shook, but she did not sound as pathetic as before.

Mathew looked at her and gloated in supremacy for a moment before he tipped his gun barrel up and smiled. "Very good. That was better." He quickly trained his gun back on the Templar. "But you know, I'm still not convinced."

Lea shut her eyes when she spoke this time. "I'm a nasty fucking girl. I'm such a dirty, slutty whore. I fucking love cock. I love grinding on thick, hard dick. I want his cock. I need his cock in me." Lea's eyes opened, accompanied by a pair of tears.

"So get to it," Mathew said, returning to his place leaning against the table.

Lea moved closer to the Templar, and their eyes met. Leon felt a fear that had never before come to haunt him. She was there right in front of him—his fantasy made real. It was all his for the taking.

He was being forced. He could have her and still keep a pure conscience; it would not count as a betrayal of his friendship with her or with Mark. Leon had to confess to himself that he wanted this. Deep down, he wanted this—craved it, even. He shut his eyes, because he could not stand the sight of the woman who slayed him so. The Templar shook with fear, adrenalin, and guilt.

Some of the Patriots assembled around them had undone their pants, already stroking themselves. Others brimmed with low, twisted laughter. "Hey. Hey, look at me," Lea said ever so gently, putting a hand on his cheek. Leon recoiled from the chill on her fingers. She withdrew her hand and warmed it with her breath, then returned it to his face. This time, he accepted her touch, his eyes were shut. "Look at me, Leon," Lea said, her voice so divine it could set the oceans on fire.

The Templar opened his eyes. He was more frightened than he had ever been in his life. Lea's hand felt so good on his face, and he hated it. He hated how comforting it was when her other hand took his and interlocked with his fingers. Leon wanted to die.

"It's okay," she said lovingly. Leon's breathing continued irregularly, shaking. "It's okay." This time, she leaned in and softly kissed the Templar on his cheek. "It's okay," she said again and again, kissing him each time. Then she let her lips linger on his skin. She pulled back and looked at Leon with perfection. "It's okay," she said one final time before she pulled him in to meet his lips with hers.

The kiss was the most beautiful thing Leon had ever experienced. He fought it at first. He denied wanting it more than he had wanted anything. He hated himself as his hand found its way onto Lea's waist and he pulled her into an embrace. They enjoyed the feel of each other's mouths for what seemed like a long time. When they parted, Lea gave a soft, floating moan and looked at Leon with inviting eyes. Electricity pulsed through Leon's body. He couldn't take this anymore.

"Nice. Now get on your knees and suck his fucking cock, bitch,"

Mathew spat among the grunts and groans of his fellow Patriots.

For a moment, they had managed to push out everything but each other. Mathew Haze had ended the intimate moment with his repugnant vulgarity. Lea slid her hands down Leon's muscular chest and firm abdomen. Once she was on her knees, she unbuckled his pants. Leon shook, convulsing. It was like he had been stuck by lightning. Lea slipped down his pants and underwear, stopping before she could put him in her mouth.

Leon had started to sob. He cried like a child who had broken a bone for the first time. Tears flowed down his face like a rainstorm. This paragon of discipline, this fearless warrior, had broken into hysterics. The sound of his crying filled the library.

The sound of Mathew Haze's devilish laughter was the next thing to overtake Leon's grief. "Oh, that is *too* good. That's too fucking good." He laughed, slowly clapping. "Okay, enough of this proxy shit. It just goes to show you can't beat a classic," Mathew blared. He tossed the roll of duct tape to Tony. "Get this limp-dick faggot out of here."

Tony bound the Templar's hands and escorted him out of the library back to the pharmacy cage.

***

As soon as the doors to the library had shut, Mathew looked at Lea with malice. He could see it in her now. He had won. Breaking the Templar had broken her. Now that they were separated, she was so much more vulnerable. He had been upset that crushing her resolve would come at the price of getting her after another man had had his way, but the Templar's emotional breakdown had given him everything he wanted. Now it was time to finish her off—to ruin her.

"Table," Mathew said with a flick of his wrist. Like a pack of wild dogs, the Patriots set upon Lea. Three of them lifted her up and forced her to the long table. One went about pulling down her pants. Lea squirmed and struggled reflexively, shuddering whenever one of them touched her bare skin.

Mathew was first. He pushed into her, long and slow, while the others held her down, taking his time with each thrust. Whenever he felt her start to drift away, he brought her attention back with blows to the face and bites on her neck and ears.

After the first few minutes, Lea finally screamed in rebellion. It only intensified the experience for the Patriots. When he neared the end, Mathew put his hand around her throat and squeezed. He put increasingly more pressure on her delicate neck until he released inside her and roared. He made her look him in the eyes the whole time.

"Damn, that's good. I'm going to take a shit now. Enjoy her, men," Mathew said as he climbed off Lea and wiped the sweat from his face. Then he went down the stairs to the restroom and left Lea screaming on the table as Tony started his turn with her.

***

"Aw, fuck. Shit," Tony exclaimed after less than a minute. He had not lasted very long at all. Several of the Patriots laughed and mocked the man's lack of sexual stamina. Tony grabbed Lea by the face and leaned into her. "I'll find you later, bitch. To be fucking continued," he growled through clenched teeth. Then he clamored off the table and pulled up his pants. "Fuck all you assholes." Tony stormed out of the library, oozing embarrassment.

Lea continued her screams, but after the fourth man had finished between her legs, those screams turned to tears. Lea was hopeless, defeated; she just wanted it to end. She didn't care if they killed her. Each time a man rammed into her, she hoped it would be the last time and someone would just put a gun to her head. She had never been a spiritual woman, but now, in her most dire hour, she prayed for mercy.

"What the fuck is this?" shouted Aaron Haze with a voice commanding righteousness and virtue.

The Sixty-Sixth Law
Only the Challenged may call for combat to the death.

Chapter 23

Aaron exploded through the library doors like a cannon, moving with an air of zealous indignation. The Congressman's younger brother was never one to act in rash or impulsive fashion, but what he saw his brothers-in-arms doing to their prisoner unchained something within his core. Normally, he would seek to assess a situation and try all peaceful means of resolution before turning to a physical solution. Peace was the farthest thing from his spirit, now.

His being burned with a primal sense of right and wrong. There were no complex ethics to debate, no extenuating circumstances to ponder. What was going on in front of him right now was wrong, undeniably wrong. Aaron Haze was a man of conscience. More than anything, he was a good man. He was going to put an end to the evil occurring before his very eyes.

None of the Patriots paid him any mind. They were all thoroughly engrossed in their savage brutalization of the helpless woman pinned to the table. Aaron was not a large man, but the strength of his conviction allowed him to achieve the incredible. With one hand, he grabbed a handful of the Patriot's hair who was bearing down on the woman. In a profound show of strength, he lifted a man nearly twice his size into the air and threw him to the ground. That act put the room into total silence save for the woman's soft whimpering.

The cold air in the library was filled with nothing but violent tension and wrath yet to be realized. Arron felt as though he stood on the ledge of a tall building, looking down at a deadly plummet to the street below. All he had to do was let himself fall.

The Patriot he just assaulted returned to his feet and shoved Aaron hard in the chest. "What the fuck is your problem? Just wait your turn."

That statement was all it took to push Aaron over the edge and send him diving into freefall. The total lack of conscience in this man was disgusting enough. The fact that he was so far gone as to assume that Aaron's first intention was to join in this abomination stung the Congressman's younger brother like frost. Aaron pulled his pistol from his gun belt and shot the Patriot point-blank in the head.

The gunshot reignited the poor woman's screaming. The Patriots gawked at the blood-spattered body spilling a growing red pool on the floor of the library. Everyone stood still as a rock save for Aaron, whose seething anger was so great he could not stop from shaking. Aaron thought to send the rest of the men in the room to join their compatriot, but he did not act on the impulse. His sense of mercy won out over his need for punishment.

"Get out! Everybody get the fuck out of here, right now!" Aaron shouted. He fired his gun into the bookcases lining the walls, and the five remaining Patriots scrambled to get out of the room. A few tripped over each other. Another fell several times during his exit as he tried to pull his pants up from around his ankles.

Aaron's gun fell silent as he reloaded the empty weapon. The woman had quieted and sought refuge against the side of the main desk. She sat on the floor, shivering and holding her knees to her chest.

A sorrowful calm found each of them. It was the same emotion but originated from separate places. The woman's physical shock seemed to dissipate, now turning inward toward her intellect. Aaron was starting to come to grips with the fact that he had just killed a man without any reasoning, rational, or attempt to find a path to peace.

"What did you do?" Mathew said from behind. His voice was stripped of its usual bravado, and there was an evident sense of anxiety in his words.

The sound of his brother's voice rekindled the frenzy that had just subsided within Aaron. The younger of the Haze brothers spun around with his weapon aimed right at Mathew's chest. "What did I do?" Aaron said with mocking resentment. "What did I do?" He raised his voice, great chunks of spittle flying from his lips. "What did I do!" He took several steps towards his older brother. "What did *you* do?" he hissed.

"Aaron…" Mathew started, putting his palms up in defense.

"Don't say my name! Don't you say my fucking name!" Aaron shouted. Then he lunged at Mathew and grabbed him by his shirt. He pushed and shoved his brother with a strength fueled by rage in its purest form. After physically dominating the man for several moments, he threw him up against a large, free-standing bookcase with enough force to send several books from the upper shelf raining to the floor.

"Did you know about this? Tell me. Say it. Did you fucking know? Come on, lie to me, you fuck! Fucking lie to me like you always do. You're so fucking good at it! Tell me you didn't know! Come on and do it! Make me believe you. Fuck you. Fuck you!" Aaron shouted so loud his voice began to crack. His stare burned into Mathew.

It was fortunate that the Congressman had just emptied his bowels. If he hadn't, he would have assuredly soiled himself right there. His eyes said it all—he was more afraid of his brother than of telling the truth. "I knew…and I raped her too," Mathew confessed.

"What is wrong with you?" Aaron said coldly before he struck Mathew in the face with the butt of his weapon. "Why would you? This is not who we are." He pistol-whipped his brother a second time. "This is not what we do." Aaron struck him again. "This is not what we do." He reared back for another strike with his gun but stopped.

"Please…" Mathew said defenselessly. He seemed completely taken aback by Aaron's outburst. His eye flicked to the woman, who still cowered by the desk.

Aaron saw Mathew's gaze drift. That act restored his raucous temper. He was suddenly hit with something greater than his hatred for Mathew's wickedness. Now, he became aware of the fact that however far the depth of Mathew's cruelty, the woman he'd violated had been scarred to an even greater level. "You do not look at her. You do not ever fucking look at her again! Never!" Aaron roared, pressing the barrel of his gun into Mathew's forehead. "I'll kill you. I'll do it. I'll kill you. I'll kill you." He repeated those three words over and over while pressing his weapon into his brother's face, harder and harder.

"No!" Mathew screamed in one long, continuous cry. The feeble plea for mercy fell on deaf ears as Aaron continued his mantra.

Aaron cocked back the hammer on his weapon and slowly applied pressure on the trigger. Mathew closed his eyes, continuing his desperate cry for pardon. Aaron nearly fired the gun when he saw the corpse of the Patriot he had shot just minutes earlier. The sight of the man lying cold and bloody sobered him of his overflowing rage. "This is not what we do," Aaron said and lowered his weapon. "Get out of my sight." He cast his eyes away from his older brother. Now, even the mere vison of Mathew made him feel nauseous.

Without a word, Mathew fled the library.

Aaron tried to swim the sea of emotions in his heart, to weather the storm of thoughts in his mind. The sound of the woman's crying pulled him out of his introspection. He saw the broken woman, and his heart suffered a wound that would never heal. His raged softened into mourning and pity.

He took a step toward her a little too quickly, and it made her jump and quake. "I'm sorry. I'm sorry. I won't hurt you. I promise," Aaron said, spreading his arms wide and laying his weapon on the floor in front of him. He felt the need to help this woman now more than anything else. "My name is Aaron Haze. I'm going to sit down here," he said and sat down on the floor. "I want you to know that you're safe now. I'm not going to touch you or come near you, but I'll be right here. I'm going to stay with you for a while. Nobody else will hurt you. I won't let them."

159

"I swear, you're some kind of stupid, boy. You can't do anything right, can ya? You're never going to be able to learn nothing. I told ya to get me a bottle, not a can. The cans ain't cold yet. Don't you back-sass me, boy. I know what I said. I said a bottle. Now quit yer hollering. It don't hurt that bad. Ya ain't no girl, so shut up and take it like a man. Danny, close yer damn mouth and stop that cryin. Now go back to the fridge and get me a bottle like I told you in the first place. And bring me my belt, too. I'm gonna show you what something to cry about feels like."

Randel Matager

Chapter 24

The pharmacy was poorly lit, especially in the back where Leon was being held in the medicine cage. A few work lights had been strung up to keep the place from falling into pitch darkness, but the pharmacy was not one of the more commonly used buildings in the village. For that reason, it had never been equipped with a proper generator. The only person with any use for the building was Michael, but he mostly used it for storage. It was a matter of convenience, really. There was not much point to relocating all the pills and bottles that already had a well-organized home. When Lea and Leon were captured and locked up, it was the first time the Templar had actually ever seen the inside of the building.

The pair had spent several hours locked up in the pharmacy before the Patriots came to take them to the library. They were grateful not to have been separated while they were held. They'd spent some of their time postulating who these people might have been or why they were here; they both agreed it was probable that they were the ones responsible for the tragedy in New Boston. They also wondered what might have become of the rest of the villagers in Northeastern Connecticut. To their horror, on the way to the pharmacy, the Templar and Lea had seen several bodies in the streets, much like the ones in New Boston. Still, they were unable to confirm the identities of many of the dead. Mark might have been among them. As they'd walked the bloody streets of the village, looking for signs of her man had been the only thing that existed to Lea. Leon had done everything in his power to strengthen her morale and resolve.

He had expected a standard interrogation when they were brought to the library. But he was not prepared for what happened inside those walls. The man had trained every day to be strong. In a matter of minutes, he realized how futile that training had been. Now he sat alone in a shadowed room with only his grief and his guilt.

Several hours later, Leon's tears finally ceased to fall. He was somewhat grateful for his solitude. He was glad that nobody else had to see him in such a vulnerable state, especially *her*. The Templar dared not imagine what was happening to Lea since he had been returned to the cage alone.

He could not stop thinking about what had just happened, his guilt twofold. First, he admonished himself for being too inept to keep Lea from harm. He replayed the events on the interstate over and over, pushing his tactical acumen to the limits, making sure his plan for escape was the best possible version it could have been. It never removed the heavy burden of failure, but knowing that he had done everything in his power to avoid it eased the weight. Still, he wondered if there had been another way or if he could have done more.

That grief was daunting, but it dwarfed in comparison to the guilt he felt for allowing himself to finally succumb to his desire for Lea. Here in the darkness, the Templar finally confessed it to himself; he was in love with her. Leon despised his heart for so cruelly betraying the rest of his being. His respect for the love shared by her and Mark was unimpeachable. So was his friendship with the pair of them. He knew that taking her there on the floor of the library—fulfilling the fantasies he never indulged— would have been a means to save them from the brutality of their captors. If he had been able to cling to his sense of duty and keep his heart from the affair, perhaps he could have seen the act through. But in those moments, he was neither a man of principle nor worthy of the title Templar Sebastian. When he held her in his arms and felt her body pressed closed to his, honor and chivalry had fled completely. All that had existed for him was the serene beauty in her old-world eyes, the indescribable softness of her skin, and the pleasure of her lips. Leon's tears were renewed, as was his hatred of himself.

The sound of someone approaching withdrew him from his sorrow. Perhaps they had finished with Lea. He didn't know if he had the fortitude to meet her gaze now. He didn't know if he could ever bring himself to look at her again. Maybe their captors were now coming to finish him. He had clearly not provided his abductors with the sport they desired to see. The men who had taken the village knew he was a Templar Sebastian and showed no evident love for that fact. He guessed that the next time he saw one of them, it would be for his execution.

Leon's resolved had cracked in regards to Lea, but he reflected on the fact that he had spent virtually all his life *after* as someone who stood up for those in need of a protector. He had put his life on the line for others on many occasions. Men and women of the new world respected and admired him for the breed of man he had become and the manor and fashion in which he lived his life. Leon swore that when it came time, he would die in the way he had lived. The Templar refused to let his enemies feel they had conquered him. He would peacefully defy them like the mountain he was. Standing, Leon made to receive whoever was coming like a man proud to wear the shield of the Templar Sebastian. When he saw the person's face, his heart caught in his chest.

"Where are the keys?" Danny whispered. He was dirty and banged up from the battle on the interstate, with a few deeper cuts on his face not fully clotted and still trickling little drops of blood.

"Daniel. I don't believe it," gasped the Templar. Sir Leon never would have believed that seeing his hapless follower could make him feel such a great measure of relief. In all honesty, Leon had forgotten about the young man until this very moment. That fact squeezed a special little stir of guilt in the Templar's heart which belonged just to Daniel.

"I hid in the trunk of a town car. I saw them take you and Lea. I didn't know how to help you. I'm sorry," Danny said.

"You don't have to apologize. There was nothing you could do. You were smart to hide the way you did. I'm impressed you were able to slip in here undetected. That couldn't have been easy," Leon said encouragingly. The Templar shouldered enough guilt for the both of them. He did not need Danny to torment himself so.

"It was just a matter of patience and choosing the right time to move. Like you taught me," Danny said in a hushed voice. He scoured the nearby cubbies and drawers for the cage key.

"They keep the keys on them. You're going to have to break the lock to get me out." Leon tried to make out anything well suited to breaking the lock on the cage.

"Okay. I think I can manage that. What did they do with Lea?" Danny asked.

The question was like a razor drawn across his skin. Just the mention of her name made Sir Leon feel weak and helpless. He could not recount the events that transpired in the library and keep his composure. "Just focus on the lock for right now. We'll get Lea once I'm out," Leon said quickly.

"Right," Danny responded as he hefted a shelf bracket that had been loosed from one of the inventory display shelves. "I think this might work."

"Maybe. They're still making a lot of noise outside with their celebrating, but you need to be as quiet as possible," Leon said, peering through the darkened pharmacy at the dancing silhouettes outside. "The lock is pretty sturdy, but the latch itself seems like it could be busted open with a few good blows."

"Okay," Danny said with a warry glance over his shoulder. He took a moment to steady his aim and get a firm grip on the shelf bracket. With a grunt, he wacked the lock on the cage. He was obviously afraid to put much power behind the blow, and the lock repelled the strike.

There was a frozen moment as Leon and Danny waited to see if any response to the noise came from the men outside. The activities outside the pharmacy continued in the same fashion. "Okay, Daniel. That was good, but you're going to have to hit it harder than that. Try again, ok?" Leon urged.

Danny checked over his shoulder again, then slammed the lock several more times. The young man put all his might into the blows now. He struck the cage lock until his arms shook, but the bracket had not accomplished much more that some dings and scratches in lock's finish. "This doesn't seem to be working," he said with a hint of demoralization.

"It's okay. You're doing just fine. We need something heavier to hit with is all," Leon said, forcing himself to sound upbeat about the circumstances.

"All right, I'll see what I can find," Danny said. He went about searching the Pharmacy for something with greater bulk.

After several moments of scrounging, Leon heard it. The front door to the pharmacy opened, and footsteps approached in the low light. Leon didn't have a line of sight on Danny, but he couldn't risk exposing him by calling out, so he tried to quickly come up with a plan.

"I hope you're ready for round two, because I'm—" Tony arrived at the medicine cage, jingling a set of keys. He stopped mid-sentence and looked upset when he saw that Lea was not where he expected to find her.

"Sir Leon, I think I need to try and make it to the firehouse for some bolt cutters. I can't find…" Danny started as he came back into view. The young man halted his words abruptly and fearfully as the Patriot turned and locked eyes with him. Only a half a second passed before the realization of what was set in motion dawned on all three men.

"Shit," Tony exclaimed as he went for the gun at his side.

"Danny! Run! Get away!" Leon shouted. The Templar banged his hands on the mesh of the cage imprisoning him.

The Templar's warning cry seemed to spur the young man into motion. Danny closed the distance between himself and the Patriot with good speed. He shoulder-checked the Patriot into the cage and grasped Tony's hand before he could raise his gun to fire.

Leon was overcome with a moment of shock. Danny had not fled; that would have been his best option for escape. The technique and speed Danny demonstrated with his rush was sound. Leon had never seen the man use the hand-to-hand technique he had been taught in a practical setting. The Templar focused his mind and removed himself emotionally from the situation. Leon's body might not have been capable of joining this fight, but he would see his mind and expertise well employed.

"Good, Danny! Good, Danny! Control his wrist! Keep him pinned on the cage. Stay on his side. Step over his leg with yours and lock his hips against the wall. Good, good, Danny. Control his wrist. You got this. He's not strong. Control him," Leon called out excitedly, watching the two men tied up in a clinch. Leon kept enough battlefield awareness to stand clear of the line of fire, watching his student quickly and faithfully obey the instructions.

"Shut the fuck up. Shut up!" Tony snapped at the Templar.

Leon allowed himself a moment of self-indulgence as he took his mind from the combat before him and responded to the Patriot. "You can suck my big fat Templar cock, you asshole!" The retort was uncharacteristically vulgar for Leon, but he had to admit it felt good to say the words. He wasn't sure, but he thought that he saw the traces of a smile on Danny's face.

"Fuck you both," Tony blurted.

"Watch your feet, Danny. Get his wrist," Leon ordered. Danny did a phenomenal job of keeping his man immobile against the cage and keeping the barrel of the gun pointed at the ground. The greatest concern was that Tony might manage to shoot Danny in the foot or even the leg.

"Yeah," Danny panted. He was beginning to tire with the amount of force he needed to keep Tony pinned.

A gunshot fired into the floor just a few inches from Danny's toe. The near miss rattled the Templar's student, but Danny was able to work through the surprise. Fortunately, the men outside were still in a wild enough way that the shot was not out of place enough to draw attention.

"Roll his wrist in. Make him drop it. Fold his wrist in half. Break his hand, Danny!" Leon shouted while he pounded the cage with his fist.

Danny did as he was told. It took effort, and Tony did not make it

165

easy, but leverage and anatomical mechanics were on Danny's side. He managed to bend Tony's wrist. The Patriot fought it savagely, but in the end, he was forced to drop the weapon or risk shooting himself in the gut.

"Yes, Danny!" Leon shouted with admiration as the gun fell to the floor. The Templar was just about to instruct Danny to break the clench and kick the weapon away, but he was not fast enough.

Danny had it half correct in his mind. Once the gun was on the ground, he sent it sliding across the floor with a sweep of his foot. Unfortunately, he performed this maneuver while still engaged with Tony. With Danny's stability compromised, Tony sent Danny to the ground and landed on top of him.

"Pull guard! Pull guard! Pull guard!" Leon shouted as he saw the men go down.

Danny hit the floor hard on his back but managed to heed his teacher's instructions, wrapping his legs around Tony's waist and getting his arms in an over-underhook position. Danny pulled his body close to his opponent's and bore down on the grip of his thighs and hands for all he was worth.

"You got this. You got this. Work your submissions, Danny," Leon ordered. The Templar assessed the position of the two men. The full guard option was a sound defensive posture but offered little in the way of offensive opportunities. It was the most neutral stage of ground fighting. "Get his hands off you and on the floor."

Like he had been shown, Danny swept Tony's hands aside and got him to put one palm flat on the floor.

"Yes, now go open your guard and Kimura. Kimura! Tear his shoulder up. Rip his arm out, Danny!" Leon ordered.

Danny unlocked his ankles and controlled Tony's body with the strength of his hips and thighs. Sitting up, he took hold of Tony's wrist on the floor. The Templar's student nearly set in the Kimura lock, but Tony was able to wiggle free from the threat. The man landed a few light punches to Danny's face and head in the exchange, giving Danny a fresh bloody nose.

"Triangle choke!" Leon called.

Danny caught hold of Tony's arm after a punch and set up the submission technique, but again Tony wormed his way out of it. Danny was starting to lose his wind.

Leon could tell the young man's stamina was nearly tapped. "Back to full guard. Get yourself some time. You're doing real good, Danny!" he cheered.

Danny fought through the blood in his nostrils and relocked his legs around Tony's torso. The Patriot tried to break free and pass Danny's guard with increasing intensity. Leon waited and studied the stalemate position. He willed Tony to try to advance his posture in hopes that the man would make an exploitable error. That chance finally came after several more minutes of grappling with neither man gaining the upper hand. Tony put his knee flat on the ground in an ideal positon for Danny to take dominance in the fight. "Sweep and roll. Sweep him!" Leon yelled.

Danny took Leon's cue and worked his lower body like a pair of scissors. With a flex of his hips and sweep of his legs Danny pulled Tony's knee out from under him and rolled him, bringing Danny to a full mount position with Tony pined to the floor.

"Beautiful sweep. Now hit him, Danny! Hit him in the face!" Leon yelled.

Danny's blow landed on Tony's mouth. The Patriot now sported a split lip. Danny paused and looked up at Leon as if lost for what to do next.

"Again! Again!" Leon yelled. Danny struck the man several more times. His punches were solid, but it looked like he was still holding back. "Hit him, Danny! Hit him again. Break his face! Go! Fucking kill him! Kill him!" Leon roared.

Danny's punches were relatively timid to start, but each grew successively harder. Tony was on the full defensive, covering up as best he could. None of Danny's punches connected fully, but even his glancing blows were enough to make Tony's world nothing but a flash of white. Danny grew wilder with his attacks, and his technique got sloppy.

Leon saw what was happening and called out. "Don't let him rock you like that. Stay focused, keep your balance. Keep your balance." It was not enough. Tony finally shucked Danny off him with some lucky timing and brute force.

In a few more seconds of havoc and chaos, the Patriot and the Templar's acolyte scrambled to their feet and sized each other up. Tony then had one of the better ideas he had managed to concoct since entering the pharmacy; the Patriot turned and made for the exit. Danny moved without thought and gave chase, catching Tony as the man stumbled for the front door. Danny grabbed him from behind and tried to bring him to the ground again. Tony kept his feet and worked himself around in Danny's grip. They found themselves in a standing clinch positon, battling and pushing each other around the empty isle of the pharmacy, crashing into shelves and whatever clutter existed.

"Hip toss him," Leon cried, seeing an opportunity for Danny to take the other man back down.

Danny executed the maneuver, but instead of sending Tony to the ground, it sent his head smashing through the cracked glass of a makeup display case. Tony came back up slowly, his face badly slashed. He took several uncoordinated steps and opened his mouth wide, like he was yawning or trying to scream, but no sound came out. Then Leon noticed the large shard of glass driven into Tony's ear. The man fell to the ground and lay motionless.

Danny stood over the body of his beaten enemy, not sure what to do and still shaking with the pulse of combat. He snapped his head up when Leon called his name.

"Danny. Danny. He has the keys on him," Leon said.

Danny knelt and rifled through the dead Patriot's pockets. After a few seconds of pilfering, he found a key ring and brought it to the medicine cage. The third key he tried opened the lock. Danny stood looking at Leon, who beamed nothing but awe and admiration back at him, and his eyes started to well up.

"It's okay," Leon said. "It's not your fault. If you didn't kill him, we would both be dead. You saved us. You did what I told you to do, and you do not need to feel any guilt for that man." He pointed to Tony's lifeless form.

The tears flowed in greater volume from Danny's eyes. "No, it's not that. I don't feel bad for killing him. It's…it's just that…this is the first time I ever felt like you were proud of me…or anyone was proud of me." Danny sniffed.

The words hit the Templar in the heart like a train. "You might get on my nerves because you don't give me room to breathe or even think, but Danny, I've been proud of you for many years. I couldn't ask for a better or braver pupil to bother me every day. Every… single… day," Leon said paternally, clapping a loving hand on Danny's shoulder. The admission only made Danny cry even more. Leon put his other hand on Danny's shoulder and looked him in the eyes. "I know. I know, but later, okay? We need to get Lea and we need to get out of here."

"Right, Lea," Danny said and wiped his eyes.

"We should take his weapons and slip out one of the windows in back," Leon stated, walking toward the body. He relived the corpse of his gun belt and combat knife, then rooted around on the floor to where he recalled Tony's gun sliding. When he found the weapon, it made him feel bitterly cold and impossibly hot all at once. Wrapped around the pistol's grip was an Arbiter's eye patch, traces of fresh blood on it. Leon held the patch and forced himself to deny the implication.

"Oh, no. Mark…" Danny murmured, giving voice to the terror running rampant in Sir Leon's own head.

"We do not tell Lea about this. At least, not until we're safe, understand?"

"Yeah. I understand," Danny said, eyes downcast.

"I think I know were Lea is. Follow me out the back," Leon stated, leaving the pharmacy. Like he always did, Danny followed the Templar.

It was dark in the village, and the pair remained inconspicuous enough that they did not draw attention from the Patriots still celebrating their conquest. Leon led Danny to the rear of the library, keeping off the main streets and sticking mostly to the shadows. They slipped into the building using the lower-level entrance.

It was deathly quiet inside the library. The silence, contrasted by the animalistic jeers Leon recalled from hours ago, only deepened his fear of what he might find. He took Danny up the stairs without making the slightest sound. When they reached the lobby, a mix of emotions filled the Templar's heart. The room had seen a lot of violence. Books were scattered everywhere, several shelves had been knocked over, and some furniture lay broken. Leon saw Lea, silent and wounded. Sitting on the floor, she shook like a leaf clinging to its tree against an autumn gale.

Leon saw one of them sitting across from her—one of the enemy. The men who had killed his friends and brothers in New Boston and Northeastern Connecticut. One of the men who most certainly had done unspeakable things to the woman Leon loved.

"Watch my back. I want to do this quiet," Leon whispered to Danny as he handed him the gun. Danny nodded in understanding. Leon slowly and masterfully made his way across the room towards the Patriot's back. Neither Lea nor the man heard anything; Leon was a silent death in the night. The Templar drew his combat knife to kill his target swift and without a sound. It would only take one cut. From out of the darkness, he struck in a flash and put a razor-sharp blade to Aaron Haze's throat.

"I see y'all got yerself into a bind. You drew a challenge from the wrong man. I guess yer choice is leave town or throw down, and I can tell by lookin at ya that one of those choices ain't gonna end up too well for ya. If y'all wanna stay, I can help ya with that. Yeah, that's right. Kinda like them Templar folk do, but not quite the same. Y'all might think of me as an independent contractor of a special sort. If y'all care to see my credentials, well then, I'll direct you to the eighteen notches on the grip of this here forty-five. Y'all can see I don't lose. Now, if you want Jane here to get number nineteen, when it comes time for yer sit down with the Arbiter, you opt to choose weapons and y'all pick pistols. Then y'all call for it to go lethal, and I'll take care of the rest. And you, sir, don't need to worry one more lick about it. I told ya I don't lose. Now of course, there's the matter of my compensation. Oh sure, y'all don't think I'll do all this for charity now, do ya? That lady over there, she yer sister? Oh, yer wife...she's real pretty."

Casey Boon

Chapter 25

He just wished it would stop. There was nothing left in his belly, but he kept retching as his body tried to vomit. Only bile came up. Mathew spat and hocked up all the saliva he could in an attempt to get the bitter, burning taste out of his mouth. Normally, when he was sick like this, it was because he had overindulged in hard liquor. This, now, was a totally different cause for his body to rebel against him. Mathew had been face to face with death earlier that night. His brother had nearly killed him—shot him dead. The Congressman still didn't know why Aaron had not decided to splatter his brain all over the library. He was not in a clear enough frame of mind to even begin dissecting his brother's motives.

Another wave hit him, and Mathew doubled over. It felt like some-one had broken open his ribcage and was using his chest as a barbeque. He hated this sensation. He was not one to be made afraid, and certainly not to the extent that it caused his stomach to lose its contents. The wave came and passed like the others. This was the last one—at least, Mathew hoped it was. After a few moments, he was sure he was done.

The Congressman stood and took several long, deep breaths. The putrid taste in his mouth lingered, but the fresh air felt good in his lungs. He groaned and wiped his face before spitting again. Mathew was glad he made it to the side street before he let the spew fly. Being seen in such an un-statesmanlike state would do irrevocable harm to his credibility with the rank and file troops under his command.

Mathew thought on the day. It had been nothing short of a roller-coaster ride, starting with what he had anticipated—the fall of another obstacle on his way to confront the Templars in Manhattan. On the march south, his Patriots had made sure that Sebastian Clarke's sympathizers would not be left alive to come to the Templar's aid. The day started to get away from him only after bringing Northeastern Connecticut under his control.

The battle on the interstate was not something he had foreseen. Mathew absolutely did not plan to lose nearly a dozen of his men taking a town that was scarcely more than an afterthought. The day might have stopped there and still been more than he had bargained for, but seeing that woman on the road was something else.

It had been at least a decade since he had laid his eyes on a woman who affected him the way she had. She was a stunning vision, and breaking her was the most pleasure he had been party to in longer than he could remember. Ruining her was like crushing ten New Bostons. Even the memory of feeling her, helpless and fear-struck beneath him, wrapping his fingers around her perfect little neck and forcing her to look him in the eye made him hard.

Then Aaron—his intervention was something totally out of all expectation. Mathew had never seen that side of his brother. There was something inside Aaron that chilled the Congressman to his very center. Mathew had always known his brother to be a naive dreamer with a tragically attuned sense of right and wrong. The thing was that Aaron lived his own brand of zeal fervently, but when it came time to butt heads with those who did not share his ideology, Aaron was always the weaker man. Mathew didn't know what his brother looked like with a backbone, but he was sure he would not care to find out precisely the quality of man Aaron was capable of becoming.

He didn't like to admit it, but perhaps Tony had been right when he'd mentioned Aaron was bound to split away. Mathew could always bring Aaron back into line with a longwinded spout of stars and stripes. He knew he would never be able to do that again. The curtain was pulled back now. Aaron knew exactly who the real Mathew Haze was. Clearly, the Congressman's brother would only be a liability from now on. Beyond trying to win Aaron's obedience again, there was the very real possibility that the man might finally find the will to actually pull the trigger next time. Mathew did not like any of the scenarios playing out in his mind.

Aaron had to die. Mathew was sure of it now more than ever. After the humiliation Aaron had visited upon him in the library, Mathew had no qualms about ending his sibling's life. His dilemma lay in the method of execution. He could not simply kill his brother outright. Aaron would be valued more as a martyr. He could be used as an icon—a symbol of the cause. Aaron could be the hero the Patriots needed. Right now, they were just pretty words about an idea of democracy and government. Mathew was the voice of the movement, but it needed a face in order to really connect with the people Mathew indented to win over after taking out Sebastian Clarke. The best part of it all was that, with his brother a dead hero of the cause, Mathew would never have to doubt his loyalty, and Aaron could be anything and everything the Congressman needed him to be. Mathew felt a little silly for not realizing that he should have sacrificed his brother some time ago.

He cleaned himself up and straightened out his disheveled-looking clothes. He ventured out into the streets and moved through his men, using his most confident and charming smiles and nods of approval.

Mathew asked several of his men who had seen Tony last. At this hour, most of them were too intoxicated or exhausted to be of any use. Mathew grew upset, searching unsuccessfully, but he needed the council of his closest aid in order to best plot Aaron's glorious demise. One of his subordinates finally told him that he had seen Tony headed for the pharmacy. The Congressman made for the building, rehearing a magnificently heroic eulogy for Aaron in his mind.

"Not a chance I let that fly. Yes, you to get to choose the time and place for the challenge, and yes, the law allows for you to set the date a year and a day out. But everyone here knows full well that Steven does not have that kind of time, and he certainly won't survive a trip all the way to Lake Michigan. Just because he's dying does not mean that he's beyond the protection and right of the challenge. You pulling a blatant move to circumvent a challenge is unacceptable. I'm using my discretion as Arbiter and making the call to set the time and place, unless you want to be more reasonable about the logistics. Really? Really? You think that right here and now is a legitimate option? You're some piece of work, I'll give you that. It's people like you who create the need for people like me. Steven openly declared the use of a personal champion. The soonest this thing plays out is as soon the Templar Sebastian show in town, and not a second before. Did it ever occur to you that you might actually have to fight in the challenge you laid down?"

Arbiter Marry Kenton

Chapter 26

"The only reason you still have a heartbeat right now is because she stopped me from slicing you up. I have no idea on this earth why she wanted me to stay my hand, but this is where we are. She just saved your life, and you owe her for that," Sir Leon growled, low and menacing. Aaron was trapped beneath him on the library floor. A few drops of blood ran down the Patriot's neck from where the Templar's combat knife had pressed into his skin. "I'm going to take my hand off of your mouth now. If you shout for help, or even speak when you're not told to speak, I will cut you open. Blink twice if you understand me,"

Leon threatened.

Aaron followed the Templar's instruction and blinked twice. Leon slowly took his hand from Aaron's mouth and grabbed his shirt by the collar. "First thing you're going to do right now is thank her for saving your life," Leon said fervently.

Aaron turned his head to look at the woman he'd spared from his monster of a brother. She did not look at him. The only words she had spoken were, "No, Leon, don't kill him," when the Templar had ambushed him from behind. Now, she had returned to her cold, withdrawn, detached state, just like when Aaron first found her.

"Thank you," he said quietly but genuinely.

Leon picked Aaron up by his shirt a little before pounding him back into the floor. "Use her name. Her name is Lea. Say, 'Thank you, Lea,'" Leon ordered, visibly shaking in an effort to keep his temper in check.

"Thank you, Lea. Thank you for saving my life," Aaron said, his voice resoundingly kind and gentle.

"Now I want you to tell me what you did to her. You're going to confess everything to me," Leon said. His dripped with a craving for retribution.

Aaron returned his eyes to meet the Templar's. A strange sensation came over the Patriot. He found an air of calm, a measure of peacefulness, realizing that, while death may be only moments away for him, he did not fear it. In fact, part of him would welcome such a thing. Aaron Haze steeled himself before he spoke. "I was looking for my brother, Mathew. I heard he was in here. I came in, and I found six of his men. They were…" Aaron didn't turn his head, but his eyes flitted to Lea as he tried to best choose his words. "They were hurting her…very much. I stopped them. Killed that one," Aaron said, nodding toward the corpse of the dead Patriot on the ground. "After that, Mathew came in. We fought. He told me that he…that he…hurt her too. I nearly killed him, but I didn't… I couldn't. I wanted to." Putting that desire into words made the Patriot understand in his head what he knew in his heart. "He left. I stayed."

"No lies," Leon sneered. "I won't listen to this. You're not telling the truth." He tightened his grip on Aaron's shirt and started to drag his blade across Aaron's neck.

"He is telling the truth," Lea interjected in barely more than a whisper, empty and hollow. But she looked up at Leon with wide eyes.

***

"Lea..." Leon breathed. As soon as she'd spoken, he stopped, like she had some kind of power over him. He couldn't begin to understand what nightmare she had been put through. Leon scolded himself for his breakdown, wondering whether, if he had just been stronger, he could have spared Lea her fate. He looked back at the bleeding man beneath him. This man might not have wronged her personally, but it sickened Leon to look upon a man who could side with such disgusting animals.

"He stopped them. Please don't kill him. Please..." Lea whispered before her eyes glazed over and she seemed to drift out of the present again.

Leon felt something push aside his anger for the men who had brought his world to ashes. It started in his heart and welled up; it could only be his love for Lea. He would move the stars for her, so a small show of mercy was a thing of little consequence. Leon got off the Patriot and returned to his feet.

"When I tell you, I want you to get up slowly," Leon said to the man, who was still lying flat. "Daniel, if he does anything aggressive, I want you to shoot him."

"Understood," Danny said with firm conviction.

"Now get up," Leon ordered. The man slowly and carefully returned to his feet. "Turn around and put your hands in your pockets," Leon continued. The Patriot obeyed. "Lea, I'm going to have to do something with him. I can't let him alert the others." A moment passed, and Leon exhaled all the air in his lungs. "I'm sorry." Then he sprang into motion.

Sir Leon wrapped his muscular arms around the Patriot's neck, bearing down and cutting off his circulation. At first, the man fought instinctively against the choke hold, thrashing his arms and grasping at

Leon's hands. It took only a few moments before the Patriot's ability to fight dwindled. "Just give in. It's okay," Leon soothingly whispered into the man's ear. The Patriot went limp, but Leon held the choke for another eight seconds longer.

Sir Leon released the man, who crumpled to the ground. The Templar knelt by the unconscious Patriot and checked to see that he was breathing regularly. "Gather up all the weapons and gear you can find in here. We need to move out extra quick. They'll be looking for us soon, if they aren't already," Leon said, searching the unconscious man for anything useful. The Templar looked at Lea, who still sat in a daze but clearly had at least some rudimentary sense of direction, urgency, and purpose. He felt the Arbiter's eye patch in his pocket. *Not yet. I can't tell her yet,* Leon thought.

"What do you think I am? I'm not some mercenary hired gun. That's not what we do. That's not who we are. Yes, we step in on challenges and serve as personal champions. But we don't do it just because someone asks us to. We champion honorable people, those who need someone to protect them. That's who the Templar Sebastian are. If you got yourself into a challenge because you want to want take property you have no claim to, you're on your own, I want no part of that challenge. Wait, hold on a second. That's too rash. I should reconsider. Who did you say you challenged again? Good. I'm going to go see if they want my help. I'll see you on the other side of the field."

Templar Maya Watson

Chapter 27

Dawn was about to break, and all the world was dipped in a cloak of blue. Lea, Sir Leon, and Danny had been on the move since they left the village. The alarm was raised before they even got out of the library, but they managed to slip into the woods before being spotted. Still, they had to move slowly. They only had one flashlight between them, and even then, they couldn't risk using it and giving away their location.

They had fifteen, maybe twenty-five minutes between them and the Patriots right on their heels. They couldn't cover their tracks and were easy prey to follow. The only thing between them and death was their marginal head start, which had only decreased in size as the night wore on. They could see the flashlights of their pursuers in the distance. That was motive enough for the three escapees to push on through the trees of Northeastern Connecticut and cast aside all the pain of burning lungs, sore legs, and sweat-soaked feet.

So far, the Patriots had not laid eyes on the fugitives. That was a great mercy. Once the Templar and his charges were spotted by the enemy, the grueling pace they had held throughout the night would seem like a leisurely stroll. They managed to scavenge enough weapons before fleeing the village, so they each could be armed. Ammunition, on the other hand, was a slim commodity. Leon and the others could return fire if fired upon, but if they got trapped or pinned down, they were as good as dead.

"We can't keep this up," Danny gasped as he stumbled over a rock.

"I know, but we can't slow down," Leon responded. He helped steady the young man and stopped Danny from falling to the ground. "We might not see the lights anymore, but they're still back there. I can feel them," the Templar continued grimly.

"We can't go any faster. My legs don't have it in them. I can't feel anything below my knees. Whoever is behind us, they have to be at least as exhausted as we are," Danny protested. "Lea, are you okay?" He diverted his attention to the third member of the party, who had scarcely said a word since being reunited. Perhaps if Lea voiced an opinion to slow the horrendous forced march, the Templar might take heed.

"I'm fine. I don't need to stop," Lea said with a hard edge to her voice. "I won't let them take me again. I won't." Her words came as a resolution to push on until they were free of pursuit or to fight the enemy to the bitter end, but in truth, her statement carried a morbid subtext. She would die before she would be a victim a second time. Even if she had to be the one to end it herself.

Leon saw her determination to keep going, but her body belied her fatigue. She could barely stand upright, and her breathing was labored and near irregular. Danny was clearly out of energy, and the Templar had to admit that his reserves of stamina were long depleted. "We can't slow down, but I agree that we can't keep up this pace. It will break us if we keep on like this," Leon said. He became aware of the sound of running water, and that helped to plant the seed of an idea. "Maybe there's another way we can lose them. Follow me."

The group came upon a shallow creek running through the forest.

The sight of it made Leon breathe easy for a moment, and he felt a stirring of hope in his heart as he finished the plan in his mind. "We're making a trail that's easy to follow. If we can mislead the men tracking us, we can get away from them. Lea, you and Danny are going to walk in the creek and head upstream. The running water will cover your movement. You might end up with a case of athlete's foot, but you'll be safe. I'll keep the trail going for a bit, then retrace my steps and follow you up the creek," Leon said, illustrating his plan with a gesture.

"No! We're not splitting up!" Lea snapped. "I don't want to lose anyone else."

"I agree with her. We should all stick together," Danny said, crossing his arms and shaking his head.

"I don't want to split up either, but this will get them off our back, or at least gain us some more distance. I'll be right behind you guys. I promise. They'll pass us over. Ten minutes, just ten minutes. Head up the creek ten minutes and find someplace to keep out of sight. I'll meet you there, okay? This is going to work," Leon said with confidence and conviction.

Lea and Danny exchanged nervous glances. They wanted to object further, but they knew Leon's plan was the soundest option, even if they didn't like to admit it. "Ten minutes," Lea said reluctantly.

"Ten minutes." Leon nodded.

"Okay," said Lea. She kept her eyes closed when she agreed to the plan. It made it easier to accept the alternative.

Leon went to cross the creek but turned back and spoke to Danny first. "Nobody hurts a hair on her head. You come between her and anyone who tries to do her harm. You protect her with everything you are while I'm gone. Promise me that."

Danny let the Templar's words wash over him, and agreed with a nod. Then he quickly lurched forward and wrapped his arms around Leon in a brotherly embrace. "I promise," he said.

Leon hugged Danny back and speedily departed across the flowing water to the other side of the creek. He made a show of scuffing up the bank and marking the path so it was easy to spot from the opposite side. Before the Templar disappeared into the woods, he forcefully pointed upstream with his index finger, as if to command Lea and Danny to get moving.

***

"Follow me. I'll go first," Danny said, stepping into the calf-high water.

Lea followed him up the creek. The pair moved silently, glancing frequently over their shoulders. They searched the tail behind for signs of their pursuers as much as for the vision of Sir Leon materializing out of the woods. Neither of those things came into view.

Danny finished counting in his head. "I think that's been ten minutes," he said to Lea.

"I think that feels about right. That looks like a good place to hide and wait for him," said Lea as she pointed to a cluster of four rocks just smaller than boulders beside a fallen tree.

They took up a vigil in the midst of the rocks on the creek bank and waited. Both scanned the woods for the slightest sign of another person, listening intently. There was nothing but the sound of gentle flowing water and abundant nature greeting the morning. Their waiting grew longer, making them nervous. Neither one wanted to voice their apprehension for fear of putting the other on edge.

Danny was finally the first to break the silence. "How long should it take Leon to get here, do you think?" he asked in a barely audible whisper.

"I'm not sure. I would think ten minutes, maybe," Lea said, unsure of her assessment.

"I guess that makes a lot of sense. Has it been ten minutes yet?"

"No, I don't think so. We'll wait until Leon comes. He's going to find us," Lea said, reaffirming her faith in her own words.

It was much longer than ten minutes before the sound of snapping twigs caught their ears. They both held out the hope that maybe Leon chose to leave the creek and start moving on dry ground, but they knew it was unlikely.

Lea's breath came in panicked spurts when she saw them through the predawn shroud enveloping the trees. Nine well-armed Patriots stalked through the woods. They did not see Lea and Danny hiding in their spot near the water.

Lea was on the verge of a panic attack. *Where are you? Where are you, Leon? I need you now. I need you so badly.* Her eyes went huge and round like a doe being hunted by a pack of wolves. The next thing she was aware of was a disarmingly calming voice in her ear.

"They will not hurt you. I'm here with you, and I will protect you from them. They're not going to find us, and if they do, I'll stop them before they lay a hand on you," Danny whispered. His voice was steady and cleansing like a drought-breaking rainstorm.

In an instant, Lea's fear was removed. She saw a measure of something great in Danny's eyes as he looked at her. She had never thought of him as strong or inspiring, but in that moment, the young man at her side embodied both of those things. The calm she felt disappeared when she saw Danny's gaze move from her eyes to something behind her. She spun around, relieved beyond reason to see Sir Leon crawling out of the water and up into the nook created by the rocks and toppled pine tree.

"That was much more than ten minutes. You should not have waited so long," Leon whispered admonishingly.

"Then you should have gotten here faster," Lea retorted, the faintest hint of the playfully joyous women she used to be interwoven into her speech.

"Seven of them?" Leon asked as he unslung the one rifle the group had at their disposal from his shoulder.

"Nine," Danny responded quietly.

"Damn. They're the reason it took me a while to meet up with you. I nearly got spotted twice," Leon said.

"They're not heading this way. They look a bit lost. I think your plan might have worked," Lea said admiringly to the Templar. It was the first time she had smiled since New Boston.

Leon blinked. "I told you. I know a thing or two," he said, seemingly hiding his feelings in humor.

The runaways silently observed the ensemble of Patriots scanning the area, looking for any sign of the trail they had lost. For a few brief moments, Lea felt all the nostalgic exhilaration of playing hide-and-seek as a little girl. It almost felt fun; the fear of death had left her mind. The Patriots started to turn and withdraw from their positon, and Lea beamed a large, victorious smile. Her joy quickly ended when she saw his face in the first rays of morning light piercing the shelter of the trees.

The last Patriot in the precession was one of them. One of the men who had forced himself upon her in the library. He'd been the fourth. Lea felt the welts on her breasts the man had made with his teeth. She felt them inside of her. She smelled them on her skin and felt their hands pawing her body. She saw the dark and wrathful eyes of Mathew Haze cutting into her. Then it quickly returned—the grotesque kind of filthy she didn't know how to be rid of or clean off herself.

Lea's stomach turned upside-down, her head swam, and her blood froze. She was on the edge of breaking again, but she clung to the oath she had sworn to herself to never be a victim. She felt the weight of the gun in her hand. It had been tucked into her waistband since the escape from the village. She had not even realized that she had drawn the weapon. Looking up at the man's face again, she felt herself drawn back into the consuming shame of her suffering. Lea refused and fought back.

"No, you don't ever touch me!" she shouted, standing and firing on the man who had wronged her. The first two bullets missed him by a narrow margin, but the next three stuck the Patriot high in his chest as he turned to face the origin of the gunfire. He fell dead to the ground.

"Lea!" said the Templar through gritted teeth as he stood and opened fire with his rifle.

Danny and the other Patriots joined the firefight. The once peaceful woods were now filled with the sound of guns blasting, bullets smashing into trees and rocks, commands being yelled, strings of profanity, and the cry of dying men's screams. It was a vicious, quick, bloody exchange, but the few moments the gun battle persisted seemed to last forever.

***

Seven Patriots remained alive, but only five of them were capable of fighting. Leon counted the rounds left in his rifle clip. He had six shots remaining and a full clip loaded in the pistol at his hip. If he made his ammunition last, he could keep laying down suppressive fire. He would be able to hold the Patriots behind the trees they used for cover while Lea and Danny retreated across the creek.

"Go! Go now. Across the creek. I'll be right behind you. Danny, get her out of here!" Leon ordered.

After the initial shock had worn off, Lea's wits seemed to return. She and Danny looked at each other before abandoning their spot in the rocks and made for the other side of the creek. Leon held his ground and kept his cool while bullets snapped and whipped by, missing him by feet and inches. He dropped his rifle after firing the last round. He then took his time and fired ten of the fifteen nine-millimeter rounds in his pistol. Until now, he had been highly judicious and effective with his ammunition expenditure. Turning around, he checked to see that Lea and Danny had made it a good distance from the firefight. Then he left the rocks and followed after his companions.

Leon was surprised to hear the lack of gunfire at his back when he waded across the creek, wondering what had caused the ceasefire. As he clambered up onto the opposite bank, he heard shouting from the area where the battle had just been fought. "Don't worry about them. We can find them later. Help me! Get his legs. We need to get him back to base camp quick. Someone get the Congressman on the line. Aaron's hit! Aaron's hit!"

The Sixty-Seventh Law
When it must fall to combat, the Challenged shall have
first option to set the principle terms of both the time and
location of the Challenge or the weapons to be used in the
Challenge. The Challenger shall set the terms of the op-
tion not selected by the Challenged.

Chapter 28

It was safe now. The Patriots had not continued their chase of Sir Leon and the others. At least, it seemed that way to the Templar. He was not about to stop and find out if their pursuers had in fact retired from the chase. The sun shone fully through the treetops of the Connecticut woods. Leon, Lea, and Danny ran from the creek with all their speed. None of them had time to stop long enough to think or catch their breath. Each exhale came like the sound of paper being torn in half.

Even though their endurance was past its breaking point, all three of them ran headlong deeper into the woods as fast as their weary legs would carry them. They didn't follow any path or rout. The only goal was to get away from the men on their backs. Leon and the others had less than ten bullets between them. They could not survive another head-to-head encounter with the Patriots. The depleted supply of ammunition was irrelevant, though. Leon and his charges were done fighting the enemy. Now they were running. They would continue to run until they made it to safety, though they didn't know where that was or what safety even looked like now. Not even two days ago, any one of them would have thought the village of Northeastern Connecticut a safe place. The last twenty-four hours had proven that to be far from the truth.

The Templar pushed out in front, leading the way, Lea right on his heels. Danny had kept pace with the other two, but as they ran, he lagged farther and farther behind. Leon didn't look back, but he knew that Danny's pace was slowing. Still, he could not allow them to stop. If they stopped, they were dead. "Come on, Daniel. We need to keep it up. You can keep running," the Templar called back.

"Sir Leon... sir... I don't think I can," came Danny's voice from the rear.

"Yes, just keep running faster. You can do this," Leon called with a slight backwards glance.

"No... I'm sorry... I can't run anymore," Danny pleaded with desperation.

Leon couldn't be angry with the man. Danny had asked more of his body in the last hours than most people demanded in a week. Still, the Templar was unquestionably frustrated. They couldn't stop. Leon needed to motivate Danny. He needed to get his student to push himself even though he had nothing else to give. Leon spun around as he spoke. "Daniel, we are all—" His voice was cut short as if severed by a sharp blade. Leon's heart crumbled, and everything in his body just let go when he saw Danny. "It's okay, Danny. We can stop. We can stop," Leon said, defeated and on the brink of tears.

Lea heard the Templar's sudden change of heart and turned to look at Danny. Her hands went to her mouth as she stifled a gasp of shock and mourning. "Danny..." Then she seemed to lose command of her voice.

"Sir Leon..." Danny said before he fell to his knees. The blood still flowed from his abdomen and had soaked the right side of his clothes solid red all the way down to his pantleg. The young man's hands were stained a deep crimson from where he had tried to stem the bleeding of the bullet wound.

Leon and Lea rushed to his side. "Lie down, Danny," Leon said, fighting tears and trying to think how he could stop the flow of scarlet cascading from Danny's body.

The wounded man lowered himself to the ground, but it ended up more like falling. "I'm sorry…I can't keep going. Please…please don't be disappointed. I… I tried," Danny said in labored, heaving pants while Lea cradled his head. Leon pressed his hands firmly against the bullet hole. Danny was the only one not crying.

"Don't. You don't need to apologize for anything. You got us out of there. You saved us, Danny. We are both…we are all alive because of what you did for us. You were braver than I ever thought you could be. I'm so proud of you," Leon said. He tried all he could to stop the bleeding. It was a lost cause. Danny's skin was already turning pale.

"It feels good. It feels good to be like you." Danny gasped between his words, his eyes fighting to stay open.

"Thank you, Danny. I'm proud of you, too," Lea managed to say as hot tears streamed down her face. "I'm so proud of you. Thank you," she quietly repeated over and over, maternally stroking Danny's face and running her fingers through his shaggy hair.

"Two people proud of me in the same day. I never had that before. Sir… Sir Leon. Nobody ever taught me anything like you. You made me feel like I belonged to something…it's all I ever wanted," Danny said. Then his eyes closed and did not open again, his breathing shallow.

"Would you like to belong to something, Danny?" Leon asked as he gripped the dying man's hand.

"Yes… I… Yes," Danny murmured.

The Templar wiped the tears from his face with the back of his wrist. It was the only part of his hand not soaked in blood. Leon cleared his throat and mustered all the formal bearing he could manage. "I, Sir Leon Scott of the Templar Sebastian, recognize your heroism and selfless defense of others. You put yourself in harm's way for the sake of those who were unable to protect themselves. I have borne witness as you took arms against those who would use strength to oppress the weak. As such, by the power vested in me by Sir Sebastian Clarke, the Northeast, and my brothers in arms, I dub thee Sir Daniel Matager, Templar Sebastian," Leon said, touching the man on his forehead then clasping Danny's limp hand in both of his.

There was silence in the woods. Lea and Leon sat with the body of their friend after he slipped away. "That was something very special you did for him." Lea sniffed. "I hope he heard it."

"I hope so too. He deserved it. I just wish I had realized it sooner," Leon said, still clutching the icy hand of his departed brother Templar.

"You were his idol. He worshiped everything about you. It must have meant the world to him to hear you say you were proud of him." Lea gave one last stroke of her fingers through Danny's hair.

It was so quiet now but impossible for Leon to think clearly. He wanted to grieve for his friend. He wanted to get moving and continue the escape from the men chasing them. Seeing the anguish on Lea's face only reminded him of the unstoppable love he felt for her. His love turned to guilt when he recalled Mark's eyepatch tucked in his pocket. He struggled with how and when he would tell Lea. He didn't know if there would ever be a proper moment to break the news.

Lea saved the Templar from drowning in his ocean of thought when she spoke. "I don't want to leave him here like this. It wouldn't be right," she said.

Leon returned to being a man of thought, reason, and logic. "I agree, but we don't have time to bury him, and we're not in the condition to carry him. We can mark the trail to come back for him and take care of him later the way he deserves. It's late enough in the season that there shouldn't be any animals to disturb him before we return," Leon stated.

Clearly, Lea did not care for the plan, but she accepted it as the best course of action. "So what now?"

"We need to get to Sebastian Proper. It's the only safe place I can think of. I say we double back up to New Boston and find a vehicle that's still serviceable there. Then we can take the long way around the village and come up on Manhattan from the south," Leon said with a shake of his head. The plan sounded ridiculous and far-fetched, but it was the least crazy-sounding scenario he could conceive.

"Walk to New Boston, cross country?" Lea asked in disbelief.

"I know, I know, but it's all I can think of. It's the best place to get a ride. It's still early in the day, and if we don't stop again, we could make New Boston by nightfall. Otherwise, it's a long way to Manhattan on foot, and we need to meet up with the rest of the Templars," Leon said removing his emotion from the crisis and speaking objectively.

A voice came from out of the woods. "If you're looking for Templar Sebastian, you're not going to have to travel as far as you think."

Lea's eyes shot up, filled with fear. Leon spun and brought his pistol halfway up. The Templar laid his eyes on a sight nothing short of divine. Four Templar Sebastian clad in head-to-toe body armor and carrying assault rifles came out of the trees. They moved like a tide of inspiration. Laying eyes on his brothers in arms lifted Sir Leon's heart from the depths into which it had fallen.

"Leon, you are one fine human being. You don't know how to lose, do you?" said the Templar at the front.

Leon recognized Sir James, one of the senior men who had been something like a mentor to Leon in his early days at Sebastian Proper. "James... I... it's been..." Leon tried to speak, but his words were all lost.

"I know it's been hell. It's over now. We're here. We're all here, and then some. This is over," said Sir James, extending a hand to help his brother to his feet.

"Lea? Lea!" came Mark's voice. The Arbiter bolted past the Templars in front of him and ran to his lover.

"Mark!" Lea shouted. As Leon's heart was lifted with the arrival of his brethren, so was Lea's with the reunion of her beloved. They embraced, and the joy at first then turned to something wicked. Lea pulled away, shaking and tearful. She looked into Mark's eyes—his one eye of perfect green and the other a mangled grey mass. "I can't... I..." she stammered, then walked away from Mark, turning her back to him. She cried like she had in the library.

"What's wrong? I'm sorry?" Mark said as his hand went to cover his blind eye. He made to follow her.

Leon understood what was happening and came between Mark and Lea. The Templar put a gentle hand on the Arbiter's chest. "Not now, Mark," he said quietly so only the Arbiter would hear him.

"I don't understand," Mark said.

Leon dug in his pocket and returned the eyepatch to its rightful owner. "We were captured by the men who destroyed the village.

They… they…" Leon thought he possessed the strength to tell Mark what had been done to his love, but he was unable to speak of it. He didn't need to say the words; Mark could read the whole graphic story in the Templar's shameful eyes.

"No, no, no…" Mark sputtered as it hit him. He drifted away and stood at a distance, obviously tormented by the inability to hold the only person he cared to hold. Even greater seemed the torment that he was unable to console her.

"We found them less than an hour ago," Sir James said to Leon as he indicated a small band of villagers trailing his team. "Not too many made it out."

"No. No they didn't," Leon said bitterly.

"We're going to take you all out and get you patched up," Sir James said. "Leon, when I said we're all here, he…he's here, too."

"Clarke?" Leon said, star-stuck.

Sir James smiled widely and nodded as he spoke. "Yes, sir. He would like to speak with you, if you're up for it. He could use whatever intelligence you might have. It's not required, and you don't have to by—"

"I want to. I'll tell him everything I know," Sir Leon said with vengeful measure. "Just one thing."

"Anything, brother," Sir James said.

Leon nodded at Danny's body. "Please take him with us."

"Last week, I came across an elderly couple. Married thirty-two years, and they both survived the sickness. Some teenage brat booted them out of their home with a challenge just because he liked the look of their place. It made me sick to hear it. I believe in the challenge. At its core, it's right. It's about putting your life on the line for what you believe is right, but there needs to be some order. I won't see it become another tool that the strong use to beat down the weak. I will build something that sees the law of the challenge serve all equally."

Master Sargent Sebastian Clarke U.S.M.C.

Chapter 29

It looked worse than it felt. When it first happened, Aaron thought he was going to die. Getting shot was not pleasant, and he was far from one hundred percent, but it could have been much worse. The bullet was a small-caliber round and had gone through and through. It didn't hit any bones or vital organs, but the hole had gushed blood like a broken fire hydrant. He did lose consciousness on the way back to the Patriot base camp, but when he came to, he was bandaged and stitched up. It hurt like fire whenever Aaron tried to lift his left arm. He quickly decided he best not push his luck after he thought he heard something that might have been a stich popping.

He rolled onto his right side after a sip of water. It felt good to get some of the pressure off his wounded shoulder. From what Aaron had gleaned and overheard in his bouts slipping in and out of consciousness, the rest of the men were still looking for the escapees. The young Patriot felt a mixed well of emotions about that news. On the one hand, he knew that prisoners escaping with information about the Patriots' armaments

192

and capabilities posed a direct threat to the cause. On the other hand, he was glad they had not been recaptured. The treatment shown to the villagers when they were in Mathew's custody was less than human. One way or another, Aaron swore that the fugitives would never have to be treated like that again.

He found himself actually rooting for their escape. Even if they were on the other side, Aaron could not reconcile what had been done to them as anything of which he wanted to be a part. That fact was a large part of the reason he had volunteered to be part of the tracking and recapture efforts. When it came time to bring them back in, Aaron wanted to be there in order to make sure they received civil treatment.

The rest of Aaron's reasoning for taking part in the expedition was the fact that it allowed him to get away from the Patriot camp, and more so, from his brother. He was still trying to process what he had seen and done in the library, let alone his complicated feeling for Mathew. Aaron wrestled with the motive behind his actions. Did he kill a man in cold blood? Was he a murderer? Did he act in the defense of someone else? Had he saved her life? All these questions bubbled to the surface in the forefront of Aaron's mind.

His thoughts turned from his actions and rested on Mathew. Even seeing his brother's face in his mind's eye made Aaron brim with anger. He reflected on the path Mathew had drawn him down since finding the weapons stockpile in Maine. Since starting the march south, Aaron had been complicit in theft, assault, murder, torture, and rape. He grew sick with the weight of his actions—or rather, his inaction. Clearly, Mathew had lost his way. Aaron wondered if all his brother's fine speeches about the cause, the restoration of government and democracy, the healing of America, were just fanciful stories and things to say in an effort to justify his whims and desires.

Aaron had been feeling a creeping suspicion growing in his belly over the last few weeks. It had started when Mathew pitted the two Templars against each other. At first, it was only a single grain of sand, but with each passing day and every community his brother destroyed, it grew. Now, it was like a boundless desert of bankrupt morality. Aaron wondered, for the first time, if he was on the right side of this war. He had become a man trapped between duty and conscience—a tortured spirit indeed.

He noticed that someone had hung an American flag on the wall across from the foot of his bed. Seeing that image helped give Aaron some clarity. Seeing the symbol of his beloved country never failed to inspire the man. As he lay there with his thoughts, Aaron worked on sorting out his emotions. Slowly, what was unclear began to take on a sharper image. After some time, Aaron felt like he knew where he stood.

The door to the room opened slowly. Aaron sat up in the bed and winced in pain as he put pressure on his left side. Anger overtook him when he saw Mathew creep through the open door. It was not the white-hot, burning anger that had possessed him the last time he had been face to face with his sibling. This variety was a low, simmering heat, threatening to explode like a volcano. Aaron stared his brother down without speaking—a disarming gaze. Dark, haunting eyes imbued with a silent wrath were a dominant family trait.

There was something different about the way Mathew looked. He was not filled with his usual swagger and confidence, his footsteps soft and timid. He held himself low with defensive body language. Aaron could almost detect an air of fear in his elder sibling, now determined to take the power in this situation. He would make his brother speak first.

"I heard you were awake. I wanted to check on you," Mathew said as he crept up beside the bed.

"I'm still alive," Aaron said. He wanted to say more. He felt the urge to lash out at his brother with harsh words again, but he stopped himself. Aaron remained cool and poised to the outside world despite the maelstrom in his heart.

"You were lucky. I thought the worst when I heard you'd been shot," Mathew pulled up a chair and sat next to his brother, oozing with the intricately masked insincerity that was his trademark.

"The worst, huh?" Aaron repeated. He figured that phrase meant something entirely different to his brother. "Does that mean you were afraid I was or wasn't dead?"

This threw Mathew. He obviously had not expected his brother to call his bluff or see through his wiles. Blinking a few times, he apparently opted to adorn a cloak of innocent obliviousness. "What are you talking about? Why would I want you dead?"

"Because the last time we saw each other, I beat you bloody, held a gun to your head, and threatened to kill you," Aaron said matter-of-factly.

The Congressman took a deep breath. "I understand that tempers were high and everything—"

"Stop it. Just stop," Aaron interrupted, frustrated. "I'm not playing these games with you anymore. I'm sick of your talking and all your manipulation."

"Aaron…"

"I told you not to say my name!" Aaron snapped before Mathew could stop his momentum. The anger with which he spoke made his shoulder hurt, and his free hand went to the bandages. The room was quiet for a few tense seconds before he continued. "I've decided something." He let that statement hang in the air, begging a question.

"What have you decided," Mathew finally asked after Aaron refused to volunteer any clarity.

Mathew had asked the question Aaron was hoping he would. He relished the slight manipulation he had exerted over his brother, admitting it felt good to pull some puppet strings. Now, he understood his brother's attraction to the act. "I'm still behind the cause. This country needs to be indivisible again. It needs to heal this fracture the sickness left in its wake. You see that?" Aaron pointed to the flag hanging from the wall. "I love it, live for it, breathe it. I love everything about it. I love what it stands for. I love who we are because of it. I love who we are. I bleed red, white, and blue…"

"That's good…" Mathew said, sounding both genuinely supportive and fearful of where Aaron was going with his proclamation.

"I'm not finished," Aaron said calmly but assertively. "I believe in this country, and I believe in the cause." He took a breath as he steeled himself for the final push. "Even if I don't believe in you anymore." He finally looked his brother in the eye.

Mathew shook, his face growing a deep shade of red as he planted his feet. "Look, it's been a long—"

"Shut up, Matt. You're done talking. For once, you're going to listen to me. We're going to Manhattan, and we're going to talk to the Templars. We're going to be reasonable and humane. We'll be there for however long it takes to come to a mutual understanding with them. Only if they're impossible and beyond any diplomatic solution will we resort to force," Aaron said, his voice unwavering. He licked his dry lips and took a sip of water. "After that, there will be an election, and the people will decide who's in charge of this country. I'm going to run against you. Now I'm done talking to you. Get out of my room."

Mathew just sat there, jaw opening and closing as if he'd lost his voice. His eyes seemed on the verge of bursting from his skull. "You…look at who decided to finally grow a pair of balls. You think you know the first thing about being a leader? You can't even piss without someone telling you to," Mathew hissed.

"I know plenty. You were a good teacher, I'll give you that. I learned a lot about what not to do from you. You're going to lose, and I'm going to make you feel it," Aaron said.

The Haze brothers stared at each other for some time. Aaron managed to exude the calm confidence his brother had always mastered, while Mathew now seemed to have lost control completely over not only his emotions, but his body as well. His fists clenched and unclenched, and when Aaron started to wonder just how dangerous his brother might be, footsteps crashed down the hall, and a Patriot stood huffing in the doorway.

"Congressman Haze, sir?" the Patriot panted, sweat forming upon his brow.

"Yes, what is it?" Mathew said, clenching his teeth.

"We spotted Templars approaching north- and southbound. It looks like all of Sebastian Proper emptied out and is coming for us."

"Well, this should make it easier. It'll save us a trip to Manhattan, and they've abandon a fortified positon. I thought Sebastian was supposed to be a calculated man. Apparently, I overestimated him," Mathew said haughtily.

"Uh, sir, I don't think it'll be quite so easy," said the Patriot.

196

"What are you talking about? Why not?" Mathew said.

"The Templars, sir. They didn't come alone."

Chapter 30

Sebastian Clarke was a showman, whether he knew it or not. Mathew Haze couldn't deny the powerful image the Templar founder presented. Alone, out in front under a white flag of parley—it was something. Mathew might have just ordered his men to open fire immediately. Sebastian wasn't exactly making it difficult to hit him. Gunning down the leader of the Templars would have sent quite the blow to enemy morale. That was a tempting prospect, but two obstacles stood in the way of that plan. First, many of the Congressman's Patriots were under the impression that once they had gotten to Manhattan, they would try to reach a peaceable solution with the Templars first. Mathew Haze had been able to keep all the zealots like his brother in line by resting on the shoulders of self-defense. So far, Mathew could claim that he only ever fired if he had been fired upon. He wanted to keep it that way.

The second issue inhibiting Sebastian's Clarke's outright assassination was the looming prospect of retribution. Mathew was prepared to face the whole of the fighting men garrisoned at Sebastian Proper. The Templars did have superior numbers, but they were not even two-to-one odds in their favor. The artillery at the Congressman's command more than made up for that deficit. It would have been a bloody fight but a highly probable victory for the Patriots if it had only been Sabastian and his Templars. But it wasn't.

The road to the Village of Northeastern Connecticut where the Patriots were entrenched was blocked off as far as the eye could see, both to the north and to the south. More than just Templar Sebastian had sounded the Patriots' alarm. The black and white flags with the iconic Templars shield flew from the vehicles in the front, but behind them was an imposing unity—the stars and bars of the Atlanta Militia; the lone star of the Texas Frontier; the cerulean fleur de lys of Sovereign Quebec; even the twin peaks of the Rocky Mountain Territory Irregulars all flew in the air over Northeastern Connecticut. Men and women had come to the northeast from halfway across the old America. An army outnumbering the Patriots by no less than twelve to one stood behind Sebastian Clarke. More importantly, that army stood against Mathew Haze.

The leader of the Patriots would have to employ the use of his gifted speech once again. He needed to try talking his way into the advantage.

Mathew drove out to meet Sebastian on neutral ground, viewed from affair by Patriots and Templars alike. Aaron rode silently with his brother. Mathew had tried everything to get Aaron to remain behind, but his younger brother did not listen to him anymore. The Patriot Jeep pulled up before Sabastian, and both Haze brothers got out.

"I heard you gentlemen wanted to meet me. So here I am," Sebastian said in a powerful, resonating, military voice. His age was starting to show, his hair equal parts silver and brown. Decades of soldiering had worn the man's face, giving it many deep lines as well as a few scars. He stood in a traditional posture of ease, hands clasped behind his back, in finely cleaned and pressed Templar combat fatigues. Obviously confident enough in his bearing and reputation, he had forgone his gun belt or body armor.

Mathew had so prepared to take Sebastian unawares on his home ground that he himself was unprepared to respond to a man so clearly equipped to handle any threat. "I am Congressman Mathew Haze, of the second district of the great state of Rhode Island," Mathew started. He quickly warmed up to his usual bravado. "I don't think you came all this way for a simple introduction. Clearly, you have something on your mind."

"Congressman! Congressman...I can't tell if you're being serious or not. Maybe you were a Congressman once upon a time. I used to be a Master Sergeant in the Marine Corps. We are not those people any-more. Congressman…don't make me…" Sebastian scoffed and shook his head at Mathew's arrogance.

Mathew forced himself to stop smiling. It had not taken long at all for Sabastian Clarke to give him the precise opening he needed to exploit. "That's where we seem to disagree. What happened to this world, this county, it doesn't mean we get to wave a magic wand and all of a sudden start doing whatever we please. This is still America, and we are still a people of laws and government. It's time we get back to the things that made this nation great," Mathew said.

Sebastian grimaced and wiped a hand over his mouth before he growled his rebuttal. "You might want to tell that to the people of New Boston. Was that supposed to be your brand of law and government?"

"Your regime is an unlawful and unconstitutional circumvention of proper government. Anyone who sided with you and your men is committing high treason, even if they're in the majority," Mathew spat back.

He turned to see Aaron looking out at those who had come to oppose the Congressman, all waving their own varied and diverse flags. Then Aaron glanced up at the stars and stripes hanging from the Patriots Jeep and frowned. "Congressman Elect. You never actually sat in office," Aaron said quietly. His soft words inflamed his older brother and brought an impish smile to the Templar founder's lips.

"What's your name, son?" Sabastian asked the younger Haze brother.

"Aaron Haze. Yes, this is my older brother…I'm sorry to say," Aaron said with disdain.

"Sounds like you have some dissention in the ranks… Congress-man," Sebastian gloated.

Mathew wanted to fight back, but Aaron was too much of a wild card at this point. He decided that his best option was just to ignore his brother and focus on the Templar. "So, is that a white flag of surrender?" he said mockingly.

"If you want to hold it, it can be," Sebastian retorted.

"I don't see why. I have all the heavy guns, if you really want to go that way. I don't want to have to kill all your people," Mathew boasted.

"Are you out of your head? Unless you have a nuke tucked away in your back pocket, I don't think you have enough firepower to stop us from coming over and wiping you off the map," Sebastian said, eyes wide in clear shock at the Patriot leader's ill-founded confidence.

"Come on, Matt," Aaron said, looking at the gathered forces before them. "This is over. We lost. Don't you see that the whole world showed up to stop us—" He swallowed, as if the words pained him even still.

"Keep on talking, son," Sebastian encouraged.

"If you go to guns now, it's just going to mean a lot of people die before you get beaten," Aaron said. He glanced at the flag's stars and stripes waving from the Patriot Jeep again. "She's gone. This is not who we are anymore."

"You should listen to your brother," Sebastian called. "He seems to have a good head on his shoulders. I'll say this, you disarm and head up Canada way—steering clear of Sovereign Quebec, of course—and none of your men will be harmed. Now, if you ever come back, I'll have you shot on sight."

Mathew trembled with rage. He knew that Aaron and Sebastian were right. He had the guns, but there were just too many men on the other side. They could win by sheer weight of numbers. If they wanted victory, he resolved to make them pay dearly for it. "Maybe you have what it takes. Maybe you do, but how many men are you willing to sacrifice? If you want to stop us, it won't be easy. A lot of your men will die," Mathew hissed.

"You can't be serious!" Aaron shouted. "Mathew, this is done! Pushing this is just going to get a lot of good men killed. I don't want to see anyone else die for no reason."

"Then they can stand down! I won't!" Mathew shouted back at his brother.

"No. No! I'm not going to let this happen. I'm going to take command from you and surrender," said Aaron with a combination of rage and desperation.

"Like Hell you will. I will order my men to fight to the last, and there's nothing you can do to stop me. If we all die, I swear we'll make it hurt before it happens," Mathew growled.

"How far up your own ass is your head? You know, you're not the only man people follow. They look to me as well. You might talk America, but I live it, and don't for one second think that people don't see that. Do you really think that if I snapped my fingers, half our men wouldn't fall in line behind me...maybe more than half?" Aaron said, pointing toward the Patriots far behind them.

Mathew knew his brother spoke the truth. It hurt to feel the power he once had over his sibling crushed into dust. "So you would just take by force, huh? After all your whining about how we killed and oppressed those who refused to join the cause and get on the right side, you'll just rest on the threat of force. Because this fuck shows up with some extra bodies, you lose your fucking balls and turn from devout Patriot and true-blooded American. You were all about the cause and the restoration of democracy, and now you're a damn traitor who will just take what he wants. You hypocrite!"

Aaron took the insult and formed a rebuttal that made Mathews skin turn pale as snow. "You know what? You're right. I still wish for democracy more than anything. So fine. We'll do it the right way. We'll let the people choose. I say we go back to the camp right now and put leadership of the cause to a vote. I will win. You know I will. You're going to lose, and I'm going to make you choke on it!"

In that moment, Mathew knew there was no hope for him. He didn't have the strength to beat Sabastian, and he didn't have the heart to beat Aaron, but would not admit defeat. He did the only thing he could think to do. "I challenge you." There was a brief mumble of surprise among those gathered, then silence. "I challenge you for command of the cause, Aaron."

"We need an Arbiter!" Sabastian Clarke shouted back to the assembly of Templars in the distance, the dangerous smile widening on his face.

**

Mark had never thought that he would have to preside over an adjudication like the one between the Haze brothers. The thing was both simple and yet epically difficult at the same time. Both men were of the same mind. Aaron had opted for the challenge to be fought here and now. Mathew had figured that any weapons used would offset the exploitable advantage of Aaron's wounded shoulder, so the challenge was to be unarmed. Neither brother had yielded as the stakes continued to rise, so Aaron finally pushed the challenge to be to the death. The Adjudication had lasted less than ten minutes.

Mark found it difficult because he was horribly ill-suited to be impartial in this matter. However, Mark Fishers was an Arbiter, and that meant he would be an impartial party and see the law of the challenge upheld. He had done his duty magnificently; Henry would have been proud of his pupil. The only thing left was to begin the challenge.

"Are you sure, Aaron? Any one of my men would be honored to fight in your stead. There's no shame in stepping out," Sebastian offered.

"No. I won't have anyone fight for me. I...I need this..." Aaron responded.

"Then your shoulder... You don't have to do this right now." Sebastian really seemed to be pleading.

"Yes, yes I do," Aaron said. "I do." He nodded at Mark, reaffirming his belief. "I'm ready, and I'm not going to lose. Just promise that if I win, none of my men will be harmed. There are a lot of good people here...they just followed the wrong man for too long," he pleaded, turning back toward Sebastian.

The Templar looked Aaron in the eye with a knightly gaze. "I know that now. I promise. Not a one who lays down arms will be mistreated. Just please do one thing for an old Marine."

"Yes," Aaron said agreeably.

"I would like the privilege of shaking your hand." Sebastian extended his arm.

Aaron took Sebastian's hand in his and gave it a firm grip. "Thank you, sir."

"No, thank you."

Aaron undid his gun belt and let it fall to the ground. He turned and stepped onto the village green of Northeastern Connecticut. The town center had been surrounded by Patriots, Templars, and their allies alike. Everyone in the Northeast was focused on the challenge about to take place. Mathew waited for his brother near the gazebo, and the Haze brothers took their respective places, waiting for the Arbiter's cue.

Mark addressed the gathered crowed. "These men have agreed to the terms set forth in adjudication. A hand-to-hand challenge will be fought until one man is dead. The winner shall stand as the leader of the so-called Patriot Cause." He looked to each man, his perfect green eye reflecting murderous contempt for Mathew but hope for Aaron. "You may begin," Mark said. Then he felt someone next to him.

It was Lea. She had taken his hand in hers—the first time she had touched him since they had been reunited. Her fingers were soft and gentle at first, but she squeezed her lover's hand passionately. "I love you," she said.

"I love you too." He'd never meant any words more in his life than those four words in that moment. The Arbiter knew, then, that the love they shared would heal all wounds. Their life was forever changed by Mathew Haze, but it would not be destroyed by him. Together, they turned their focus to the two brothers engaged in combat.

Mathew made the first move, obviously aiming to press the advantage of Aaron's wounded shoulder. Aaron kept his distance and made Mathew chase him down. He took a southpaw boxing stance and fired off lots of quick right jabs to keep Mathew off him. They worked as a deterrent, but none of the blows made it past Mathew's guard. Aaron's right arm quickly seemed to tire, his pace slowing.

Only minutes into the brawl, Aaron's show of confidence had almost fled completely. Mathew had been a relentless attacker. The elder Haze brother kept Aaron on the back foot the whole time. Aaron found it more and more difficult to throw jabs. His pace slowed, and soon he struggled to even keep his hands high enough to protect his face. Mathew came at him with jabs of his own, and Aaron scarcely managed to dance out of their way. Quickly, Aaron's feet fumbled on the ground, dragging. His speed and agility—the advantage he'd once held over

Mathew—had now vanished. He went from evading blows to deflecting blows to absorbing them.

Mathew rocked his younger brother with a well-placed jab, giving him a bloody nose. Another follow-up jab bloodied Aaron's lip. Mathew went in for a powerful overhand punch, and Aaron's legs were too heavy to evade it. The left-hand counterpunch Aaron through seemed purely reflex, but it connected hard with the side of Mathew's torso. The Congressman's blow did not land, but Aaron howled in agony, clutching his left shoulder. When he brought his hand back down, it was covered in blood from where his stitches had ripped open.

Mathew recovered from the body blow and seized the advantage. He landed several heavy punches to Aaron's upper body and a few glancing blows to the side of his head. Aaron nearly went down, scrambling away from his brother.

Watching the spectacle was something akin to watching the games in Rome's Coliseum—though what had started as a contest between two mighty gladiators had degenerated into something more like a sacrifice of slaves and convicts to the lions. The area fell strangely silent. Nobody offered any cheers of encouragement to their favored fighter or insults to his opponent. The air around them felt almost like they watched some kind of sacred ritual. Sebastian clenched his fists tightly at his sides. Mark and Lea held each other's hands firmly and lovingly. Sir Leon acceded to Aaron's position at every moment and thought of what he would do in his place.

***

Mathew and Aaron went to the ground, and Mathew ended up on top of his brother. Aaron's resolve had nearly disappeared. He'd started to accept defeat as he felt Mathew's hands clamp around his throat, the life squeezed out of him bit by bit.

"Fuck you," huffed Mathew. "I don't fucking lose. I don't…"

Aaron had started to black out from the lack of oxygen. Between two waves of blackness, he saw Lea's tearful face. In the blink of an eye, Aaron was back in that library, reminded of the monster his brother had become. More than that, Aaron remembered the man he was capable of being himself. He whispered something inaudible, repeating it over and over as Mathew bore down on his neck. His chant grew louder despite the deadly choke.

"Shut up! Shut the fuck up!" Mathew spat on his brother, incensed by Aaron's refusal to die. The elder Haze had become sloppy, reckless, and his balance on top of Aaron waivered.

Aaron had a perfect moment of clarity as he kicked out and connected with Mathew's groin. He felt a rush of fresh air fill his lungs when Mathew's grip was broken. Then chant Aaron had been repeating grew to a booming proclamation for all to hear. "I'll kill you," he roared.

Mathew was shucked form his perch on top of his brother. The Congressman fell to the cement flagstones leading up to the gazebo and cracked his skull, disorienting him. Aaron turned the tide and climbed atop his brother, all the while screaming with righteous zeal. "I'll kill you. I'll kill you," he shouted with renewed strength. He struck blows to Mathew's face with a maddened ferocity, opening cuts on his brother with his hands and forearms.

The impact to his head had made Mathew dazed and all but helpless. "Please…" he murmured.

"Shut up!" Aaron screamed. "Stop talking!"

"Please don't kill me," Mathew begged, trying to regain control of his body.

"Shut up! You don't talk! Stop talking!" Aaron bellowed. He punched Mathew in the face several more times, oblivious to the free-flowing blood and pain coming from the wound in his shoulder. All the while, Mathew asked for mercy. Aaron had none to give. He could not stand the sound of Mathew's voice anymore. Putting the heel of his right hand on Mathew's mouth, he began to push. "I hate it…your words…you don't…talk…" Aaron babbled in a rage as he pressed his hand into Mathew's mouth harder and harder. "Shut up…you…all my life…I hate it…your mouth…" He put more pressure on his brother's face. Mathew's lips parted, and his teeth dug into Aaron's hand until they cut through his skin. "I'll kill…die…you won't ever…your fucking mouth…" Aaron panted and huffed.

Mathew gagged and choked on Aaron's blood flowing from the cuts on his palm. Teeth cracked and shattered as Aaron kept on pushing. "This…this is what it feels like to lose… You hear? This is what it feels like." Mathew Haze's garbled screams filled the air, the grotesque sound of his retching stopped by the sound of bone splintering as his lower jaw was separated from the rest of his head. Then there was nothing—only the quiet.

Aaron Haze got off his brother, who convulsed, bleeding profusely. He walked aimlessly in a fog, his spirit in turmoil. Lost in a world he didn't understand—different and foreign—Aaron saw a great, varied people assembled before him. Without the cause, he didn't know what his life looked like. The idea of a united world had driven him; he'd followed a path leading to unspeakable things.

The younger Haze brother looked out at the diverse flags of the different people who had come together in opposition of his brother. They were the majority—they were many people who had spoken in one voice. Aaron wondered what could be a more beautiful demonstration of democracy than a nation coming together and reinventing itself? For all its harshness and deviation from traditional American politics, the Law of the Challenge was what the majority of people chose to follow.

The newly anointed leader of the Patriots wandered over to his Jeep. Aaron Haze looked up at the stars and stripes hanging from its antenna. It was one of the hardest things he had ever done, but Aaron said a silent goodbye to the country he loved so dearly. In his grief, the man pulled the flag from where it was affixed and ripped a long, thin piece of red, white, and blue cloth. He wrapped the trappings of a defeated nation around his bloody left hand.

Aaron went to his gun belt and put it back on. Everyone watched with intense focus. The Patriot drew his combat knife from its sheath and looked over the faces of the crowd. "This is who we are," he said solemnly. Shutting his right eye tightly, he buried the tip of his blade into his left. His scream of torment rose above the terrified gasps of shock from those gathered. Then he pulled the knife from his face and opened his right eye. For the very first time, Aaron Haze saw a brand new world.

Epilogue

Mathew Haze's body was taken to the beach near his childhood home in Rhode Island. It was buried in an unmarked grave overlooking the Atlantic Ocean. Few people ever spoke of him.

The Patriots disbanded and went their separate ways. Some remained in the Northeast and built peaceful live for themselves. Some even performed the Blinding and went on to serve as Arbiters. Others were taken in by the Templar Sebastian. A few zealous fanatics refused to give up the cause and disappeared into the south, where they plotted the return of the America before.

Sir Daniel's ashes were scattered over the entrance to Sebastian Proper in Manhattan. He was posthumously awarded the Templar's Shield—the greatest honor that could be bestowed on a Templar Sabastian, awarded for outstanding heroism and selflessness in the defense of others.

Sir Leon struck out for the Rocky Mountain Territory. He never returned to the Northeast. He thought of Lea every day.

Mark and Lea moved to New Boston, where they helped rebuild the city into an outstanding testament to society's will to thrive in the face of tribulation. They had three beautiful children. Their youngest two, Henry and Michelle, had the majestic green eyes of their father. Their eldest, Danyelle, also had the eyes of her father—dark and wrathful.

Aaron Haze went on to become a hero of mythic proportions—a man of Legend in the world *after*. His was an amazing story to be told.

About the Author

Photo by Leah Sharae Photography

Jason Pere is a born-and-raised New Englander. He always had a passion for the arts and creative storytelling. At the age of thirteen, Jason took up the craft of acting for film and theater. He pursued that interest for over a decade until refocusing his medium of expression into writing.

At first, Jason took a causal interest in writing, starting with poetry and journaling. Over time, he honed his direction and finally began writing larger works. In November of 2012, Jason self-published his first book, *Modern Knighthood: Diary of a Warrior Poet*.

Since then, Jason has continued writing on his own, mostly short stories and poetry. *Calling the Reaper* was his first experience committing to a full-length Fiction title.

In early 2015, Jason became affiliated with Collaborative Writing Challenge (CWC). Since then, he has joined many other writers on numerous collaborative projects. Jason is a regular contributor to CWC and is scheduled to have multiple pieces of his work appear in their publications.

You can find out more about Jason Pere's involvement in collaborative fiction at:

www.collaborativewritingchallenge.com

Thank you so much for taking the time to read World After Death. If you enjoyed it, please don't forget to leave a review at your favorite retailer and let us know what you thought.

Jason Pere

https://www.facebook.com/jbp.author/
http://teamcovenant.com/category/ashes-rise-of-the-phoenixborn
jbp.author@gmail.com